It's Wrong for Me to Love You, Part 2:

Renaissance Collection

It's Wrong for Me to Love You, Part 2:

Renaissance Collection

Krystal Armstead

www.urbanbooks.net

Urban Books, LLC
300 Farmingdale Road, NY-Route 109
Farmingdale, NY 11735

It's Wrong for Me to Love You, Part 2:
Renaissance Collection
Copyright © 2017 Krystal Armstead

ISBN 13: 978-1-945855-80-1
ISBN 10: 1-945855-80-0

First Mass Market Printing November 2018
First Trade Paperback Printing November 2017
Printed in the United States of America

10 9 8 7 6 5 4 3 2 1

Distributed by Kensington Publishing Corp.
Submit orders to:
Customer Service
400 Hahn Road
Westminster, MD 21157-4627
Phone: 1-800-733-3000
Fax: 1-800-659-243

It's Wrong for Me to Love You, Part 2:

Renaissance Collection

by

Krystal Armstead

Acknowledgments

Of course, I have to thank my homie, Racquel Williams, for taking me under her wing. Without her, none of this would have been possible. When she told me that Carl Weber (thank you, Carl Weber) was picking up a few of my books, I cried tears of joy. This is my moment, and best believe, I'm gonna take it. Third contract and counting. You're stuck with me foreva (in my Cardi B voice).

I also give thanks to Robin Watkins for keeping my spirits up when I want to give up. There are days when I don't want to get out of bed, when I'm just ready to give it all up and throw in the towel. But then, Robin curses me out, and I have no choice but to keep going. I appreciate ya, homie, for giving me that push that I need.

I can't forget about my homies in my reading group, Krystal's Motivation. Michelle Neal,

Acknowledgments

Mesha Turner, Elysia McKnight, Octavia Carter, Glenda Daniel, Nicki Ervin, Kasey Smith, Monique Franklin, Fallon Hampton—these are my motivators. There have been days where I was too sick to get out of bed. One of them would message me on Facebook or text my phone, asking me, "Where the hell is my book, Krystal?" Even when I feel like giving up, even when I'm crying my eyes out over the daily stresses in my life, this crew always manages to put a smile on my face. I appreciate you all. There are too many to name, but just know I appreciate the love.

Thanks to my mother and father, Jennifer and Conrad Artis, Jr.

I would like to thank my cousins Latrese Washington, even though she has "deemed me uncousined" a few times. Muah. Love you, cuz.

This book is also for my four beautiful children, Jada, Adrian, Jordan, and Angel. A life without you four is not worth living. This book is also for my beautiful stepchildren, Jamie, Jasmine, Anglie, and Little James. I love you all like you are my own. Never forget that.

And last but definitely not least, my husband, my jerk, my asshole James. You gave me just the frustration that I needed to keep writing. Appreciate that, I really do.

Thank you all for your support. Thank you, God, for the opportunity. A'ight, y'all, let's do this *again!*

Chapter 1

Reaction

Charlene

You already know I wanted to beat the fuck out of Ne'Vaeh's ass when that receipt fell out of Aaron's jacket pocket. I didn't give a fuck about Karma's bitch ass. All I cared about was the fact that my so-called best friend was doing something to have my man buy her a dress that cost damn near $400. The way he touched her, the way he held her, the way he looked at her, and the way she looked at him at her birthday party let me know that something was going on. I didn't need to see the receipt for the dress to let me know that they were fuckin'.

I called Aaron for hours after he left the party. My girls were in the club, dancing, having a good ol' time. Where the fuck was I? Outside the club, blowing up Aaron's phone, cursing him out on his voicemail.

I screamed aloud, shoving my cell phone in my purse after calling the phone about fifty times within a fifteen-minute period. It was about 3:15 in the morning. I should have been home, asleep in Aaron's arms. Instead, I was up calling and looking for him . . . when I already knew where he was.

"Shorty, what you doin' out here?" I heard a familiar voice over my shoulder.

I turned around to see Jamie walking toward me, dressed in a totally different outfit than he was dressed in a few hours earlier. I rolled my eyes. "Oh my goodness, Jamie—you gotta wear a different outfit to each place you go to? You go to the store in one outfit, you go the gas station in another outfit, and you go to the bathroom in another outfit. Arrogant and ghetto-fabulous as a muthafucka." I shook my head.

Jamie grinned at me. "What—you mad because you can't afford to do shit like this unless your parents pay for it for you?"

I rolled my eyes. "Whatever, Jamie. I don't have time for your shit tonight, okay? I have better things to do than stand here and go back and forth with you. Go on now. Get!"

Jamie looked at me. "What better thangs? Calling your man, seeing which hotel he's at with your best friend?"

I looked at him. "What are you talking about?"

Jamie took a pack of Newports out of his pocket. "Yeah, shorty, one of my niggas said he saw your boy at a party at the Marriott Hotel in Alexandria, Virginia. That was about 11:00. Said they seen him there with this cute li'l brown-skinned chick."

I shook my head, eyes watering. "Jamie, Ne'Vaeh isn't the only 'cute li'l brown-skinned chick' in the world, okay?"

Jamie looked at me. He laughed a little. "Wearing a sexy, tight, Coogi dress?"

I folded my arms. I really didn't want to hear any more. "Jamie, look, I don't really wanna be hearing all of this shit, okay? It's bad enough that I had to find the receipt to that fuckin' dress in Aaron's pocket, but now I have to hear that the muthafucka took her to a party at a fuckin' hotel? What time did they leave the hotel?"

Jamie shook his head, lighting his cigarette. "They didn't. Dude said they got a room there. A fuckin' suite."

My eyes immediately were swollen with tears. "Oh my God." I covered my mouth, tears sliding down my face. "How—how could they do this to me, Jamie? Jamie, I love him. I changed who I was for him. I never loved anybody like I love him. I can't take this shit. I won't take this shit." I took my keys from my purse.

Jamie grabbed my arm. "Shorty, what are you doing?"

I pulled away from him, pushing him off me. "What am I doing? Are you seriously asking me that shit? I am about to go beat a bitch's ass. She has no right to fuck with my man."

Jamie's eyes searched my face. "She doesn't?"

I folded my arms across my chest. "What me and you did ain't got shit to do with her. She's old news to you, Jamie. The only reason why you and I even slept together is that I needed to get laid. Aaron wasn't touchin' me, kissin' me, fuckin' me, lookin' at me, holdin' me—doing nothing to me for months."

Jamie scoffed, nodding his head. "Oh, okay. But you weren't using me, huh? 'Cause that sure as hell is what it sounds like, Charlie."

I shook my head. "No, I wasn't using you. You really came through for me; I needed you."

He shrugged. "Well, shorty thinks she needs him too."

"This can't be happening to me!" I screamed out. "He's gonna leave me for her, Jamie!"

Jamie looked at me, shaking his head. "Nah, shorty, your boy must just be goin' through somethin'. You were goin' through some shit when you slept with me. What makes you think Aaron isn't goin' through it too? I'm not sayin' what he's doing isn't wrong, shorty. All I'm sayin' is people go through thangs. My girl got tired of my shit and broke up with me a few weeks ago. She said I had too many hoes. I told shorty from jump that I wasn't ready to settle down. There really is no point in fallin' in love with a nigga like me. Told shorty from the start that I was no good."

I just looked at him. "Jamie, what the fuck does that have to do with me?"

"I'm sure you saw some sign in the beginning that Aaron was feeling your girl, and you just decided to ignore it. He ignored it too, obviously. Must have been something you said or done to make dude decide to holla at your girl now, some three years later." Jamie exhaled smoke from his nose.

I looked at him. I wanted to shove that fuckin' cigarette down his throat . . . until I actually thought about what he said. Aaron asked me what I thought about marriage. Without even thinking, I shut the boy down, telling him that marrying him was the last thing on my mind.

That was only because I was pregnant with Jamie's baby.

I looked up at Jamie. I wanted to tell him about the baby, but I couldn't. I wanted Aaron. I needed Aaron. I loved him. Yes, I was attracted to Jamie. Who wouldn't be? He was beautiful, he was sexy, he was fine, he was charismatic, and he was amazing. My heart was broken because I let my feelings for Aaron go unspoken. I never really told him how I felt about him. I never really told him how much I loved him, and because of that, he lost interest in me and found it in Ne'Vaeh. He called her "Heaven." He avoided her on every occasion, probably because he was trying to suppress his feelings for her. I'd made a mistake that I couldn't take back.

"Well," I sighed, "I think he was thinking of proposing to me. I blew it when he asked me what I thought about marriage."

Jamie exhaled smoke through his nose. "What did you say?"

I looked at him. "I laughed in his face."

Jamie laughed a little to himself. "Why did you laugh?"

I shrugged. "I guess I was in shock that he even brought the topic up. He'd never talked to me about getting married. We had just started having sex again after not having sex for months,

Jamie. He'd finally started touching me again. He'd finally started kissing me again. He finally started holding me at night again. When he asked me how I felt about spending the rest of my life with somebody, I guess I felt guilty because I knew that I slept with you."

Jamie's eyes searched my face. He flicked his cigarette into the street. "Yeah, shorty, love will have you feeling all types of ways. That's the reason why I make it known off the gate that if you're looking for love from me, you might as well make it easy and leave, shorty."

I rolled my eyes. "You talk all that good talk when you're with a female, and you expect her not to feel anything for you? Jamie, you're amazing. You can't tell me that you didn't feel anything when you saw Ne'Vaeh dancing with Aaron."

Jamie just looked at me, hands in his pockets.

"You use other women to suppress the feelings that you have for Ne'Vaeh." I glared at him. "You used me, Jamie, and you know it."

"The same way you used me to alleviate the pain you felt from your boy neglecting you?" Jamie's eyes searched mine.

"Jamie, I just told you that I didn't use you," I exclaimed. "Yes, I wanted to get laid, I'll admit, but no one has ever touched me the way you did.

I love Aaron, but everything that you do, it feels like making love, Jamie. You know what to do, what to say, what a girl wants, what a girl needs. You know the shit you do drives a girl crazy. Like right now, I was out here, minding my own business, trying to find out where my man is, and you got me here thinking about sex."

Jamie grinned a little. "I'm just trying to get you to really think about what you're thinking about doing to your best friend, shorty. What she's doing with your boyfriend is fucked up, true, but you can't act like your shit doesn't stink as bad as hers does. You wanted your boy, you should have told him. You were too busy, you were too pretty, you were too popular, you were too independent, you were too comfortable, and you were too proud to tell the dude how you felt about him a long time ago. You can't blame this entire situation on him, shorty. I think you both have some talking to do. Obviously, it's not happening tonight, so you might as well take your ass home."

My lips trembled. I stood there, arms folded across my chest, hair blowing in the wind. I was really hurting. There was no telling when Aaron was going to go back to his apartment. He was avoiding me. It was almost four in the morning. I knew he was in bed with her, probably just finished fuckin'. He was holding her, kissing her, running his fingers through her hair—all the things he used to do to me when we first met.

Jamie watched me jiggling my car keys in my hand. "You takin' me home with you or nah?"

I looked at him, heart jumping in my chest. "I thought me and you discussed this back in August, when I confronted your ass at that hotel?"

Jamie grinned. "After a night like this, wouldn't you like some company? I know what you saw tonight fucked your world up, shorty."

I knew he was just as mad as I was about the situation. He hated seeing Aaron with Ne'Vaeh, though Jamie was better at covering up his feelings than I was. "What do you think he's doing to her, Jamie?" My eyes searched his.

Jamie just looked at me. "Probably the same things that I wanna do to you."

I shook my head, looking up at him. "He's making love to her, Jamie. You don't make love, remember? 'No love' is what you make. Jamie, I need my man back." I started crying.

Jamie sighed. My depression was depressing him. He took out another cigarette. "Shorty, you and I already had this discussion months ago. I told you to leave dude alone, but you decided to stay anyway."

"So, I brought this shit on myself?" I exclaimed.

He shook his head. "Nah, but you could have avoided it. You stayed with dude when you knew neither one of y'all were happy. You knew he would eventually go looking for whatever he felt he wasn't getting from you. Now he found it in your best friend. And I know that shit's eating you up right now."

Depressed, I said, "I don't even know what to say, Jamie."

Jamie held my hand. "Let's get outta here. My car is at my aunt's crib. I caught a ride with my homie. Just take me to your crib so I can get some sleep, yo. I won't touch you if you don't want me to. I haven't slept in a few days. Been up partying; I just need a break."

I looked up at him, drying my tears. What damage could have been done that wasn't already done?

I drove him to my two-bedroom apartment in Baltimore. He made himself right at home on my beige sofa. He took off his jacket and kicked off his shoes.

"Did you want something to drink?" I walked into the kitchen, tossing my keys on the granite countertop.

"Nah, I'm good. Man, shorty, you gotta nice li'l place here." Jamie laughed a little to himself.

"Well, it's no mansion in southern Maryland, but it is comfortable, and I paid for it myself, without my mother's help, thank you." I opened the fridge, taking out a bottled water.

"Oh, so you heard I bought a house here?" Jamie was surprised that people still talked about him.

"What? Who hasn't heard about you moving back here next year? Everyone knows you signed a contract with the Ravens, Jamie. Why you picked them out of all the teams who wanted you, only your heart knows that, right?" I walked over to him.

Jamie just looked at me as I came over and sat on the sofa next to him. "Let me ask you somethin'. You been with Aaron since you were sixteen, going on three years now, and y'all not living together? I don't see shit in this apartment that belongs to your boy. No jacket, no shoes, no pictures. Where is the love, shorty?"

I looked around my apartment. He was right. Nothing about my apartment said that I even had a boyfriend. Everything around my apartment centered on dancing or cheerleading. I had a china cabinet full of trophies from dance and cheerleading competitions. I had pictures of my sorority and dance team all over the wall. You knew that I loved dance by coming into my apartment, but nothing about my apartment said that I loved Aaron. Aaron didn't so much as have a toothbrush at my apartment. At least Aaron did have a picture of me sitting on the table next to his nightstand. Come to think of it, I can't even really count that picture, because he probably only cherished it because it was a picture that I'd taken with Ne'Vaeh.

I opened the bottle and took a long sip.

Jamie looked at me as I licked the water from my lips and screwed the top back on the bottle. "Dude has no idea that you love him, shorty. He went to Ne'Vaeh looking for the love that you never showed him. I've been with shorty. She knows how to love. She loved me, and I was too afraid to accept it." Jamie's mind wandered for a few minutes. He was mad at the situation, the same way that I was.

I looked at him. "Sounds like tonight has you feelin' some type of way too, Jamie. How did you feel when you saw them dancing together?"

He looked at me. "It—" he hesitated as his words faltered. "It made me really miss her. And I'm not even the type to tell someone that I miss them."

My eyes sparkled. It seemed like everyone was in love with Ne'Vaeh, and that made me really hate her at the moment. She didn't have to do anything to get someone to love her. Seemed like I was doing the most, and it still didn't get me who or what I wanted. My life seemed easier when I was doing whatever I wanted. I was good at being bad. Seemed like I always got what I wanted. As soon as I changed my lifestyle and stuck to one man, my entire life had fallen apart. Maybe Jamie did have the best solution to a happier life.

I stood from the couch, undressing down to my black bra and cotton boy shorts.

Jamie's eyes traced my curves. "Damn, shorty, you getting' thick as a muthafucka."

I looked at him. He noticed my weight gain. I didn't have a belly yet, but my breasts were bigger, my hips were spreading, and my thighs and butt were getting chunky. "What? What do you mean?" I hesitated.

He looked into my face as I sat back down on the couch. "You picked up a few pounds, and it looks good on you, shorty. Got-damn." He pulled me closer to him by my hips.

I sighed as he slipped his fingers under my panties, tickling my clit. "I just—let's just kiss and touch. I just need to feel something tonight. I don't need to go all the way. I just need to feel your lips on me. That's it." I was already breathless from his first touch.

Jamie nodded, unbuckling his belt with his free hand. "That's cool. I don't have any condoms with me tonight anyway, shorty. I'm done with that raw shit. I got a shorty down in Mississippi pregnant a few months ago."

I swear my heart damn near stopped. "What?"

Jamie watched the horrified expression on my face. "Shorty went and had an abortion at six weeks pregnant and didn't tell me until afterward. I can't go through that shit again, Charlene. I felt bad for shorty, but I'm not ready to be a father."

I immediately pulled his hand from my panties. "Okay, ummm, I think you should go."

Jamie laughed a little. "What, you want me to go get some condoms?"

I shook my head, standing from the couch. "No, Jamie, you need to just leave. Doing this with you isn't gonna win Aaron back. This isn't gonna get back at Aaron, because he doesn't give a fuck about me. This is wrong. Even if Aaron is out there somewhere with Ne'Vaeh, this is still wrong. This shit right here is the reason why Aaron doesn't love or trust me. I tried to change, I tried to be the perfect girlfriend, and now, I'm standing here damn near naked with a guy who made it perfectly clear that a relationship is something he is not ready to be in. You could never love me, no matter what I did for you. I might still have a chance with Aaron. I love Aaron, and this is wrong. So you need to go."

Jamie laughed. Nothing ever seemed to faze him. He always laughed everything off. "A'ight, shorty, you want me to leave? A'ight, I'll go. You know my number." He stood from the couch.

Tears slid down my face as I grabbed my cell phone from the end table, and then handed it to him. "Actually, I don't have your number anymore. I threw it away the day that you gave it to me at the airport."

He grinned and entered his contact information in my phone. "You didn't think you'd see me again? Didn't think you had to face me again? We've known each other a long time, Charlie. You can't get rid of me just because you throw my number in the trash can, shorty." He handed my phone back to me.

It was excruciating holding in the truth for so long. I wanted to tell Jamie about the baby. There was no better time than right now to tell him that I was having his baby, especially when I was losing Aaron anyway. After hearing him say that he wasn't ready to be a father and that he'd had some other chick in the hospital getting an abortion, I couldn't bring myself to tell him that I was having his baby.

"I know, Jamie, and I'm sorry. I'm just really vulnerable right now. I'm so mad at Aaron, and then you show up tonight at the club. Seeing you just does something to me sometimes." I dried my tears.

Jamie looked down into my face. He gently kissed my lips. Oh, I felt like I was floating on a cloud. His lips stroked mine until I gently pushed him away.

I looked up at him, watching him lick his lips. "You have my heart racing, Jamie. Stop it," I whispered, with my hand over my heart.

He grinned a little as his cell phone rang. "What's up?" he answered the phone after eyeing the caller ID. "I'm in the city, man; what's up wit'cha?"

I sighed, picking up my clothes from the floor. Jamie had stayed in the streets ever since I've known him. I think what he liked most about Ne'Vaeh when we were growing up was that she never had a problem with who he was. There was no changing Jamie, and she never tried. Jamie really loved her for that. No one cherished Jamie the way that she did. Ne'Vaeh once worshipped the ground that he walked on. She was sprung, and now I know why.

I walked into the kitchen, wishing I could drink that bottle of Cîroc that was in my refrigerator. I hated myself right then. I was trying my hardest not to fall for Jamie, but he was making it a challenge. His heart was even more unattainable than Aaron's, so I wasn't stupid enough to believe that he'd ever have a relationship with me, but at least Jamie showed interest in me. It didn't hurt that we'd been friends since elementary school. That was probably why he cared about me so much.

It also didn't help that Jamie was sexy as a muthafucka. The way he looked at me, the way he smiled at me, the way he kissed me, the way he touched me, the way he talked to me—everything about him touched my heart. He had everything that I wanted in Aaron. The only thing that I hated about Jamie was the one thing that he had in common with Aaron—Ne'Vaeh.

Jamie pressed END on his cell, and then put the phone back in his pocket. He looked up at me. "Shorty, my nigga, Andre, is about to pick me up at the Exxon gas station on the corner."

I nodded, sitting down on the bar stool at my barista table. "Okay, boo," I whispered.

"You have my number now, Charlie. If you want me to come back over, I will." Jamie walked toward the door.

Tears slid down my face as I watched him leave.

Chapter 2

Caught

Charlene

I spent the next day and a half calling Aaron and trying to keep Jamie off my mind. I didn't bother going to class. I sat in the school library, dialing Aaron's number on my cell. I must have left thirty voicemail messages on his phone that Monday morning. Dude had the audacity to cut off his phone after I called the tenth time. I was hurt; I couldn't believe Aaron would do me the way that he did. He knew I'd find out where he was. He knew I had eyes and ears everywhere. Jamie wasn't the only person to let me know where Aaron was. My nanny's daughter, Martha, was a housekeeper at the Marriott where Aaron and Ne'Vaeh were. She called me that morning and told me that she'd walked in on Aaron naked, asleep, holding 'some li'l black girl.' The manager at the hotel dated my cousin, Tasha. He told me that he saw Aaron's Impala parked outside the hotel. He said he knew by Aaron's license plate that it was his car. There weren't too many "PhuckIt" license plates around.

You could imagine how pissed I was when Martha called me around 4:30 that afternoon telling me that another housekeeper walked in on Aaron and Ne'Vaeh having sex in the bathroom. She said there were condom wrappers everywhere. She said they looked like they'd been fuckin' all muthafuckin' day. At around 6:00, I received an automated call reminding me of my monthly checkup. I called Aaron another twenty-five times that night. Still, straight to fuckin' voicemail. Aaron didn't want shit to do with me. He didn't even wanna hear my voice.

Around 9:00, my cell phone rang. I hesitated to pick it up, but I looked at the caller ID. Kelissa, Dana, and Danita had been calling me all fuckin' day. I didn't feel like talking to any of them. All they cared about was dancing or me getting them into some club. They didn't care about my life or that things were going downhill with Aaron.

I didn't recognize the number on the caller ID, but I answered the phone anyway. "Hello?"

"What's up, Charlie?" You can imagine my shock when I heard Aaron's voice on the other end.

I was furious. "Aaron? So you finally decided to pull your dick outta the pussy and call me? I've been calling you all muthafuckin' day. I've been calling you since you left Ne'Vaeh's party. Do you think I don't know where the fuck you're at or who the fuck you're with?"

Aaron sighed. "Charlie, I just needed some air. I needed some space. I'm sorry. I never meant to hurt you. We need to sit down and talk. We need to work this out some type of way. I know you hate me, but you need to hear me out."

I exhaled. "I don't have time for this shit, Aaron. I have a baby checkup appointment tomorrow. You wanna talk to me? Well, you can come with me to my appointment. My appointment is at 9:30. Meet me at my apartment."

"Charlie, I—"

I interrupted him. "Aaron, I really don't wanna hear shit you have to say right now. I've been calling you for two days. You call me from some number that I don't even recognize like I can't figure out that this is the phone number to your fuckin' hotel room. The shit you do to me is fucked up, Aaron. You treat me like I'm shit, and I'm sick of it. If she's the one that you wanted, then that's the bitch you should've been with. I love you, but you love her, and you have no idea how much that shit hurts. Whatever you have to say to me doesn't even matter. Keep your lies and your sorry-ass apologies to yourself, asshole."

I hung up the phone.

At 4:30 in the morning, I was still up. I held my cell phone in my hands, trying to resist calling Jamie, but I needed him. I needed to feel some version of love, even if it wasn't the real thing. When I dialed Jamie's number, he answered after the third ring. "What took you so long to call, shorty?" he answered, loud music in the background.

My heart rattled in my chest. Oh my goodness, it felt so good to hear his voice on the other end. "Where are you, boo?"

"Club Toxic," he spoke over the music.

"Are . . . Are you with someone, Jamie?" I hesitated to ask. When wasn't Jamie surrounded by bitches?

He chuckled. "Nobody I can't leave to come to you. You at the crib?"

"Yes, Jamie." Tears began to slide down my face. "You comin' over?"

"Let me just let my crew know I'm leavin'; then I'm out, shorty. Stop cryin', Charlene. I'm comin' to you, a'ight?" Jamie assured me.

I hung up the phone. He was killing me, sending all sorts of mixed signals. He didn't want anyone to fall in love with him, yet he said and did all the right things. He was so affectionate. Though he was the guy who said what he had to say to get in the drawers, he made it sound real good. That muthafucka.

It was about 5:30 that morning when Jamie showed up, dressed to impress in a chocolate-brown Armani suit. I looked him up and down in awe as he walked through the door. A trail of Armani cologne trailed behind him. He looked like he jumped straight out of a fashion magazine. He looked like a piece of chocolate wrapped in a suit.

"Whoa, excuuuusssee me," I exclaimed. "I feel like I crashed a party. Look how you're dressed. What did I interrupt, Jamie? Oh my goodness, you look so good."

Jamie grinned, turning to face me. "A charity event. It's cool, shorty. Too many groupies were up in that club."

I rolled my eyes, closing the door behind him. "Must have been some chicks you've banged already. Used goods, huh?"

He nodded, "Yeah, a few of 'em, I'm not gonna lie."

I walked past him over to the couch. I had wine, cheese, grapes, strawberries, warm melted chocolate, and crackers on the coffee table. My glass was filled with grape juice. I was dressed in a black lace camisole and bikini panties.

Jamie followed behind me, smacking me on the butt. My butt jiggled. "Thick as a mutha-fucka," he whispered.

I tried not to smile as I sat down on the couch.

Jamie took off his jacket and laid it across the recliner. He grinned, looking at everything I had set up for his arrival. "Wow, all this for me, shorty?" He kicked off his dress shoes.

I smiled up at him. "Why not? I mean, you actually answered my phone call. You came when you knew I needed you. I don't get that type of treatment too often."

"It's been a long day, shorty. Meetings, physicals, conferences, clubs, charity events, checking on my dad, ordering furniture for the new house, class assignments online. Exhausting-type shit; I hate to admit, but I was waiting for you to call me, shorty." Jamie's eyes searched my face.

My eyes misted over as I poured him a drink. "Well, you deserve a drink."

"Still no Aaron, huh?" Jamie sat down beside me, unbuttoning his shirt.

A tear slid down my cheek as I attempted to roll my eyes at the thought about Aaron. "Well, he called me from the hotel around 9:00. Said we needed to meet tomorrow morning. I went damn near two days, Jamie, without a fuckin' word from him. What kinda man leaves his girl alone for two days? No call, no text, no stopping by, not shit."

"The kind of muthafucka who's not worried about someone else snatchin' her up." Jamie tossed his shirt over on the recliner.

My heart skipped a beat as I handed him the wineglass. "Am I the kinda girl you'd snatch up, Jamie?"

His voice hesitated. "I gave my heart once, Charlie; I won't do it again. Yeah, I fuck around with different females, but my heart belongs to her. I'm not gonna sit here and lie to you, shorty."

I drank from my wineglass with both hands. Man, I wanted a real fuckin' drink. Nobody wanted me, and I felt like shit.

"Nobody wants me. I'm not the kinda girl that anybody likes. I'm just the kinda girl who everyone wants to fuck, right?" Disgusted, I shook my head.

"Nah, shorty, don't take what I said that way. Everything about you is beautiful, Charlene. I'm going through a lot, shorty, and when I need you, you always seem to know what to do to take the edge off."

I nodded, "You just confirmed what I said, Jamie. I know how to suck and ride the dick. That's all I'm good for. You don't wanna love me, Aaron doesn't wanna love me—nobody wants to love me. Aaron can't stand me, which is why he's out there fuckin' her."

Jamie shook his head, taking a few sips from his wine. "Shorty, your man's coming home. You just have to give him some time. Trust me, baby, you don't wanna love me."

I sighed. "But I just want someone to love me, Jamie."

"We've known each other for a long time, and you know that I have always loved Ne'Vaeh. I'm not gonna lie to you and tell you that I can love anybody else, because that's it. One shot, one kill. That's all my heart can take. Now, if you want a man who'll come around when you need some late-night action, I'm your boy. We can go out to a club, go dancin', go get some drinks, have fun, but I'm not the one to love you, shorty. We have a connection because we've been friends for so long. I care about you, shorty, but my heart is hers." Jamie drank the rest of the wine from his glass. "Trust me, someone will love you like that someday, Charlie. Don't rush it."

I set my glass on the table, wiping my lips. That hurt like hell, but at least the boy was honest with me. I reached behind my back to unhook my bra. I slid the straps off my shoulders, and then pulled the bra from my body, tossing it to the floor.

"Got-damn." Jamie's eyes traced my body as I stood, sliding off my panties. "Look at that phat pussy. Can I bite it, shorty?"

I nodded. "If you don't wanna take my heart, can you at least take my body tonight? Can you just love my body? Please, Jamie," I cried.

He pulled me closer to him, drying my tears. "C'mon, baby, stop crying." He gently kissed my lips, sucking on my bottom lip just a little.

"H-how did you know I was crying on the phone, Jamie?" I whispered in between kisses, unbuckling his belt buckle.

"Because I can feel you, shorty, trust me; I feel your pain. I know how it feels not to be wanted." Jamie held my body up against his. "C'mon, shorty, let's relieve some of that pain for a little while."

Then, relieve some pain is what he did. He kissed, and sucked, and licked warm melted chocolate from my entire body. He worked my body until my legs went numb. He didn't stop until I came twice. It was hard as hell to separate love from sex with him. He said he couldn't love me; what he was doing to me, however, felt like love. He kissed me, he held me, he made me come, he made me squirt, he made me scream out his name, and he had me in tears. Homeboy put in work; I'm talkin' overtime; shit, time and a half.

At about 7:00, the phone rang. The ring tone was "Come and Talk to Me." It was Aaron. Jamie and I were still getting it in. He was working the shit out of me. He had just come inside of me, dick still throbbing when the phone rang. He looked into my face.

"You gonna get that, shorty?" He reached for the nightstand and handed me the phone.

I hesitated as I pressed "talk" on the phone. "H-hello?" I stuttered.

"Charlie, I'll be there around 9:00, a'ight? You hungry? You want me to bring you anything?" Aaron asked.

Jamie sucked and kissed on my neck as he slid out of me. He sat up, sitting on the edge of the bed.

"Ummm, no, Aaron, I'm good. I can't really talk right now. I'm about to get in the shower. Just get here when you get here." I hung up the phone. Didn't much feel like talking to him; not just because Jamie had my heart racing and my body glistening in sweat, but because my heart was really broken. I knew what I was doing was wrong, but what Aaron was doing to me was wrong too. If he didn't want me, he should have dumped me in the beginning, instead of stringing me along. I only slept with Jamie because he was giving me the attention that I craved from Aaron. The only person I was hurting by sleeping with Jamie was myself.

I sat up in the bed, tossing the phone on the nightstand, looking at the clock. Then I looked at Jamie.

He looked at me. "Your boy on his way over?" he asked.

I nodded. "He'll be here at 9:00."

"Shorty, I gotta get goin'. I gotta take a shower and meet my people over at my sister's crib at 9:00." Jamie stood from the bed, dick dangling between his legs. I couldn't help but gaze at it. Shit, you would have too. Big, chocolate, juicy thang. Looked like a fuckin' king-sized Snickers.

I looked up at him. "You can change here." I got up, walking over to my closet. I opened it, taking a Footlocker bag off the floor. Then I walked over to Jamie, handing the bag to him.

He laughed. "What's this?"

I shrugged. "Well, you said I didn't have anything here that said I was in a relationship. I had this bag in my closet for months, hoping that Aaron would spend the night, but he never did.

It's just a tank top, sweatpants, long-sleeved white Nike shirt, Nike slippers, a pair of Nike socks, and a pair of Hanes boxers. I'm sure you can fit everything."

Jamie grinned at me. I think he was a little impressed, but he wouldn't admit it aloud. Motor Mouth was speechless for once.

I nodded, smiling up at him. "Yeah, soap, washcloth, towels, everything you need is in the closet in the bathroom."

I slipped into a tank top and sweatpants and made a quick breakfast while Jamie was taking a shower. Bacon, eggs, and toast. Just thought I shouldn't send the boy about his day hungry. I found a spare garment bag in my closet for his suit. I couldn't help but smell his clothes before placing them neatly in the bag. I hung the clothes on the closet door in my living room.

"Wow, she can make me come and make me breakfast," Jamie said, walking down the hallway into the kitchen. "Just in case you didn't know, shorty, you're the fuckin' best."

I smiled a little, setting the butter and jelly on the barista table. "Just thought you'd want something to eat; can't send you outta here hungry. I hung your clothes over there on the closet door."

Jamie sat down at the table. "I'm gonna have to take this plate to go, shorty."

I nodded, tears in my eyes. "I know. Thanks for coming over when I needed you, Jamie. You're a great, great friend."

He smiled a little, eyes glistening. "Any time, shorty. Oh, damn, I almost forgot my dirty clothes in the bathroom. You think you could wrap this plate up to go for me, Charlie?" He got up from the table, walking to the back.

I sighed, getting a roll of plastic wrap out of the kitchen drawer. As I wrapped his plate, the doorbell rang. I had no idea who would be ringing my doorbell at 7:40 in the morning. The doorbell rang again. I walked to the door, not even looking through the peephole, and opened it. There stood Kelissa, Ashton, and my cousin Tyra.

My mouth dropped open, but nothing came out.

Tyra threw her arms around me, hugging my neck. "What's up, cuz? Ready to go eat?" She walked past me, with Kelissa and Ashton following behind her.

"Wh-what are you guys doing here?" I exclaimed, still in shock.

Kelissa eyed the Armani suit hanging on the closet door. She looked back at me. "We were in the area, so we just decided to stop by."

I looked at her. "In the area? At 7:40 in the morning?"

"There's an awards breakfast this morning at Morgan State. I thought we talked about this a few days ago?" Ashton spoke up. He smelled bacon and eggs in the air. "Bacon and eggs?" He looked at me. "Since when do you cook breakfast, Charlie? Your idea of cooking breakfast is pouring water in instant oatmeal. This is a first. Aaron's got you up cookin'? My nigga must've put it down."

I hesitated, just when Jamie came out of the back with his dirty clothes in a plastic bag.

Kelissa, Tyra, and Ashton were in shock. Kelissa damn near jumped out of her skin. Tyra nearly stumbled over her own two feet, backing up against the wall. Ashton stood there, hands in pockets, laughing to himself.

"That's not Aaron," was all Tyra knew to say.

Jamie looked at me, watching the tears start to slide down my face. He didn't seem fazed by the situation, though he knew I would have some explaining to do. "Shorty, thanks for letting me use your shower while they're working on the pipes at my sister's crib. Where's my suit?" He walked up to me.

My lips trembled. I was so embarrassed. I didn't even know how to play along with him.

"It's hanging on the closet door, fool." Kelissa rolled her eyes. "You know, I'm gettin' about sick and tired of catchin' you two muthafuckas."

Tyra looked at Kelissa, then back at me. "What is she talking about?"

I looked at Ashton. Ashton didn't have shit to say to me, but I knew he was pissed. He looked at me, then back at Jamie.

Jamie went over to grab his suit.

I rushed into the kitchen to grab his plate; then I went back into the living room, picked up his dress shoes from off the floor and walked up to Jamie, handing him the plate and the shoes. I looked up at him, drying my face, not really sure what to say.

Jamie kissed my forehead. "You're the best, shorty. Don't you forget that." He opened up the door, and then left, closing the door behind him.

I hesitated to turn around to face my three friends.

"What the fuck was Jamie G. doing at your apartment?" Tyra's light eyes grew even bigger than they already were.

Kelissa rolled her eyes, sitting down on the couch. "Girl, you know they were fuckin'. I don't even know why you asked that stupid-ass question. These two muthafuckas have been fuckin' for the past damn near three months. This is the second time that I walked in on those two. The first was before school started. I walked in on the two fuckin' in the bathroom at the Q-Club. And Alisha said the two muthafuckas have been fuckin' ever since our dance squad's retreat in Miami."

Tyra looked at me, sitting down in the recliner. She was a short, fair-skinned girl with waist-length, curly brown hair. We were a few months apart in age, though she had her life together a lot better than I did. She was already married to the man of her dreams, she already had her dream job, and she already had the house on the hill. She never understood why I lived my life the way that I did. When I met Aaron, she thought I had cleaned up my act, but seeing another man in my house while she knew I had a boyfriend confirmed that nothing about my lifestyle had changed.

Tyra shook her head at me. "Where is Aaron?" she asked.

I folded my arms across my chest. Finally an excuse for my behavior. "Why don't you call the hotel where he's been with Ne'Vaeh since Saturday night and ask him?"

Kelissa and Tyra looked shocked, but Ashton didn't look shocked at all. He just leaned back against the wall with his hands in his pockets.

I looked at him.

He looked at me.

My eyes widened. "Ashton, how long have you known about this?"

Kelissa shook her head in confusion, "Wait, Ashton, you knew about this?"

Ashton got defensive. "Eh, man, don't turn this shit back around on me. Yeah, I knew about Aaron and Ne'Vaeh. I walked in on them Sunday morning."

Disturbed, I shook my head, "How the fuck could you keep this from me?" I approached him.

Ashton looked at me as if I were a fucking lunatic. "What the fuck? How did this conversation turn from you fuckin' with Jamie to me knowing about Aaron and Ne'Vaeh?" he exclaimed, his light skin turning red. "You wanna get mad at someone, huh? Get mad at your man for fuckin' your best friend. Or better yet, get mad at yourself for fuckin' your best friend's man two months before your man even attempted to cheat on you."

I just looked at Ashton. Dude was pissed.

"What the fuck did you think was gonna happen when you barely spent time with Aaron? What the fuck did you think would happen when you tried to cover up your past and the nigga found out? I told you that this shit would catch up with you years ago. I found you passed out in your own vomit hundreds of times, Charlie," Ashton exclaimed. "I picked you up from random niggas' houses, naked, not knowing where the fuck your clothes were or how you even got there. I picked you up from the hospital, bruised and sexually assaulted and you couldn't even file a report, because you had no idea how you got to the hospital, no idea where you were, no idea what you drank, no idea what drugs you took, or no idea who did the shit to you."

"Thanks for making me feel like a true ho, Ashton. Thanks." I rolled my eyes, trying to play off the fact that his words hurt me to my soul.

"Charlie, you fuckin' that nigga? Jamie Green? Seriously?" Ashton exclaimed.

Tyra and Kelissa looked at me for an answer, though they already knew.

"Ashton, that's none of your fuckin' business." I dried my face.

He nodded. "None of my fuckin' business?"

I nodded back at him, rolling my neck and my eyes. "No. None of your got-damn business."

Ashton was pissed. "Oh, so it's like that? I've been your boy since elementary school and all of a sudden, your life is none of my business? I just wanna know how the fuck you went from crying because Aaron didn't want anything to do with you, to being pregnant by your best friend's ex-boyfriend."

Kelissa nearly fell off the sofa. "What!" she exclaimed.

Tyra just shook her head. "Cousin, are you serious?"

I pushed Ashton in his chest. "See? This is why I don't tell people shit. What the fuck, Ashton?"

Kelissa got up from the sofa. She couldn't bear to hear any more. "Yo, I'll be in the car, Ashton. This shit is crazy. I can't hear any more. I don't wanna be a witness to shit." She walked past us and out the front door, slamming it behind her.

I looked at Ashton. "Thanks a lot."

"You think no one is gonna find out? Your belly hasn't started showin', but look at your ass and your titties and shit. I've noticed the change, and I know everybody else has. Jamie should have noticed the shit too. Does Jamie even know about this?" His temples twitched.

I looked away, not able to say anything.

"He doesn't know. Charlie, you have to tell dude he has a baby on the way." Ashton pulled on my arm.

I pulled from him. "I'm not gonna tell him that he has a baby."

"Why not?" Ashton exclaimed.

"Because I already told Aaron it was his," I cried out.

Ashton and Tyra just looked at me.

"You did what?" Tyra stood from the recliner.

"Aaron was trying to break up with me. I didn't know what else to say to him to keep him, so I told him that I was pregnant. Tyra, I love Aaron," I cried.

"Then why was Jamie here? Why are you pregnant with Jamie's baby if you're so much in love with Aaron?" she exclaimed.

"Jamie's the type of man you want, Charlie? Do you know how many bitches he fucks every night? He's not the same Jamie you knew four years ago, Charlie. He's a fuckin' celebrity. He's got groupies in every state and probably some overseas. He doesn't give a fuck about you. What the fuck has the man done for you that Aaron isn't doing for you, besides fuck you? Pay you some damn attention? Spend a little time with you? Tell you that you're beautiful, when you already know you're fine as a muthafucka? Tell me what Jamie is doing for you that I haven't done for you?" Ashton yelled at me.

Tyra looked at Ashton, and then looked at me.

"I have saved you from fights, picked you up from strange niggas' houses, covered for you with your parents, and performed CPR on you when you passed the fuck out at your own birthday. I even held you up in the shower, washing you off after finding you passed out in the men's locker room in the eleventh grade. Ain't no tellin' what you let them niggas on the basketball team do to your ass!" Ashton was really hurt, but he didn't have to go off on me like that, though. Damn.

I looked at him. This conversation had gone all the way left on me. "Ashton, we have never had this conversation, and we are not about to do this shit now. What difference does it make to you who I chose to be with or chose to have sex with? This is my problem, and I'll fix this shit myself! Get out!" I pushed him. "Both of you, get out!"

Ashton laughed to mask the pain. "I've always been on your team, Charlie. You haven't heard me say one fuckin' bad thing about you, or even confront you about your lifestyle until now. I've supported you when no one else would. I've always had your back. Even when my girl told me that you weren't shit but trouble, I stuck by you. You want me out of your life? A'ight, I'm gone."

Ashton walked out the door, slamming it behind him.

I sighed. "Oh my gosh, he has some fuckin' nerve. He's fuckin' off on Alisha; then he has the nerve to call me trifling?"

Tyra approached me, wrapping her arms around me. "Cousin, why did you do him like that? You know the boy has had a crush on you for years."

I pushed her arms off me. "Oh, whatever. Ashton just can't stand Jamie, that's all. If you're gonna lecture me, you can save it, okay? As a matter of fact, I thought I just told you to get out with Ashton."

Tyra shook her head at me. "Whatever, Charlie. I ain't gotta go no-fuckin'-where. I don't know what's going on with you. I'm just here because your mother wanted me to come with you to your appointment today. She seems really excited about you having Aaron's baby. The woman wrote down a list of boy and girl names that start with 'A.' You can't get away with telling Aaron this is his baby for long. For one, the baby is probably gonna look like Jamie. And number two, you just told a few people that you're pregnant with Jamie's baby. Jamie's either gonna find out from hearsay or from you. It's your call."

Defeated, I walked into the kitchen. "Tyra, I didn't mean for any of this to happen. Aaron found out about my past, and he started treating me different. When I went to Miami with the Morgan Girls, I ran into Jamie. One thing led to another, and we ended up sleeping together. We slept together again a few months ago and after getting pissed at Aaron on the phone last night,

I called him, and he came over. He gives me the attention that Aaron doesn't. I may be wrong, but I'm not wrong by myself. Aaron has been at the hotel with Ne'Vaeh's ass for two days."

"That doesn't make what you're doing right, Charlie. You need to tell Aaron that baby's not his, so you both can move on," Tyra explained, just when the doorbell rang.

"Come in." I rolled my eyes. I really didn't give a fuck who it was at that point.

Renée walked in, wearing the cutest Burberry coat and leather knee-high boots. "Hey, Charlie, Tyra."

I was in shock. Renée almost never came by my apartment. The last time she came by my place had to be my housewarming and eighteenth birthday party. "Hi, Renée. No offense, but why are you here at 8:00 in the morning? Why are you here, period?" I questioned her.

"Well, I've been trying to find Ne'Vaeh for a few days, and she's not answering my calls. I thought you might know where she is or have at least heard from her." Renée hesitated, watching the irritated look on my face when she mentioned the bitch's name.

"Ummm," I pushed my hair from my face, "well, yeah, I know where she is. She's with my man at a hotel in Alexandria."

Renée stopped in her tracks on the way to sit down on the couch. She looked at me. "Hotel with Aaron?"

I nodded. "When was the last time you saw your cousin? I'm pretty sure you saw her after she left the party. Didn't you drive her back to Howard?"

Renée hesitated. "No, I took her to a karaoke bar with Alisha. I'm not sure where she went after that."

I looked at Renée. "Look, everybody here knows that Ne'Vaeh is fuckin' my man. It's no secret what's going on between them. You don't have to sit here and lie to me about not knowing your cousin is fuckin' my man, Renée. You probably just came here to rub the shit in my face."

Renée sighed, "Look, I don't know what the fuck is goin' on. Don't try to put me in the middle of that bullshit. Don't go assuming shit until you ask questions, Charlie. I know you're mad, I know you're upset, I know you're pissed right about now, but you need to find out the truth, and then let it go. Because in the end, both people involved are at fault. Ne'Vaeh didn't fuck herself, Charlie, if that's what's going on."

The bitch was really getting on my nerves. I folded my arms. "You tell me why a nigga would buy a bitch a $400 dress. When the fuck have you ever seen Aaron buy me a sexy dress like that? Even when the muthafucka had some liking for me, the only thing he wanted to do was buy me lingerie. All he wanted to do was fuck me. He brought her a dress because he cares about her, wants to see her walking around in some shit that he bought her, and wants the whole world to know how he feels about her."

Renée shook her head at me. "That's all circumstantial evidence."

"My nanny's daughter caught them fuckin' at a hotel. She said she has pictures of the shit. Is that shit circumstantial evidence too?" I exclaimed.

"Hey, don't confront me about this shit. I didn't fuck your man or your best friend," Renée snapped back at me.

"Well, don't try to come at me like I'm stupid, Renée. Don't take up for your cousin when she's in the wrong. I swear to God, I'm gonna make your cousin pay for this shit some way, somehow." I felt my skin turning red.

Renée was adamant. "If you think you're just gonna whup my cousin, you have another think comin' to you, sista, I'm tellin' you. Ain't gonna be no fighting over a nigga. If he cared anything about either of you, he wouldn't even put y'all in this situation. Your beef is with the nigga, not your best friend. Have you seen these alleged pictures of them fuckin', Charlie?"

I hesitated. "No, I told Martha to delete the muthafuckas. I didn't wanna see the shit. Aaron's on his way over here, and I really don't wanna face him this morning. I'm so fuckin' pissed." Tears slid down my face. "Three months pregnant, and my man is cheating on me with my best friend? Life can't get any worse than this."

Tyra looked at me, shaking her head in disgust. I knew she wanted to bust me out about Jamie in front of Renée, but she kept it inside . . . for the moment.

Renée had a sympathetic look on her face. "Well, hon', when do you plan on facing Aaron to confront him about all of this?"

I sighed, pushing my hair from my face. "He's on his way over here, but I don't even know if I want him to go with me to my appointment. Can y'all come with me?"

"Honey, you have to confront him alone. You can't avoid this," Renée said.

Tyra said, "Cousin, you look like you've been up all night. I'm pretty sure you haven't showered. Go take a shower and get yourself together before Aaron shows up. You're gonna have to confront him about everything, whether or not you're ready to."

I took a thirty-minute shower that morning while Tyra and Renée waited in the living room, watching reruns of *Love & Hip Hop*. I wasn't sure if they were staying to be fuckin' nosy or to make sure some crazy shit didn't go down when Aaron showed up. They knew my temper. They knew I was going to show out when Aaron got there. I threw on a tank top and Victoria's Secret pink shorts. I pulled my wet curly hair up into a ponytail. As I began to brush my teeth, I heard my cousin greeting Aaron at the front door. I immediately stopped brushing my teeth, wiped my lips, and tossed my toothbrush in the sink, storming out of the bathroom.

Aaron stood at the front door in a hoodie and sweats.

I was so pissed, my whole body was trembling. "Aaron, I just wanna know one thing." I approached him.

Tyra and Renée stood alongside me ready to grab me, because they knew by my clenched fists that I was ready to fight.

Aaron looked down at me, eyes damp.

"Do you love her?" I looked up at him.

Before Aaron could even get halfway through "Charlie, it's not what you think—" I slapped him dead in his face. Instantly, Tyra and Renée pulled me away from him, trying to calm me down.

"How the fuck could you do this to me? With her of all fuckin' people?" I cried. "I took care of that bitch, took her into my home when she didn't have shit, and this is how she does me? And you knew the shit I did for her. You knew how much I was there for her. You knew that she was like a sister to me. You knew how much I loved her. You gonna go and fuck the only real friend I thought I had? Why, Aaron? If you were in love with that bitch, why the fuck did you ask me out? Why did you tell me that you loved me?" I dropped to my knees on the floor, bawling my eyes out.

Aaron cried too, but I'm pretty sure the tears weren't over me. "Could y'all leave us alone?"

Tyra looked at him. "Dude, she just smacked the fuck out of you. I'm not leaving you and her alone. There's only so much a man can take, and I'll be damned if you put your hands on my cousin."

He shook his head. "Nah, man, I'm good. Just give us a few minutes." Aaron dried his face. "I need to talk to her alone."

Tyra peeled me up off the floor and helped me over to the couch. "Sweetie," she kissed my forehead, "we'll be right outside if you need us."

Tyra and Renée walked out of the apartment, closing the door behind them.

"Aaron, I really don't wanna hear shit that you have to say," I sobbed. "I found the receipt in your jacket pocket for that fuckin' dress that you bought her."

He took a deep breath. "I loaned my cousin the money to get the dress a few weeks ago. She bought the dress without trying it on, and the dress didn't fit. You know you can't return that shit to the store. My cousin tried to give the money back for the dress, but I couldn't take it. I just took the dress, telling her I'd find someone to give it to. You are thick as hell, and I knew you couldn't fit the dress. Besides, you don't even wear that brand. Ne'Vaeh was the only one I knew who was small enough to fit the dress, so I gave it to her. She's always rockin' Coogi, so I knew she'd like it. Yeah, I gave her the necklace and the earrings too. She didn't want any of it at first. But I told her I couldn't take any of it back. I ain't got no reason to lie to you, Charlie."

I looked at Aaron. It was the first time he didn't call her Heaven. "My nanny's daughter said she caught y'all fuckin' at the hotel, Aaron. What excuse do you have for that shit?"

"Charlie, I'm not cheating on you." Aaron sounded like he was trying to convince himself more than he was trying to convince me.

I stood from the couch, about to walk out of the room. "Okay, Aaron, I'm done. I don't have time for your lyin', cheatin' ass. How you just gonna lie to me? People were calling me on my phone and shit tellin' me that they saw you with that bitch, Aaron. Housekeepers even walked in on y'all fuckin'."

Aaron caught my arm, pulling me back to him.

I pulled from him. "Aaron, let go of me," I screamed, pushing him off me. "You wanna be with that bitch? Then go ahead. I told you that I can take care of this baby by myself. I don't need a man who's obsessed with another bitch, who would sneak off to be with her in a hotel for two days at a time. Who would lie to me in my face about fuckin' the bitch. Who thinks I'm stupid enough to fall for his lies."

"Charlie, I was confused." Aaron finally admitted the truth.

"Confused about what, Aaron? You either love her or you don't. You either love me or you don't," I cried.

He shook his head. "It's really not that simple."

I looked at him. He was right. I loved Aaron with every inch of me, but my body was craving Jamie at the moment. I was having a hard time erasing the memory of Jamie from my head, of him sucking on the insides of my thighs. I didn't know what I had gotten myself into.

I dried my face, looking up at him.

"I'm gonna tell you something that you don't know about me, shorty, so you can feel me when I say what I am about to say." Aaron took a long, deep breath. "You were my first, Charlie."

I was stunned for a minute. "First what? First girlfriend?"

He shook his head. "Shorty, c'mon, don't make me say it again. Saying it the first time was embarrassing enough."

I looked into his face, still in disbelief of what he had just said. "First what, Aaron? First time—first time having sex, Aaron? But you're a fuckin' basketball player."

He shook his head. "Charlie, don't get me wrong, I have had my dick sucked on many occasions back in California. I have played in some pussy, but I didn't like anyone back home enough to have sex with, Charlie."

My eyes watered. I felt even more like a ho. I should have known Aaron was a virgin when we first met. I did most of the work when we first started dating. But after the first few times, after he got the hang of what I liked to do in bed, he took the lead. We must have had sex four or five times a day the first three or four months that we were dating. It wasn't until he heard the rumors about me that he lost interest in sex with me altogether. He was hurt. I was his first, and he found out that he was just one of many.

"When I heard all that shit about you fuckin' damn near every athlete at school, random dudes at clubs, random chicks in college, teachers, coaches, scouts, and shit, man, I was hurt. I didn't want shit to do with you; I can't lie. It hurt like a muthafucka when I found out my teammates were laughing at me. Every nigga I knew told me that they either had sex with you or you sucked their dick. How the fuck do you think that shit made me feel? Do you know how many fights I got into over you, Charlie?" Aaron's eyes watered. "I can't lie, Charlie—Ne'Vaeh was my first choice back in high school. She wouldn't give me the time of day, but you would. I'm sorry if me saying that hurts, but it's the truth."

Hearing that he had feelings for that bitch really pissed me off, but I held my composure.

I shook my head. "No, what hurts is that I was such a ho and you have every right to be mad at me, Aaron, but if you wanted Ne'Vaeh, you should have just gone after her instead of choosing to ask me out. Yeah, she was into Jamie back then, but she would have budged. You crushing on her and trying to have a relationship with me would never have worked, no matter if you heard the rumors about me or not, Aaron. I love you, Aaron, but I can't make you love me."

His eyes searched. "Charlie, we have to fix this. This baby inside of you can fix us, baby, I know it can."

I shook my head. "Aaron, I can't do this today." I tried to walk away, but he grabbed my hand. I already had a gut feeling of what he was about to ask me. I knew Aaron's family. I knew their reputation was the most important thing to them, even more important than their son's happiness.

"I called my parents. They are coming into town tomorrow." His eyes searched my face. "My grandmother's diamond ring is in my aunt's safe. I'm asking her for the ring today."

My heart pounded in my chest. I backed away from him. He had just had sex with my best friend. I had been having sex off and on with my best friend's ex-boyfriend for over three months, and I was pregnant by the muthafucka. We had all done wrong. We were all at fault. Aaron was a good man, and I deserved that he was sleeping with that girl—but I was still pissed. Everyone that I loved was in love with her, but despite the way that Aaron felt for her, he was trying to do what he had to do to bring us back together. He didn't know that the baby that I was carrying wasn't his. How long was I going to be able to carry that secret before the truth came out?

"Aaron, we have to head to the OB/GYN in a few minutes," I whispered.

"Charlene Campbell, marry me." Aaron held my hand in his and pulled me closer to him.

I looked into his face, shaking my head. "Aaron, we made some horrible mistakes. Marriage can't make up for that."

"We need to make this right," he whispered.

"Marrying me won't make you love me, Aaron," I exclaimed. "You don't have to do this shit just because your parents would want you to. Fuck them, I'm sorry."

He shook his head. "I did wrong, Charlie, but you're having my baby. I'm man enough to admit that I was wrong. I was confused. I lost my sanity for a minute, but I'm back now. It's out of my system."

"Is she out of your system, Aaron?" I asked, already knowing the answer, even if I knew he wouldn't admit it.

His eyes searched my face. "Yes," he forced himself to say.

If I married that boy knowing that I was pregnant with Jamie's baby, I would have been wrong, right? If I told Aaron that the baby wasn't his, he'd leave me, wouldn't he? He'd go after Ne'Vaeh. She'd win again; I couldn't have that.

Disgusted, I shook my head. "Aaron, I hated when you called that girl Heaven. The shit has driven me crazy for almost three years. Promise me that you'll never touch that girl again."

He nodded. "I promise." He dried my tears.

I dried his. "Aaron, I love you, and I'm sorry if I hurt you."

"I want you to have my baby, and I want us to be a family. Will you be Mrs. Aaron Carter Whitehaven?" Aaron gently kissed my lips. I hadn't felt his lips on mine in months.

Everything that happened those past few days completely escaped my mind once Aaron started kissing me. We made love that morning on the couch. I had to reschedule my doctor's appointment.

Chapter 3

Jealous

Charlene

Dinner with Aaron's parents the following evening at his aunt Rose's house went very well. Aaron proposed to me with a beautiful eighteen-karat, white gold, round halo-styled diamond ring. It was a part of a wedding ring set, passed down from his great-grandmother on his father's side. The ring was worth about $20,000 and Aaron was giving it to me. His mother cried as he slid the ring onto my finger. I cried, not because I was happy, but because I was going to have to work hard to keep my secret about the baby.

The tea that Aunt Rose made had my ass racing to the bathroom every ten minutes or so. Upon leaving the bathroom, I stumbled across voices coming from the library in the hallway. Up until that point, everyone was hanging out in the family room, so hearing voices coming from the library seemed suspicious. Whoever was talking didn't want anyone else to hear their conversation. I inched my way closer to the library, realizing the voices belonged to Aaron and his father, Avery. The door was cracked open a little, so being the nosy person that I am, I stood at the door, peeping inside of the room.

Aaron sat on the arm of the sofa.

Avery handed Aaron a glass of liquor. Aaron refused, that was, until he looked up to see the stern look on his father's face.

Aaron took a deep breath, taking the drink in his hands.

"I'm sure you had enough to drink these past few days," Avery smirked, taking a sip from his drink. Aaron's father was a good-looking, tall white man with chiseled features, dark hair, and bright blue eyes. He had a heavy, sexy British accent. The way his wife clung to him at the table let me know that she craved his attention. He was very arrogant, and everything about the dude screamed playa. Other than inheriting his father's good looks, Aaron was nothing like him.

Aaron shook his head. "Nah, Dad, I'm good." He drank from the glass. "It's just my mind is clouded enough."

"Why is your mind clouded, son? Because you think you're in love with this girl?" Avery looked down into his son's face.

Aaron looked up at him. "Think, Dad? I slept with this girl knowing that my 'fiancée' would find out where I was. I didn't care if the whole world saw us together at that hotel. Dad, the housekeeper caught us fuckin'."

Avery was outraged. "Keep your voice down."

Aaron stood from the couch. "Dad, I love this girl."

"And you're having a baby with her best friend. How do you think that is going to work out in your favor, hmmm?" Avery asked, in his son's face. "You have a beautiful woman out there, in the family room, waiting for you. No, she may not be whom you want to be with for the rest of your life, but she is having your child. You can't walk away from her, especially not for her best friend. You made this bed, so you have to lie in it. We've all been there, son, trust me. I understand your pain, I really do. But this is for the best." Avery gripped his son's shoulders in his hands. "Son, you will be okay."

"Eavesdropping, are we?" Mrs. Whitehaven's voice echoed over my shoulders.

I jumped at the sound of her voice, turning around as she pulled me away from the door by my hand. "Uhhhh—"

Mrs. Whitehaven rolled her eyes, leading me back down the hallway toward the family room. "Not every conversation is meant to be heard by others, sweetie." Her voice was so calm and eloquent. She was so beautiful and reminded me of one of those glamorous women in those old black-and-white movies.

I slipped my hand from hers, stopping in the middle of the hallway, outside of the family room. "Mrs. Whitehaven—"

She smiled, perfect teeth gleaming. "Call me Ella."

I sighed, not really in the mood for the show she was putting on. "Ella, they were in that room talking about me. I have the right to know what they were saying."

Ella's green eyes searched my face. "You're pregnant, yes?"

I hesitated.

Ella nodded. "There. That's what they were talking about. You're not the only woman to become pregnant before she walked down the aisle. It will stay between us four, if that's what you wish, dear."

I looked at her. She was actually happy that I was having "his" baby. I'm sure she spoke with her son in private. I'm sure that she knew that he was in love with Ne'Vaeh.

I sighed. "He's in love with that girl, Ella, you know he is."

Ella laughed aloud. "The little black girl?"

Ummm, bitch, you're black, is what I wanted to say, but I didn't.

"Well, apparently, she's not some 'little black girl' to Aaron. He's infatuated with that girl, Ella," I exclaimed.

Ella shook her head at me. "There is a reason why my son rejects us. His father's family doesn't accept him because they don't accept me. I will not let my son's heritage curse him any more than it already has."

"So, you're ashamed of who you are?" I looked at her. Talking to her made me feel like I'd stepped back into the 1800s. No wonder he was in love with Ne'Vaeh. She was forbidden fruit.

"No, but I'm ashamed of what I've done to my son. I want my son's children to resemble their English heritage." Ella put her hands on my face. "You're beautiful, you're light, and your family is rich. What more could my son ask for in a mate?"

I took her hands from my face. I was insulted by her ignorance. "So, your son's status means more than his happiness? The only reason why I get to marry your son is that I'm light-skinned? That's the stupidest shit I've ever heard. He's only marrying me to appease you and his father.

I love Aaron, but I don't want him to marry me just so he doesn't disappoint his family. He deserves to be happy."

"And so do you, Charlene." Ella's eyes glistened.

I shook my head at her. "Was Avery in love with you when you were married?"

Ella laughed to herself, shocked that I would have the audacity to get in her business, the way that she was getting into mine. "What sort of question is that?"

"You don't have to tell me how you two met, and that's fine. All I'm saying is that despite how Avery's family felt about you, he married you. Did he marry you because you were pregnant with his baby, I don't know. But I saw the way you were clinging on to him, practically begging for his attention," I exclaimed. "I can recognize a cry for love when I see one. Your husband is gorgeous. I know women chase that man, probably in front of your face. If you want to be ashamed of anything, Ella, be ashamed of that. Not ashamed of the color of your skin, some superficial shit that shouldn't even matter in 2014."

"I have everything that I ever wanted in Avery. Love doesn't pay the bills. Love doesn't let us take long vacations. Love doesn't pay for our four houses in California and two in England. Love doesn't ensure that your children all go to the best private schools. Love doesn't ensure that your children ever have to work a day in their lives if they chose not to. Love doesn't love anybody, Charlene, and the sooner you realize that, the better off you'll be." Ella held my hand in hers.

I just looked at her, lips quivering.

"Yes, I was pregnant when Avery proposed to me. He was sleeping with several women at the time, yes. I was the only one dumb enough not to use protection. When his family found out that I was pregnant, they were furious. The only reason why they forced him to marry me was because my family is rich. My family practically sold me to the Whitehavens, Charlene." Ella cried. "You have no idea what it is like to be forced into something that you know you're not supposed to be a part of. Do you love my son?"

I hesitated, "Yes, but—"

She interrupted me. "Then take this ring my son gave you and stop complaining."

Aaron's mother didn't waste any time helping me to prepare for the wedding. The fact that Aaron spoke to his parents about his feelings for

Ne'Vaeh really had me feeling some type of way. I never gave him the slightest clue that I knew about his feelings for her. While his parents were around, I didn't even get the chance to be alone with him to tell him, even if I wanted to. Before his parents left Maryland, Ella ordered wedding invitations. They arrived that Thursday morning. I had the girls from the squad hand out the invitations for me, making sure two were given to Renée, so that she could break the news to her cousin. The only dancers on the squad not entirely happy for me were Alisha and Kelissa. I was surprised the two hadn't spread the word about Jamie's baby, but I didn't put anything past Alisha. She had something up her sleeve, or maybe she was waiting on me to hang myself.

I wasn't formally invited to Jamie's party. His publicist sent invitations to the basketball team. Aaron invited me along with him. I wasn't sure if he was inviting me because he knew I wouldn't like him going to one of Jamie's parties at Purple Panties, or if he was inviting me because he was afraid he'd bump into Ne'Vaeh. Regardless, I wanted to confront that bitch, so I was going, whether I hated that fuckin' club or not.

Yeah, I confronted Ne'Vaeh's ass in front of her family, friends, and my dance team. I didn't really care about her feelings that night. I made sure to flash my ring in her face. I made sure to let her know exactly what I thought about her. The only reason why she had gotten an invitation was that she needed to know that her actions didn't ruin my life. Aaron was mine, and whatever she felt for him was irrelevant to our plans. She was throwing dirt on my life, so I had to throw a little on hers.

Yeah, I called her Jamie's groupie, even though I knew she wasn't. When Jamie was with Ne'Vaeh, she was everything to him. He never cheated on her, never lied to her, or mistreated her. They were best friends. I was always jealous of their relationship, though I never admitted to it. She needed him in those days. She needed us all. She was really going through a lot. Internally, Ne'Vaeh was dead, but that was still no excuse to steal the only joy that I had in my life. True, I struck the first blow by sleeping with Jamie in Miami, but she should have kept her damn hands off my man, no matter how irresistible he was. Deep down, I knew by the way that she looked at him, when she first looked into his eyes in Mr. Porter's Black History class, that she was in love. However, I forced myself not to care, because I wanted him to myself.

"You know that was fucked up what you said to that girl, Charlie." Kelissa approached me that night at the bar in Purple Panties.

I looked up at Kelissa's sparkly ass that night under the club lights. She looked just like a damn stripper in her tiny li'l purple dress, titties and ass popping out all over the place. She fit right in with the strippers at Jamie's party.

"Kelissa, kiss my ass." I stuck my middle finger up at her as I took a sip of ginger ale from my glass.

"You're the one fuckin' a man who doesn't want you, a man who'll never love you, a man who loves your best friend. Looks to me like you're the groupie." Kelissa rolled her eyes at me.

I looked up at her, watching her as she pranced away. I wasn't sure if she was talking about Aaron or Jamie. Either way, what she said was pretty fucked up. Before I could get up to go after the bitch to confront her, I felt the softest hand pull my arm in the opposite direction.

I looked up into those soft, inviting, brown eyes of Jamie Green. I sighed, not really sure what to say.

Jamie grinned. "So," he spoke as he sat down at the bar, "why didn't I get an invitation to your 'engagement party'?" Jamie's eyes strolled over my entire body.

I rolled my eyes, sitting back down on my stool. "It's not like you invited me to this here party either, Jamie. And I don't think Aaron would appreciate you over here talking to me."

"Congratulations, shorty. You deserve this. Not sure whether to call you crazy or desperate, but regardless, I'm happy for you." Jamie's eyes searched mine.

"I see your little groupie is here," I smirked.

Jamie looked at me. Guess he didn't like that joke. "Groupie? You marrying a dude who made it obviously clear to you that he didn't give a fuck if you knew he was fuckin' your best friend in a hotel for two days. You marrying a dude who has probably been in love with your best friend from the day they met. And you marrying a dude who's probably only marrying you because she won't marry him. But you wanna call her the fuckin' groupie?"

I folded my arms, weight shifting to one leg. "Oh, so you can call me a fuckin' crazy, desperate bitch, but I can't call a girl who lost interest in you years ago a fuckin' groupie?"

Jamie looked at me as he lit a cigarette, putting it to his lips. "You need to watch your mouth, shorty. Talk too fuckin' much."

"Oh, so you're mad now?" I rolled my eyes. "I talk about Ne'Vaeh, and it bothers you? As long as I don't say shit about your groupie, then we're cool?"

Jamie stood from the chair, looking down into my face. "Let's get something straight—that big-ass fuckin' ring you got on your finger doesn't mean that nigga loves you. Just because I had sex with you doesn't mean I don't love her. You got your man back and now you think you're better than her? A'ight, we'll see. You say she lost interest in me, huh? Well, watch me get her back." Jamie turned and walked away from me.

I sighed. Everybody hated me at that moment. Making an enemy out of Jamie was something that I really didn't want to do. He was a great guy. It shouldn't have hurt that he was defending Ne'Vaeh, but it did. The fact that I had sex with him didn't mean shit. Sex was something that he got on a daily basis. Love was what he was craving, but he wasn't craving it from me.

I caught sight of Ashton sitting by himself at a table, twirling a stirrer around in a glass. He looked handsome in his suit and tie.

"Well, boo, don't you look handsome as ever." I approached him.

Ashton looked up at me, light eyes searching my face for a few seconds; then he looked away.

I sighed, sitting down at the table across from him. "Aww, are you still mad at me?"

Ashton still didn't look at me. "Man, I have other shit to worry about than whose dick you decide to put in your mouth, Charlene. This shit ain't nothing new. Your mouth has always been like a Snickers bar, ya know . . . packed full of nuts."

I threw my hands up. "You know what? Forget this shit." I had had enough of everyone's mouth that night. I turned to walk away.

Ashton jumped up and grabbed my arm. "All right, all right, I'm sorry."

I pulled away from him, frowning. "Look, I really don't need you judging me, Ashton. Not you. I don't have any friends at the moment. Everybody hates me. I can't have you hating me too."

His eyes searched my face. "I don't hate you, Charlene. I'm more like disappointed. I'm just tired of playin' myself."

I looked up into his face. "What do you mean?"

Ashton looked over at Alisha, who was out on the dance floor with a few girls from the squad. "She looks good tonight, right? Can't even tell that she has a wig on."

I looked over at Alisha, then back at him. "Since when does Alisha wear a wig? Her hair is about as long as mine." I had dark brown hair that touched where my bra latched, and Alisha's was just about as long. Homegirl looked like a black Playboy Bunny Barbie, if there was such a Barbie.

Ashton looked at me, eyes watering. "Nah, the chemo makes her hair come out in clumps, so she shaved it off yesterday."

My eyes widened. "Wh-chemo?" I exclaimed.

Ashton put his finger to his lips. "Shhh! Damn, why you gotta be so fuckin' loud?"

"I'm sorry, but chemo?" I shook my head, confused

Ashton nodded. "Yeah, she hasn't told anybody. Y'all been thinking she's been going to all of these dance auditions and shit. Nah, she's been going to get treatments for cancer. She's dying, Charlie. She has a brain tumor. It's in a part of the brain where they can't operate. There's nothing more that they can do for her."

I looked over at Alisha who was dancing and having a good old time as if she didn't have a care in the world. That was why she hated me so much. I was healthy and throwing my entire life away. As long as she's known me, I'd lived a reckless life. She was smart, she was talented, and she was sexy. She even volunteered down at the homeless shelter and at the orphanage. There I was, sleeping with everybody, and the worst that I ever contracted was crabs.

"How long does she have?" I looked back up at him, eyes tearing up.

Ashton looked at me. "We don't really know. She found out back in tenth grade that she had this tumor. You probably don't remember, but she used to get these terrible migraines just about every day, and she would stay up all night throwing up. I shouldn't even be telling you this. She made me promise not to tell anyone, especially you."

I looked at him. "So, that's what you meant when you said she couldn't have sex? I'm sure all of these treatments have killed her sex drive altogether."

Ashton took a sip from his drink. "Yeah."

I just looked at him. He was holding himself together pretty well; to know he w as losing his girlfriend had to be devastating. "Are you okay, Ashton?"

Ashton shook his head, eyes glistening. "Nah, man. Hell, nah, I'm not okay. I'm losing my baby. I'm on the verge of a nervous breakdown. Alisha said she wasn't going to have any more treatments a few days ago, which didn't matter, because the doctor called today and said that chemo wasn't working for her anymore. I watched my baby cry, shaving all of her hair off. Here my girl is dying on me, and I can't get your stupid ass off my mind."

I looked at him, lips trembling.

"My girl, who has been my best friend since middle school, is dying on me. She's had my back for years, even when I didn't deserve it." Tears started sliding down his cheeks. "That girl loves the fuck out of me, Charlie. And here I am, in love with you. And I don't know who the hell you love, but I know the muthafucka ain't me."

Tyra was right about Ashton. I was too blind even to notice that the boy was in love with me all those years. Other than the time I sucked his dick in middle school, Ashton never approached me, never even mentioned having any feelings for me. Alisha had to know how he felt about me, and I'm sure the fact that she was dying, leaving him on this earth around the likes of me, made her hate me even more.

I just looked up at Ashton, not even sure what to say to him, except, "Ashton, you're my best friend, and you know I love you, just not like that."

He nodded, drying his face, and taking a sip of his rum and Coke. "Yeah, I know. Even if you did, I'm not disrespectful enough to fuck with my roommate's girl—Nah, my bad, his fiancée. The fiancée who's pregnant by her best friend's ex-boyfriend. I'm not getting mixed up in all that drama, Charlie. I'm just telling you, Charlie, you're gonna need me and you just better hope that when you do, I'll be around." Ashton walked away from me.

I just stood there for a moment looking and feeling real stupid.

You can imagine how pissed I was that night when Ne'Vaeh hit the stage and started singing. She didn't get through the first verse when Aaron grabbed my hand, leading me out of the club. He was ready to leave, but I wanted to stay. Guess he just needed a breather. He never heard Ne'Vaeh sing. Yeah, the bitch sounded like an angel. The fact that her voice fit her name wasn't helping. Aaron already had a taste of that bitch, and I'm sure he wanted more. He was trying to do the right thing by me, and I commended him for that. I'm pretty sure that Aaron would approach her before she approached him. The bitch wasn't crazy. She knew I was three Red Bottoms steps away from stomping a hole in her ass. Yeah, I know, I was in the wrong, but that bitch didn't know that. I wasn't sure how long I was going to be able to keep it that way either.

I sat back and watched as Jamie and Ne'Vaeh got back together. I'm not so sure that Ne'Vaeh wanted anyone to know, but Jamie announced that shit to the world. He wanted everyone to know that he had his girl back. Since he wanted to flaunt his relationship with that bitch, I flaunted my relationship too. I made sure to bring Aaron to Mr. Green's funeral, just to piss the two of them off. I know, I know, it wasn't the place or the time to bring my drama to a funeral, but I hated hearing that Jamie had moved that bitch into his mansion. I know; she had heart issues, another detail of her life that she neglected to tell me. I didn't know shit about her, and I was supposed to be her best friend.

I hadn't spoken to her, other than our encounters at Jamie's party and Mr. Green's funeral. It was November 26, the day before Thanksgiving and the day before my engagement party. I know, Thanksgiving was a hell of a day to have an engagement party, but I figured that since everyone would already be in town visiting family, they'd have no excuse not to show up. Everyone and their aunt Mae Mae was invited. We were having the engagement party at the National Harbor. We had spent an extravagant amount of money on food, gifts, and decorations to spend too much on the room for the party. We rented the ballroom at the Gaylord, which was fuckin' expensive enough.

I had just about all of the Morgan Girls helping me prepare for the engagement party. I needed some to help pick out the dining sets, others helped with the décor, a few helped with seating, while several others helped with menus. I was going crazy, and we were months away from the wedding, which was January 1. Aaron just sat back in the cut while I put everything together. He had enough pressure. He still hadn't decided on which team he was going to sign with, and he didn't have much time to make a decision. I didn't care which team that he decided to go with, as long as I was going with him wherever he went. I was almost fifteen-weeks pregnant, and hiding my baby bump with busy patterns and dark clothing. Surprisingly, the only people who knew about my pregnancy were those that were present when Ne'Vaeh passed out in the bathroom at Jade Allan's restaurant on the day of Ne'Vaeh's birthday party, Kelissa, Alisha, Ashton, Aaron, and Tyra. Only four out of the people who knew actually knew the truth about who the child's father was. I planned to announce my pregnancy at the engagement party. I was trying to hold myself together and not fall apart. It took every bit of strength I had not to tell Jamie that he was my child's father, but I wasn't so sure how much longer I could hold it in.

Everyone heard about Jamie's wild parties the week that he was allowing his nurses to care for Ne'Vaeh. I just knew that Ne'Vaeh would go running for the hills as soon as she was confronted with Jamie's life, but no. The bitch stayed right there and didn't budge a bit, and when Jamie saw she wasn't fazed, he wiped his entire plate clean. You didn't see him at one party, at one club, at one event if Ne'Vaeh wasn't with him, and I was pissed the fuck off.

"Charlie, why are we helping you put up these damn decorations when you have fuckin' interior decorators and a got-damn wedding planner?" Dana asked, damn near falling off a stool while trying to help hang decorations. "Why does your rich ass need our help?"

"Okay, Dana, that's crooked." I backed up a little, trying to get a bigger view. "Because, Dana, my wedding planner has enough chaos going on and my decorators are on the other side of the room hanging jewels. I really appreciate all y'all's help."

Kelissa rolled her eyes, setting Victoria's Secret gift bags on a table, next to each place setting. "Girl, whateva. You need to let go of some of that pride and call Ne'Vaeh. Your best friend is supposed to be helping you with your wedding, not some bitches who barely even like your ass."

I looked at Kelissa.

"Seriously, though, Charlie, who the fuck is gonna be your maid of honor? Ain't none of these bitches honorable. Like Kelissa said, most of them don't even like you," Tyra chimed in. "Most of these muthafuckas—family included—are only here to see if Aaron actually goes through with this bullshit. I mean, wedding."

I looked around the room. They were both right. About fifty people filled the room, helping me decorate and set up for the party. The only people there who gave a damn about me were my mother, my sister, my brother, my grandmothers from both sides, and Tyra. My other family members, who were there to help, probably didn't give a fuck about me. They were only there to make sure I really got married to Aaron, so they could stick their hands out.

"It's bad enough that I'm gonna miss Thanksgiving with my family in New York, but now I'm stuck here, handing out perfume, lipstick, and shit, instead of somewhere snuggled up with my man." Kelissa looked at her watch. "And I have to go pick up Alisha from the airport in about an hour."

I looked at her. I hadn't seen Alisha since Ashton told me about her dying. I didn't have the chance to speak with her. I really wanted to apologize to her for being a bitch all those years. I finally figured out why she hated me. She gave me such a hard time, because I didn't deserve to have a great boyfriend and have her boyfriend lusting after me.

"Look, girls, I thought we were a team. I have sat through boring-ass weddings; bought shit for some of y'all's baby showers; paid for some of y'all's prom dresses and shit . . . and I can't even get a little help with my engagement party without people complaining?" I shook my head. "Why am I always doing the most for people and everyone wants to do the least for me?"

"Well," Lailah threw her long, vibrant hair over her shoulder, "it's not that we don't wanna help you, it's just a holiday, Mami. We support you, you know we do; it's just, well, we have shit to do too."

"Looking nice in here, ladies. Keep up the good work." I heard the sexiest voice over my shoulder.

I turned around to see Jamie walking toward me. Why did he have to show up, looking like a fuckin' million bucks? He always showed his face when I was feeling the most vulnerable. It's as if the dude could hear my heart when no one else even bothered to listen.

"What are you doing here?" Kelissa said, as all of the Morgan Girls in my vicinity gathered around me.

Jamie smiled, hands in his pocket, baseball cap covering his eyes a little. "I just came by to see the color scheme, so I could make sure the outfit that I plan on wearing tonight matched the occasion."

I rolled my teary eyes. "Cocky muthafucka," I said to myself under my breath. "What do you really want, Jamie?"

"My sister and a few cousins are here to help, shorty. We found out you were short on hands. My sister and fam' needed a ride, so they called me." Jamie's eyes searched my face.

Tyra nudged me in the side.

I looked at her. She'd been bugging me all month to talk to Jamie about the baby. I knew I had to tell him sooner or later. I just wasn't so sure it was the right time.

I looked back at Jamie. "Can we talk for a minute?" I looked at everyone around us. "In private. Damn."

The crowd scattered, going about their business, still keeping an ear in my direction, though.

I didn't trust the scene. I knew someone would get an itch to move closer to the conversation. I held Jamie's arm, pulling him off to the lobby.

"What's up?" he spoke, once we got to the center of the lobby, facing each other.

"So, how are things?" I looked up into his face.

Jamie nodded, confidently. "Everything's all good. You're kinda fuckin' up my plans with this engagement-party-on-Thanksgiving thang. I planned on cookin' with shorty at my place tomorrow. Since we can't do that, we're having a little get-together at my place with a few friends tonight."

I faked a smile. "So, back together again, huh?"

Jamie smiled a little. "Yeah. I guess."

I made a face. "What do you mean, you guess? She's either your girl or she's not."

Jamie shrugged. "Not really that simple. She's not too convinced that I have my shit together. I've been bustin' my ass trying to get her trust back. It's almost like she's waiting on me to leave her again. I can't seem to erase that thought or image from her mind. Shorty won't even move in with me. Shit, I even offered to add her name to the got-damn deed to my house, but she didn't wanna do that."

The bitch was crazy.

"Well, some girls just don't know when they have something good, I guess."

Jamie grinned. "This is what you wanted to talk in private about?"

I hesitated. "No."

"So, what's up then?"

I took a deep breath. "I'm . . . I'm jealous."

Jamie laughed aloud. "Jealous of what?"

"Of you and her," I admitted, though that wasn't what I was supposed to say the day before my engagement party.

"Okay, let me get this straight: you're about to have damn near a half-a-million-dollar engagement party to a nigga who's already from a rich-ass family and who is about to join the NBA, yet you're in your feelings about a nigga who made it perfectly clear from the first kiss that he wasn't the nigga to love?" He looked down at me, hands in his pockets.

I knew what I was saying was stupid, but it was the truth. I just wasn't one to lie to myself. Yes, I loved Aaron, and we had done some serious making up over the past few weeks. However, I couldn't shake Jamie from my mind to save my own fuckin' life. From the time that he entered my body on that sandy beach in Florida back in August, to the time he kissed my tattoos in my apartment a few weeks earlier, that muthafucka stayed on my mind. I tried not to fall for him, but my heart ignored me.

"I'm sorry, Jamie, if I shouldn't be saying this, but I had to be honest," I whispered, shaking my head at my own stupidity. "I have been waiting for this moment, to marry Aaron, to live happily ever after. And now that it's here, all I can think of is you."

Jamie laughed to himself, probably to keep from cursing me out. "Unbelievable. You're fuckin' unbelievable, shorty. Leave the past where it is and don't try to relive it." He backed up and walked away from me.

I panicked. I couldn't just let him walk away. He wasn't going to make me fall for him and just diss me as if I wasn't shit. Especially to be with a girl who was ruining my fuckin' life.

"Jamie, I'm pregnant!" I called out to him.

A few of the decorating staff stopped and looked at me, then quickly got back to work.

Jamie stopped in his tracks. He turned around, watching me as I walked toward him.

Tears began to slide down my face.

Stunned, Jamie said, "And you're telling me this shit because?"

"I found out I was pregnant about four weeks after I left Miami." My eyes searched his face, looking for just the smallest amount of sympathy. I didn't find any.

"So, what did you tell your man, shorty?" He looked for some common sense in my eyes. Guess he didn't find any.

"That this baby is his," I cried.

Jamie chuckled. "Well, then, shorty, that's the story that you need to stick with. You've been keepin' the story going for damn near four months, shorty. No use trying to change the story now."

I pushed him in his chest. "Jamie, I'm tellin' you this shit because this baby inside of me is yours."

He looked like he wanted to push me back, but he didn't. "And what the fuck do you expect me to do about that? You have been holding this shit inside for damn near four months, shorty. You had time to tell me about this shit way before you got engaged to your man and way before I got Ne'Vaeh back. Oh, I get it: you're doing this shit to break us up."

I shook my head at him. "No, no, this doesn't have shit to do with her."

Jamie nodded. "The hell it doesn't, Charlene! You had ample opportunities to tell me about this baby, but when the fuck do you decide to tell me? When I get back with Ne'Vaeh—that's when. You knew I wanted this girl back. You knew how hard I was going to work to get her back. And as soon as you find out that we're working things out, you decide to tell me that you're pregnant with my baby." Jamie was so angry his damn face was turning red. "You're selfish as a mutha-fucka for this! You're gonna hurt Aaron. You're gonna hurt Ne'Vaeh. You're gonna hurt me, just because you wanna be happy. This whole time, this whole situation that everyone is in is because people have been bustin' their ass just to make sure that you are happy. Aaron fucked up, but he's making amends with you, trying to give you the wedding of your dreams. And you're out here in the lobby of this expensive-ass, muthafuckin' hotel tellin' me how much you love me, how much you wanna be with me, and how much you're jealous of my relationship with your own best friend. You know she needs me, shorty. How am I supposed to tell her this shit? How am I supposed to explain to her that I got her best friend pregnant months before we even started dating again?"

I watched the tears race down his face. I was devastated. I didn't want to hurt him, but he had to know. Yes, a small part of me wanted to get Ne'Vaeh back. Okay, a huge part of me wanted to get her back, but I didn't want to hurt her at Jamie's expense. Despite the fact that he was pissed at me at that moment, he was so good to me over the past few months. I was the idiot who had stopped taking birth control after Aaron's and my sex life had slacked off months before. I didn't even think to tell Jamie to use a condom that night in Miami, because I hadn't used condoms the entire time that Aaron and I were together.

"Jamie, I fucked up. I'm sorry. But what do you expect me to do?" I cried.

He dried his face. "Get married."

"Wh—what are you gonna do?" I wiped my tears, looking at him.

Jamie shook his head at me. "Find a way to tell her without hurting her. Shorty is gonna hate me. Fuck!" His eyes searched mine. "Who else knows about this? I'm pretty sure your friends know."

"The people who caught us and my cousin, Tyra. They haven't said anything, and it's probably because they're waiting on Karma to kick my ass. Jamie, I'm sorry." I watched him backing away from me.

"Nah. This shit is my own fault. Pops told me to stop this shit before it got out of control, but I wouldn't listen. He told me that I'd lose her before I even got her back." The tears started rolling again. "Fuck, I just got to the point where she would let me hold her. I should have known this shit would catch up with me, but why did it have to be with my girl's best friend?" He walked away from me.

Jamie was so upset with me. He was so upset with himself. He had just gotten Ne'Vaeh back. She was the girl of his dreams. As long as I had known him, he had been in love with that girl. Yes, I was jealous because no one had ever loved me the way that he loved her. Both the men I cared about were infatuated with that girl, and for that, I hated her. Jamie was right; telling him that the baby was his at that time was to hurt Ne'Vaeh. I didn't intend to hurt him, though.

Chapter 4

The Checkup

Charlene

"To us." I held my glass up to Aaron the following evening at our engagement party.

"To you." The guests held up their glasses to us. Applause and cheers scattered around the room.

Tears slid down my cheeks as Aaron stood from his chair to hug me and gently kiss me on the lips. The night was going smoother than expected, considering my run-in with Jamie the afternoon before. Dinner was great, dessert was great, dancing was great, and opening gifts was great. The house was packed. Everyone was there, including Ne'Vaeh and Jamie. Watching those two together, smiling, laughing, happy, was driving me fuckin' insane. As I made my way over to them that night, Alisha made her way over to me.

"Charlie, how are you?" She approached me before I could get to Ne'Vaeh, who sat, drinking a glass of wine with Jamie.

I glanced at Ne'Vaeh, and then back at Alisha. "Hey, Alisha, what's up?"

Alisha grinned. "I just wanted to personally say congratulations."

I folded my arms across my chest, not really sure how to accept a compliment from her. "What, no 'bitch, you must be crazy marrying Aaron' or 'how the fuck could you make me miss Thanksgiving dinner in New Orleans'?"

Alisha laughed a little. "Nah, girl. I didn't wanna go back home to New Orleans this year anyway. Them muthafuckas too stuck up for me. I don't feel like dealing with my mama's people this year. And I have nothing negative to say about you and Aaron. Your business is your business, Charlie. We've been beefin' long enough, don'tcha think?"

I looked at her, trying not to cry. "Alisha, I just wanted to say—"

Alisha could tell by the whimper in my voice that I knew about her illness. She laughed to herself a little. "Ashton told you, didn't he? I told him—"

I cut her off. "Alisha, he was just trying to make a point to me about ruining my life. He's worried about you, girl. I am so sorry about this."

Alisha said, "Girl, don't, okay? All you need to take from my experience is that you have time to clean up your life before it's too late. You have been living reckless for too long. You did something great by getting involved with Aaron. You exploited yourself, sweetie. It wasn't me; it wasn't my friends; it wasn't the Morgan Girls. It was you. You had every opportunity in the world to tell Aaron the truth about your past, and you decided not to. It's a little too late to go defending yourself after Aaron hears the news about your past from everyone but you. Apparently, you didn't learn your lesson this time around either. Look at them." She looked over at Ne'Vaeh and Jamie, laughing together. Then she looked back at me. "You're gonna ruin that. That shit with Aaron and Ne'Vaeh is over. They don't speak, they don't look at each other, and they don't have shit to do with each other. Meanwhile, you haven't even told Jamie that you're having his baby."

I sighed. Man, there was no changing her. Dying or not, she still had to make me feel like shit. "Alisha, first of all, you are not in my skin. You aren't with me twenty-four-seven to tell me what I haven't talked to Jamie about. I'm trying to make amends with you, and here you are, minding my business again. This is my engagement party, Alisha. It's supposed to be my day. Why is it always about her?"

Alisha grinned. "Oh, I'm sorry, Charlie. I didn't mean to insinuate that there were more people living in this world than you. Ne'Vach is finally happy. I haven't seen that girl smile this much since junior high. Think about Ne'Vaeh and all the bullshit she's been through. Watching her mother OD every fuckin' night, watching her sister repeatedly getting raped, muthafuckas trying to rape her, finding her brother dead in his bed, watching her mother going to jail, her sister ran the fuck away, running away from foster care, having to move in with you; then Jamie leaving her. She has been through fuckin' hell, and your bitch ass isn't making it any better. I'm fuckin' dying, Charlie! I don't even know how long that I have left to live. You have so much life left to live, and you're throwing it all away. You let this shit get too far, Charlie. You need to try to fix this shit before it's too late." Alisha walked away.

I took a deep breath. I had to talk to Ne'Vaeh. I'm not going to lie; I missed talking to her. Yes, she slept with Aaron. Yes, I was pissed. Yes, she was wrong, but I was wrong too. Jamie was right when he said that I pushed Aaron to Ne'Vaeh. Instead of talking to Aaron about my feelings, I went to Jamie for comfort. It was hard not to fall in love with Jamie. When everything a person says or does to you makes your heart smile, you can't help but fall for him. If I was going to get to him, I was going to have to get to Ne'Vaeh.

Tyra was right when she said that I needed a maid of honor. I needed Ne'Vaeh to help with my wedding. Yes, I wanted to rub my marriage in her face, though I wasn't so sure where Ne'Vaeh's heart was. Alisha was right; Ne'Vaeh kept her distance from Aaron once the truth came out about the two. She was probably taking things slow with Jamie because his lifestyle was no secret. However, even more than the hoes, Ne'Vaeh was nervous about him leaving her again.

I made my way over to the two, who sat laughing together in the far corner of the ballroom, away from everyone. Their laughter faded as they saw me approaching them. Jamie looked up at me. You should have seen the look on his face.

Surprisingly, Ne'Vaeh stood from the table, throwing her arms around me, genuinely giving me a congratulations hug. That made me feel even more like a slut bucket.

"Congratulations," she squealed, squeezing, then letting go. She smiled from ear to ear, "This place looks amazing."

Jamie cleared his throat, standing from the table. "C-congratulations, shorty." He hesitated. He reached for a handshake.

I smiled, shaking my head, giving him a hug instead. Oh my, he smelled so fuckin' good. I got a quick whiff in before letting him go. "Thank you both so much." I looked at Ne'Vaeh, who stood there looking amazing in her beige, slinky cocktail dress. "I really appreciate you both coming, even after all the bullshit we've been through since last month. I just wanted to let you know that there are no hard feelings, and I wanted to ask you, Ne'Vaeh, if you'd like to be my maid of honor."

Jamie looked at me. He wasn't sure of my motive for asking her to be a part of my wedding, but he knew I was up to something.

Ne'Vaeh hesitated. "I—I'm honored, but with all that's happened between us, I don't really think I'm the best choice."

I guess she wasn't over Aaron. She couldn't quite handle a front-row seat to our marriage. I shook my head in disagreement. "What do you mean you don't think you're the best choice? Who would be a better choice than you, Ne'Vaeh?"

Ne'Vaeh shrugged. "I don't know. Kelissa, Dana, Danita, your cousin Tyra, your cousin Kimba, your little sister—you have plenty of ladies to choose from. Shit, even Alisha is a better choice than me. I don't deserve that title, Charlie, and I'm really not sure that I even want it." Ne'Vaeh looked at Jamie, her brown eyes coated in tears.

"Ne'Vaeh, I am trying to be civil here. You are the only person on earth that I want to be my maid of honor," I exclaimed.

Ne'Vaeh shook her head. "Charlie, I slept with your fuckin' soon-to-be-husband. I'm flat-out telling you that I slept with him, whether or not the boy wants to admit the truth to you. It was a mistake, and it never should have happened. Even when I told the boy flat-out no, we shouldn't be doin' this, stop, he still wouldn't listen. If you still wanna marry the muthafucka after knowing the truth, that's cool; that's your business. Regardless of how, what, why, when, or where it happened—a friend who would sleep with your boyfriend is not fuckin' maid of honor material."

I sighed. I was glad the bitch admitted the truth, even though she was basically saying that my man made her sleep with him. Regardless, I was just as wrong as she was. When I slept with Jamie on that beautiful beach in Miami, I gave Aaron unspoken permission to sleep with whomever he wanted, best friend included. What happened was my fault. Though I took full responsibility for what happened between Aaron and Ne'Vaeh, I was pissed at Ne'Vaeh for sleeping with him. Yes, I admit, I wanted to get the bitch back. Yes, I was falling for Jamie. And, yes, I wanted to ruin her life the way that she was ruining mine.

"Sweetie, that's all water under the bridge." I took her hand in mine. "Please, Ne'Vaeh, don't make me ask Kelissa's ass to be my maid of honor. That bitch doesn't even like me, but she did look bad as hell in that dress she picked out for the wedding."

Ne'Vaeh's eyes searched me as she slid her hand from mine. "Charlie, do you really want a groupie to stand beside you at your wedding? How would that make you look, associating with a woman who couldn't keep her fuckin' legs closed? Who was fuckin' around with the groom?"

Ouch. She was still mad at me for calling her a groupie. I knew she would never forgive me for that.

I sighed. "Ne'Vaeh, you know I didn't mean it. I was just pissed at what—"

Ne'Vaeh put her hand up. "Ya know, Charlie, find someone else. Jamie, are you ready to leave? I'm really not feeling so well."

Jamie looked at her, taking her hand in his. "Yeah, shorty. Let me just holla at Charlie real quick. Wait for me in the lobby."

Ne'Vaeh nodded, and then looked at me, tears lining her lashes. "Congratulations again, Charlie."

When Ne'Vaeh was out of sight, Jamie turned to me. "Charlene, what the fuck are you doing?"

I played innocent. "What do you mean? I'm just trying to make amends with my best friend."

"Nah, you're fuckin' with her, and you need to stop. Back the fuck up off of her, Charlie," he whispered as guests walked by.

I waved goodbye to a few guests that were calling it a night. "No, Jamie, I'm not fuckin' with your girl." I looked up at him. "I want my best friend to be my maid of honor."

"First, you wanna rub the fact in that you're marrying the dude she was in love with for a few years, and now you wanna rub in the fact that you're having my baby. You're so obsessed with you winning and her losing, and the shit is fucked up. You need to focus on getting married and leave my girl out of it." He walked away from me.

***

"Good morning, Baltimore! It's your girl, Janae Paterson. And if you weren't tuned in before the commercial break, we are sitting here with the new quarterback of the Baltimore Ravens, Jamie Green. Welcome, Jamie!" Janae Paterson welcomed Jamie to WJMZ 99.1, a popular XM radio station in Baltimore City, that cold morning of Christmas Eve. The interview was prerecorded a few days earlier. I missed it the first time around. Every football groupie in Maryland was talking about Jamie's interview, so I had to see what the fuss was about.

"Thank you for having me. It's a pleasure to be here." I could hear Jamie smiling. His voice sounded amazing.

"Okay, fellas, enough with this damn NFL talk. The ladies ain't really trying to hear about all that," Kylie Hall, the flirtatious cohost chimed in. "Now, what the ladies of Baltimore really wanna know is . . . Are you seeing anybody?"

Jamie laughed a little. "Yes, I am."

"You, a new NFL player, and a dude who has been making sports headlines since junior high school, tied himself down to just one chick?" Raphael Lawrence, the host of the morning show, was shocked to hear of Jamie's relationship status.

"This one is special, Raphael. She's smart, she's sexy, she's funny, she's talented, and she's everything I need. She's this short, beautiful black woman with a milk chocolate complexion, deep dimples, and hips, thighs, and legs that'll make you say got-damn. Ass so juicy it makes you wanna just take a bite out of it," Jamie proudly exclaimed.

I rolled my eyes. "Oh, puh-lease."

The radio staff laughed.

"So, I guess I don't have to even ask if the sex is good or not?" Raphael Lawrence said.

"Man, that pussy be sayin', 'Come inside, it's fun inside.'" Jamie laughed.

The hosts were laughing their asses off.

"OMG, Jamie, the Mickey Mouse Clubhouse song, really?" Janae Paterson laughed. "I watch that show with my two-year-old. Okay, I'm never gonna look at that cartoon the same way again. There's no doubt that you love this woman. What do you like about her the most?"

"She's amazing. Seriously, on the real, the best part about her is—" Jamie laughed a little, "she doesn't even know how fine she is. She doesn't know her walk is hypnotizing. Doesn't know her kisses make me weak. Doesn't know her touch drives me fuckin' crazy. Doesn't even know that her smile can get me to do just about anything. I met her when I was three years old, and I have been in love ever since."

"I wish a muthafucka would talk about me like that," Janae Paterson responded. "She must be someone special."

"So, no side chicks? You know, I don't mind being on the sidelines." Kylie Hall was throwin' the pussy at him.

Jamie laughed. "No offense to you or anyone who chooses to be with you, but it would take about ten of you just to make one of her."

"Oh, it's like that, huh? Okay, okay, I'll keep it in the jar." Kylie laughed off her embarrassment as the radio staff had a hard time keeping down the laughter.

"I mean, I'm not trying to offend anyone. It's just I'm in love, shorty. When you have someone who you want to spend all your time with, who you wanna fall asleep and wake up next to, who makes you smile even when you're angry, and who still makes your heart flutter in your chest after sixteen years, then you'll feel me, shorty. She's my air, my heart, my soul. Without her, there is no me." Jamie sighed.

"Well, I heard from a little birdy on the street that you're not a one-woman man. In fact, the little birdy that told me that also said that she had been in several threesomes with you, sometimes even four or five women," Janae Paterson remarked.

"Damn, playa," Raphael Lawrence cosigned.

Jamie laughed. "I'll admit, I was a—"

Kylie felt the need to cut him off, getting her lick back. "A ho."

"Ladies' man," he corrected her. "But I've changed. I gave it all up for her. Like I said, it takes multiple women to even come close to her. No woman makes me feel like she does. She's a keeper. I think I found me one, y'all."

"Uh-oh, sounds like I hear wedding bells in the very near future." Janae Paterson tried to pry.

"Let's make it through next season before we start talkin' about marriage, shorty." Jamie laughed.

I rolled my eyes, switching the station. "Let me turn from this bullshit."

Hearing Jamie talk about how much he was in love with Ne'Vaeh made me sick to my stomach. I was having his baby, and there he was talkin' about Ne'Vaeh. An entire month had gone by since I'd broken the news to him about being pregnant with his baby, and he hadn't called me once. He was in denial. He didn't want to face the fact that he was having a baby with his girl's best friend; but the truth couldn't stay hidden for long.

There I was, twenty-one weeks pregnant, and just one week from my wedding. It was getting harder and harder to keep up with Aaron. Not only were two teams bidding over him state-side, there were a few teams overseas that were also interested. Aaron spent more and more time with his agent than with me. That was to be expected. It seemed like everyone was too busy to help me out with anything. Nothing I did was good enough to accommodate my family or my so-called friends for my wedding. Each brides-maid wanted her dress a different style. No one could agree on the main course for the recep-tion. I couldn't get in touch with Ne'Vaeh to ask her to get Darryl to hook me up with a sexy male R&B singer for my wedding. She hadn't said too much to me since I asked her to be my maid of honor. She was purposely avoiding me.

I was on my way to my prenatal checkup. At my sixteen-week checkup, the baby had his or her legs closed so we couldn't tell the sex of the baby. I was excited about finding out what sex the baby was, so I could finally name the baby, instead of calling it "The Baby." Aaron wasn't answering his phone, and he knew that I had the appointment that afternoon. It was getting real annoying going to visits alone. I guess God was trying to tell me something.

I walked down the hallway to the lobby of the hospital to check in, and you already know whom I ran into—Jamie. I was a little relieved to see him. I hadn't seen him since my engagement party. He grinned when he saw me approaching him.

"Happy Christmas Eve, Jamie." I smiled up at him.

He grinned. "What's up, shorty?"

"What are you doing here?" I asked.

"Just picking up Ne'Vaeh's medicine from the pharmacy." He looked down at my belly that was finally starting to round out. Then he looked back up at me. "How have you been?"

I sighed. "Well, I would be doing fine if Aaron would actually show up to an appointment with me every once in a while. How are things with you and Ne'Vaeh going? I heard your radio interview."

Jamie chuckled. "Well, shorty, Ne'Vaeh didn't. I'm not really sure how things are going with us. She never spends the night. Still won't admit to herself that I'm really here. I have all this free time on my hands, since I don't start training until next year. I'm spending all of my time with her, but she still doesn't see me, Shorty. We have sex; it's amazing, no words to describe it, but when it's over, she gets up and leaves. She's been staying with Renée. I'm ready to commit to her, Charlie, but she won't let me. I'm not one to give up, but I'm not sure what else to do."

I smiled. "Guess she's just serving you with a little bit of your own medicine." He knew he was good at fuckin' a bitch, and then dismissing her. Yeah, I know my timing was always off with the jokes, but he needed to hear that he'd treated girls like shit for years for that girl.

Jamie looked at me, not really in the mood for my shit. "Charlie, you never know when not to throw punches."

"Jamie, you know I'm just joking with you. She'll come around." I smiled, though I hated to hear that he was so sprung over that girl.

"Shorty, I bought her a ring, and I'm scared as a muthafucka to give it to her."

My eyes immediately coated in tears. *What the fuck?* Shit was about to get real.

"Charlene Campbell." The radiologist walked through the double doors to the lobby, calling my name.

I looked up at Jamie. "You wanna come with me, find out what the baby is?"

He hesitated. He didn't want to acknowledge or admit to himself that my baby was his. However, I wasn't going to give him a choice. I grabbed his hand, pulling him off to the back with me.

"Well, are you ready to find out the baby's sex?" The radiologist seemed more excited than I was. "Are you nervous?" she smiled at me.

I grinned as the doctor squirted more warm gel over my belly. "Yes." I looked over at Jamie.

Jamie sat on a stool, a few feet away from me. He seemed nervous, looking at the distorted images on the sonogram monitor. He watched as the radiologist began to glide the transducer probe across my belly.

The radiologist looked at Jamie. "You nervous, Daddy?" She could tell by the frustrated look on his face that he was the father, and may not have wanted to be.

Jamie looked at her, then back at me. "Her fiancé couldn't be here, so I'm just here for emotional support, shorty."

My eyes teared. He was still in denial, even when faced with the truth.

The radiologist laughed nervously with this 'I'm-not-even-going-to-ask-questions' look on her face. "Okay. This is the head. That's the abdomen. There are the baby's little feet. And, wait for it—it's a boy." She was so excited.

Tears slid down my face, but I quickly dried them away. I looked up at Jamie.

Jamie was already in tears. He stood from the seat. "I'm—" He choked. "I'm gonna go smoke a cigarette, shorty. I'll be outside." He left the room.

The radiologist looked at me, her own eyes watery as well. "It's none of my business, Charlene, but Daddy doesn't seem too happy about this."

I nodded in agreement. "Yeah," I whispered. "Guess I'm not the person he really wanted to share this moment with."

Jamie stood at the curb at the end of the sidewalk, exhaling smoke from his nose. He turned around to face me when he heard the heels of my boots clattering against the cement. He looked down at me as I approached him; then he shook his head, tears gliding down his face.

I reached to dry his tears, but he pushed my hands away, shaking his head at me.

"Chantelle is the name of the girl in Mississippi that I got pregnant. Shorty was devastated after she had the abortion. Hates herself, and she hates me; said she got rid of the baby because she knew that I would never be able to love her or the baby." Jamie flicked his cigarette into the street. "I would have loved that baby. The baby shouldn't have had to pay for our mistake. She just thought that since I couldn't love her, then I wouldn't love any part of her."

I looked up at him. "What are you saying, Jamie?"

Jamie dried his face. "I'm gonna be honest with you, because this is just who I am. I'm the realest nigga you are ever gonna meet in your fuckin' life. Charlene, I don't wanna have a baby with you. This is the most fucked-up situation that I have ever been in. You could have told me that you were pregnant before I worked my ass off to get Ne'Vaeh back. How the fuck am I supposed to tell her this shit?"

Jamie was furious with me when he should have been with himself. What he said to me hurt like a muthafucka; he had absolutely no feelings for me, when I was at the verge of telling Aaron that the wedding was off, because I wanted to be with Jamie.

"Oh, so you're pissed at me for keeping this baby. Is that what you're saying?" I folded my arms across my chest.

Jamie laughed bitterly, shaking his head. "The fact that people are gonna get hurt hasn't even crossed your selfish-ass mind, has it? I bought this girl a fuckin' ring. I want this girl to be my wife. My firstborn son was supposed to be with her, not with your ass, Charlie."

Tears slid down my face, but I quickly dried them away. "Well, it's too late to be angry, Jamie.

You can't un-fuck me. You can't undo what happened these past few months. Yes, I regret lying to you and lying to Aaron, but I don't regret how you made me feel. It felt so good to be with you, Jamie. No one has ever made me feel the way that you make me feel. No one. You don't remember telling me that my pussy was the softest place on earth? You don't remember tellin' me that shit, Jamie? I can't believe that you're gonna stand there and lie to me and tell me that it didn't feel good."

Jamie looked down into my face. "Yeah, it felt good, but it feels so much better with her, shorty."

The muthafucka was breaking my heart. I never knew my heart could feel so much pain. Hearing him telling me that I didn't mean shit to him hurt worse than it did when I found out that my nanny's daughter caught Aaron and Ne'Vaeh fuckin' in that expensive suite at the hotel.

Defeated, I said, "You're sayin' this shit just to hurt me, Jamie, and it's not cool." Tears slid down my face.

Jamie shook his head. "Nah, I'm not sayin' this shit to hurt you, Charlene. I'm sayin' this shit because it's the fuckin' truth. This situation is fucked up, shorty. Tell me what you're gonna name this baby. My baby, my firstborn son."

I looked up at him. "August Carter." August because it was both my favorite month and it was the month that he was conceived, though Aaron didn't know that. Carter because it was Aaron's father's family tradition to give it as the middle name to the firstborn son.

"Whitehaven, Campbell, or Green?" he asked.

I hesitated for a few seconds. I really hadn't even thought about whose last name that I was going to give my baby. It would look suspicious as hell giving him my last name if I was marrying Aaron. It would be deceiving to give the baby Aaron's last name when I knew the baby wasn't his. And I couldn't give the baby Jamie's last name for obvious reasons.

My lips trembled. "I—I don't know, Jamie." Tears streamed down my cheeks.

"Charlene, do you wanna marry Aaron?" His eyes searched my face. "Because if the answer's yes, you can't tell the muthafucka that this baby is mine. You gettin' married in eight days, shorty. I love Ne'Vaeh, and because I do, I'm gonna have to break up with her. I can't be with her, knowing I have a baby with you. It's killing me, keeping this secret from her. She's holding back from me, because in her heart, she knows something's not right." Jamie started crying, backing away from me.

"Jamie, everything is gonna be okay." I cried with him.

He shook his head. "Nah, it's not, shorty. You play too many fuckin' games. I think you actually like this shit. When you thought your man was leaving you for her, you tricked him into thinking this baby was his. And now that you know that I wanna be with shorty, you tell me the baby is mine. I was supposed to be sitting in that doctor's office, holding her hand, listening to the radiologist tellin' Ne'Vaeh that we're having a boy. Not you, Charlie. Not you."

With that, he left me standing there on the curb alone.

Chapter 5

The Visit

Charlene

You know I had to fake my way through Christmas Day. My parents' house was packed with guests that afternoon. My mother's entire family paid us a visit that day. I saw family members that I hadn't seen in years. Uncle Carlito's wife and kids came to visit. I was so happy to see them. It was their first Christmas without Uncle Carlito. They needed all the love and comfort that they could get. Aaron's sister and aunt paid us a visit. Even his parents flew in from California to spend time with us. Ashton stopped by with Alisha. She had lost so much weight in just a month's time. She was dying, but she kept a smile on her face. The Morgan Girls stopped by that afternoon. Even

Renée paid me a visit. I was shocked to see her walking through the door that afternoon, dressed in all white from head to toe.

She hugged me around my neck, after handing me a Christmas card. "Merry Christmas," she whispered in my ear.

I hugged her back, then let her go, looking down at the card. The card said: *From Juanita.* I looked at Renée. "Juanita sent me a Christmas card?"

Renée shook her head. "No. She sent it to Ne'Vaeh. It came in my mail the day before yesterday. I couldn't give it to her. She's already having a bad enough Christmas as it is. Jamie broke up with her last night."

My eyes widened. I don't know why I was so shocked. Jamie always did what he said that he was going to do. He was a cold mutha-fucka, breaking up with the girl the day before Christmas, as if her life wasn't fucked up enough. "Are you serious?" I exclaimed.

Renée folded her arms across her chest. "Yeah. Do you know anything about that?"

I looked up at her. She knew something. I wasn't sure how much she knew, but she knew something. "No. Why would I know something about Jamie breaking up with Ne'Vaeh?"

"I don't know, Charlie, but I'm starting to think there's some truth to what Alisha's been saying about you. If you didn't know anything about Jamie breaking up with Ne'Vaeh, tell me why I saw you talking to Jamie outside of Johns Hopkins Medical Center yesterday." Renée's eyes searched my face for a reaction. "Dude was crying. You were crying. Y'all muthafuckas were cursing each other out, out in the open." Renée struggled to keep her voice down.

I shook my head. I forgot the bitch did work mids at the hospital. She was probably just getting off work when she saw us. I apparently wasn't careful enough hiding the truth. "Renée, I don't know what you think you know about this, but—"

Renée put her hand in my face. "I don't wanna know shit about the games that you're playing. My cousin is hurting right now, and I know got-damn well that you're the cause of it. I could dig deep into this shit if I wanted to, but I don't wanna be a part of it. All I want you to do for me is go visit Juanita at the prison this afternoon. I put your name on the visitation list. Visitation starts at four." She looked at her watch. "It's two-thirty now, so maybe you better be on your way."

Shaking my head, I said, "Renée, no. Why the fuck would I wanna visit Juanita? The bitch killed my friend's brother. Why would I wanna speak to her?"

"Because she may say something that your ass needs to hear." Renée walked past me, her shoulder shoving against mine.

Tyra drove me to the Maryland Correctional Facility for Women in Jessup. I seriously wasn't ready for a visit with that woman. I hadn't seen the bitch since I was thirteen. Back then, Juanita was gone. She wasn't in her right frame of mind. She was strung out on all types of drugs. I think I even got high with her a few times in those days. If you wanted to get high, drunk, or fucked up, she was the one to go to. I think she even introduced me to the first guy that I had sex with. My mother couldn't stand her for those very reasons. The only reason she even let me go anywhere near that woman was because she had a soft spot for Ne'Vaeh.

I didn't want to go into the prison alone. Tyra didn't want to go in at all, because she didn't want to see Juanita's face. Why Renée thought I should talk to the bitch, I had no idea. But I knew Renée played dirty. Whatever she knew about my situation, she would air my dirty laundry if I didn't do what she asked.

I checked in with the front desk. There were so many people there that Christmas Day. Little children, husbands, mothers, fathers; it was a very depressing scene. I sat down at the phone in the visiting station, waiting for Juanita to sit across from me. You could imagine the look on her face when she approached her seat, seeing me sitting across from her. Juanita looked good to my surprise. Her dark hair fell below her shoulders. Her caramel skin glistened under the prison lights. Her eyebrows were perfectly arched. Dark, luminous lashes surrounded her bright hazel eyes. Dimples pierced her cheeks, though she wasn't smiling. She was a beautiful sight to see.

She slowly picked up her phone.

I picked up mine as well.

She hesitated to speak. "Well," she choked, "Charlene Campbell, how are you?"

My lips trembled. I didn't even know what to say to her, except, "I don't think I've ever seen you sober before."

Juanita laughed a little. "Sobriety looks good on me, huh?" She always had a joke or two to lighten the mood.

I laughed a little. "Yeah. Wish your daughter could have seen a little more of it growing up."

Juanita's smile faded. She cleared her throat. "H-how is she?"

I shook my head. "Not good."

"Yeah, by the look on your face, I'd say you may be playing a small part in that." Juanita's eyes penetrated my soul.

I just looked at her.

She nodded. "Trust me, babe, I have eyes all around my baby. Not to mention Jamie came to visit me last month on Thanksgiving."

My eyes widened. I shouldn't have been surprised. Jamie came from a fucked-up family. He was always searching for answers from women who abandoned their children. He was pissed at all women right about then. Ne'Vaeh was the only woman in his life who didn't treat him like shit. Ne'Vaeh should have been more fucked up than all of us, after the shit that she'd seen. It was no wonder she had heart problems. The people who she loved the most had broken her heart repeatedly.

"Jamie has been visiting you?" I exclaimed.

"Just once." Juanita's eyes watered. "He's feeling guilty. Says he wants to marry my baby, but he can't because of you."

I shook my head. "I didn't fuck myself, Juanita. So before you go listening to Jamie, you should realize that there are two sides to every story."

Juanita laughed at my sarcasm. "He admitted that he slept with you a few times. He admitted that he slept with a lot of women. He didn't deny that he had made a mistake. He didn't deny that he has lived a fast and dangerous life. He never denied that he slept with about fifteen girls or more a week. He fully took responsibility for his fuckups. I have seen that boy all over the television. I have been following all of his football games since he was in middle school. I knew that he loved my baby. I knew he would show her the love that I couldn't." Tears slid down her cheeks. "He really loves that girl, Charlene. And the shit bothers you, doesn't it?"

In denial, I shook my head. "I'm getting married. Why should that bother me, Juanita?"

"Bullshit!" she yelled out. "He said that you waited until he had gotten back with my daughter before you decided to tell him that you were pregnant. Why? Why did you do that shit to him? You knew he wanted to be with her. You know my daughter needs that boy. You could have any nigga you wanted, so why would you fuck with him?"

My cheeks wet, I said, "You know, Juanita, you can't sit here and try to play the holier-than-thou role, when the reason why you're up in this bitch is because you murdered your own fuckin' son. The daughter you now all of a sudden give a fuck about found his body, black, blue, and lifeless in his bed the morning after you suffocated him. You beat him lifeless, but you have the fuckin' nerve to ask me about what I chose to do with my life and how it affects your daughter? How the fuck do you think what you did affects your daughter, Juanita?"

Tears gushed down her face, but she quickly dried them. "I have owned up to what I did to my children. I'm stuck in this bitch for life. I'm gonna die in this bitch, Charlene. I'm living day by day with the guilt of what I did to my children. Don't try to twist the blame back around on me, Charlie. I know I fucked up my daughter's life. You were the one who tried to help make it better. She looked up to you. She trusted you. Whatever happened with that muthafucka Aaron wasn't her fault, and you know it. The muthafucka practically forced himself on her, even after she told him no. Did the muthafucka tell you that? My baby loved you, Charlene, and you are letting your jealousy fuck up your life and hers too."

"Well, what do you expect me to do, Juanita? The damage is already done. He broke up with her yesterday, according to your niece, Renée."

Juanita was stunned. "What?"

I nodded. "And it's my fault. I made him go with me to my sonogram visit. I ran into him at the hospital yesterday, and I made him see the sex of his baby. We're having a boy."

Juanita laughed, shaking her head. "How do you think that boy feels having his firstborn son with a woman he doesn't give a fuck about?"

I cried aloud, standing up from the stool. I wanted to slam that phone right through the window into her face, but what would have been the point in that? She wasn't wrong about anything that she was saying.

"Charlene, sit down," she demanded.

"Fuck you, Juanita," I cried, sitting back down, screaming into the phone. "Bitch, you have no right to judge me. Nobody loves me; nobody gives a fuck about me. All everyone cares about is Ne'Vaeh and whether she's happy. Well, what about me? The bitch stole my family, she stole my boyfriend, and she stole Jamie's heart, when I have been trying to get it since we were fuckin' kids." I finally admitted my feelings for Jamie. I had never once vocally expressed how I felt about him.

Juanita sighed. "Well, you need to tell Ne'Vaeh that she has a nephew on the way."

I was confused. "A nephew?"

Juanita said, "Have you ever asked your mother why she hated me so much? Why we haven't been friends since senior year in high school? I haven't spoken to your mother since she was having you in the hospital, July 6, 1995. She got pregnant by your father in October of 1994. And I got pregnant by your father in January of 1995."

My eyes widened. I was in shock. I shook my head at her. "You're lying, Juanita."

She grinned. "No, I'm not lying. I loved your father with all of my heart. Your parents broke up that month. Your father and I got drunk at this party and ended up sleeping together. One thing led to another, and we slept together for months before he decided to get back with your mother. By the time he got back with her, I was already four months pregnant. He begged me not to tell her. I only told her just to hurt him. Your mother was seven months pregnant and whupped my ass at senior prom." Juanita's stared at me. "Don't tell me that you didn't do this shit to hurt Jamie for not loving you. I have been where you are, so I know firsthand what it's like to love a muthafucka, who loves your best friend. Karma is a bitch, Charlene. Y'all can't let these men come between you two. Y'all are more than best friends—y'all are sisters. And you owe your sister an apology."

I was stunned. Ne'Vaeh and I were sisters? My mother knew all along. That was the reason why she loved Ne'Vaeh so much. That was the reason why she replaced my father with Ne'Vaeh when he passed away. I was having my sister's nephew by a man who she was in love with. Oh, I had fucked up more than I knew.

I didn't even tell Tyra what Juanita told me that day. Instead of going straight over Ne'Vaeh's house, I went straight back to my mother's. The house was still full of guests. The Christmas party was nowhere near being over. My mother was in the kitchen, asking one of the caterers if there was any more champagne.

"Mama, we need to talk," I spoke to her.

"Honey," my mother brushed me off anxiously, "I don't really have time right now. We are out of champagne, and the kids are breaking shit all over the house. I don't know why your aunt Stacen thinks I'm her got-damn babysitter. And where is your sister? She's supposed to be helping me serve." She set wineglasses on the countertop frantically. She was always stuck serving guests alone without any help.

"Mama, why the hell didn't you tell me that Ne'Vaeh was my sister?" I exclaimed.

My mother stopped in her tracks, looking at me as if I just told her someone had come back from the dead. She cleared everyone out of the kitchen; then she turned to me. "Who told you this?" she hesitated, gripping a wineglass in her hand.

"What? Who told me? Why the fuck didn't you tell me?" I shouted.

My mother approached me as if I'd gotten loud with the wrong one. "Look, I'm only asking you one more time to watch your mouth, Charlene. Being pregnant doesn't mean you have an 'S' on your chest."

I sighed. I don't know why Mama had it in her head that I was just gonna still let her whup me with a belt—old people.

"Ma, is it true?" I looked into her light eyes.

She hesitated. "Charlene, there's a lot you don't know about me, and I really would have liked to keep it that way. While I was dating your father, he was also sleeping with Juanita. She claims that she only slept with him after we broke up, but I didn't and still don't believe her. Regardless, it was wrong for her to sleep with him, knowing I was pregnant with his baby. Once we got back together, she waited until prom to tell me that she was pregnant with his child. We haven't been friends ever since. I really loved Juanita. We were best friends since the first grade; I never trusted anyone else after her. You know, your father didn't want anything to do with Ne'Vaeh. I think that was really what made Juanita start living the way she did. She came from a broken home; her own father tried to sleep with her, her own mother abandoned her. She looked for love anywhere that she could get it." Tears wet Mama's cheeks as I forced her to relive her past. "Ne'Vaeh was the sweetest little girl. She had her father's smile and her mother's eyes. I fell in love with that little girl, even though I hated her mother for ruining my life. When your father died, I held all my children close, and maybe I held her a little closer, because I knew she needed love a little more than you kids did. You know Ne'Vaeh needed love, Charlene."

My cheeks were wet right along with hers. "Yeah, but so did I, Ma. I have resented that girl for so long, because of everyone's love and affection toward her. I was heartbroken when Dad died, Ma. Do you know how many men I slept with? Do you know many women I slept with? Ma, do you know how fucked up I am? Do you know I'm not even pregnant by Aaron?"

My mother was stunned to silence. She wasn't sure what she could say to me at that moment that would make the situation any better.

I sighed. "I'm pregnant by Jamie, Ma."

I didn't even see it coming. My mother slapped me right across the face.

I just looked at her, lips trembling, hair covering my face.

"Jamie? Ne'Vaeh's Jamie?" she cried. "You are getting married to Aaron in one week, Charlene. Why would you do this to your best friend? Why would you do this to Jamie or Aaron or to yourself?"

Pushing my hair from my face, tears sliding down my cheeks, I never felt so stupid. "Mama, I love him."

Mama dried her face, her ivory cheeks turning bright red. "Who, baby? Jamie or Aaron?" Disgusted, she walked past me. "Charlene, I was so proud of you when you and Aaron sat down with me a few weeks ago. Aaron was so nervous asking for my blessing, for me to accept his proposal to you. He gave you a beautiful ring that had been passed down through generations in his house. I don't know anything about what you two are going through, but what I do know is that Aaron cares enough about you to marry you, despite your faults. True, his family doesn't believe in getting a woman pregnant outside of marriage, but he didn't have to follow that tradition. He could have bailed on you. He could have done you the same way that your father did Juanita when he found out that she was pregnant. He married me right in front of her face, just to prove to her that she didn't mean anything to him." Mama slammed the wineglass on the kitchen counter, breaking it at the base, slicing the palm of her hand right down the middle.

"Mama!" I rushed over to her, immediately taking her hand in mine.

"Honey, just wet a towel." She cried as I rushed over to the sink to wet a towel.

I hurried back over to her, wrapping the wet towel around her hand. Tears slid down my face as I held her hand in mine, applying pressure to her wound.

Mama watched the tears slide down my face. "Does Jamie know?"

I nodded, not able to look at her. "He's really hating me right now, Mama."

"Does Ne'Vaeh know?" She hesitated to ask.

I shook my head. "No. I don't think so. I'm not sure. All I know is that Jamie broke up with her last night. I never meant to get pregnant by Jamie. I was stupid, and I was careless. It's my own fault that Aaron has a hard time loving me. When I found out that I was pregnant, I told Aaron it was his. I never meant to hurt anybody, Mama." I looked up into her sad blue eyes.

Mama was upset with me and had that same disappointed look on her face the day she stopped me from having the abortion. "You're gonna ruin a lot of lives this week, sweetie. You're gonna ruin a nice young man's life if you marry Aaron, knowing that he isn't the father of this baby. You're gonna ruin your sister's life by telling her that you're carrying the baby of the man who she's waited four years to have back in her life. And you're gonna ruin Jamie's life, a man who went from nothing to something, in hopes of making his mother finally see him and the love of his life know that he didn't leave her in vain. January 1, 2015, marks the beginning and end of your life with the people who you love the most. You can't have them both, Charlene. Figure out a way to fix this, Charlie, before it's too late."

Chapter 6

Can't Find the Words

Ne'Vaeh

Jamie kissed the "J" tattoo on the back of my neck before peeling his body from mine that chilly morning in November. The way he woke me up in the morning was amazing. Every time we would have sex, it always felt like the first time. Everything that boy did sent chills up and down my spine. I never knew someone's touch could make me feel so good. I loved everything about him. From the way he ran his fingers through my hair, to the way he made love to me, to the way he kissed my lips, to the way he undressed me, to the way he said my name. He gave me that I'm-about-to-get-my-tax-refund feeling. He was perfect, too perfect.

Jamie wasn't lying when he told me that he could change for me. There wasn't a place that he went that he didn't invite me to go with him. Every night with him felt like we were at the Grammy's. The hoes didn't back off, even when they saw us together holding hands. The fact that he had a girl made them try even harder to get his attention. Girls would show up to his autograph signings in nothing but bra and panties. Others would show up to restaurants that we were dining at wearing nothing but a raincoat and high heels. Nurse Helen's feelings were hurt when he ended things with her. She claimed she had no feelings for him, but I knew when I first met her that she was in love with Jamie.

Jamie did everything he could to try to get me to move in with him. As soon as we got back from Tennessee, I moved in with Renée. I hated every minute of living with her only because she thought she was my mother and because her boyfriend (or should I say "Fuck Buddy") slept there on the couch every night. Either the two were having sex out in the open, or they were at each other's throats. Jamie didn't want me in the midst of that drama, but I wasn't ready to move in with him. My heart and mind were at war with each other from the moment Jamie stepped foot back in Maryland.

Jamie had gotten my name tattooed over his heart. I was a little skeptical about getting a man's name on my body that wasn't promised to me forever. I got a fancy "J" tattooed on the back of my neck, the very place that I loved to feel his lips. I hesitated every time Jamie went to hug or kiss me. After sex, I would barely let him hold me. I hadn't spent the night with him since before his father passed away. Since I moved back in with Renée, Jamie made it a habit to show up every morning at 7:15 to wake me up for class. He spoiled the hell out of me with clothes and jewelry. He even let me drive his baby, his black, chromed-out Cadillac Escalade. Jamie was crazy about his cars, and there was no way he would let just anyone drive them. But he let me. Me, the girl who had a hard time loving him back. Here it was, the day before Thanksgiving, and I couldn't even admit to myself that Jamie was back in my life again.

"Are we gonna talk about this, shorty?" Jamie sat down on the edge of the bathtub and lit a cigarette as he watched me undress in the bathroom at my cousin's apartment that morning.

"Talk about what?" I slid off my panties, going over to the shower to turn the water on.

He looked at me, exhaling smoke from his nose. "You leaving your cousin's apartment and coming to stay with me."

My eyes grew misty, but I wasn't going to cry in front of him today. I rolled my eyes as I climbed into the shower. "Jamie, just yesterday, you asked me to meet you at your mansion. As I walked up to your mansion, some bitch shows up in her red Corvette asking me if you were home. When I told the bitch you weren't home, she was like, 'You must be Ne'Vaeh, his childhood sweetheart. Sweetie, when he gets home, could you ask him if I left my panties by the pool a few weeks ago?'"

Jamie laughed nervously. "The Puerto Rican chick?"

I nodded, "Yeah, Jamie, the li'l Puerto Rican chick." Vexed, I stood underneath the showerhead, washing my hair. "These groupies are gonna make me catch a case, I swear. I'm trying to hold it together, but you know my temper when it comes to you. My love for you is a very lethal weapon, Jamie. This is why I was telling you in the beginning that I wasn't ready to be sprung like this." I closed my eyes, rinsing my hair.

"Well, shorty, I saw your boy, Aaron, the other day. Every time I see that nigga, I wanna knock his ass the fuck out. We both are feeling some type of way about the past; it's normal, Ne'Vaeh." I felt cold air as Jamie swept the curtain back and climbed into the shower.

I wiped the excess water from my face before grabbing the bottle of shampoo that sat alongside the bathtub. "What? How can you even compare the two, Jamie? My past is across town, minding his own fuckin' business. Meanwhile, your past shows up at your mansion, your events, autograph signings, radio appearances, to my fuckin' classes at school, and to restaurants while we're fuckin' eating, Jamie. Yeah, Aaron showed up to your father's funeral, for what I don't know. But you don't have to constantly be reminded that we slept together. I can guarantee you right now that at least three groupies are gonna show up to your dinner party tonight."

Jamie exhaled loudly, taking the shampoo bottle from my hands. "Ne'Vaeh, bae, I promise you that no unwanted guests will show up tonight. I'm through with the hoes, Ne'Vaeh, I promise you. You know I never make a promise that I can't keep." Water trickled down his body as he poured shampoo into his hand. He set the bottle back down on the edge of the tub, and then pulled my body closer to his before lathering my hair.

My body trembled up against his as his fingertips massaged my scalp. Everything he did to me made the insides of my thighs throb.

"Hopefully, you can learn to trust me enough to add a few more letters to that 'J' on your neck." He gently kissed my lips. "I love you, Ne'Vaeh. You be having a muthafucka goin' crazy. You see my ass is over here every morning, shorty. It feels good as fuck makin' love to you every morning, noon, and night. It would feel even better if I got to wake up next to you every morning, instead of comin' by your cousin's crib to see you. I don't know how I'm gonna make it through football training camp. Shit, I'll probably pay to have you fly out to a hotel close by." he chuckled. "You got a muthafucka goin' crazy."

I blushed, eyes misty. "You already said that, Jamie. Trust me, I feel the same way. Sex every day, sex every night. Every night is date night. Every night we're going somewhere different. Every day, a new outfit or a pair of shoes or a necklace or a bracelet. Yesterday, you bought me a new Apple iPad. You're spoiling the hell out of me, Jamie. I'm not used to shit like this. You don't have to buy my heart, Jamie, because it's already yours."

Jamie backed me under the showerhead a little more to rinse the suds from my hair. "I'm just trying to give you all of the things you deserve, and more. I've been gone a long time, shorty. And now that I'm back, I'm trying to find a way to make it up to you. Seeing you laced with nothing but the finest is the only way I know how to show you how much you mean to me. Let me spoil you, shorty. I like seeing you in expensive clothes and fine jewelry. You're the best, and that's what you deserve."

"You make me feel like I'm the most important person in your world, Jamie. You make me feel so beautiful," I whispered to him. "I never felt like this before."

Jamie's wet lips pressed against mine. He sucked on them a little before saying, "You are beautiful. So beautiful to me."

"This feeling scares me because I'm afraid you're gonna take it all back. I would be so hurt if you took all of your love away from me again." I felt like crying. I didn't cry, but I wanted to.

Jamie shook his head. "Baby, I'm not going anywhere, believe that. Only God can separate us, shorty. You're mine, I'm yours, forever and ever." He gently kissed my lips, gripping my hips in his hands.

OMG, I love the way that he touches me. He backed me up against the wall of the shower, then lifted my body up, wrapping my legs around his waist. We must have devoured each other's lips for a good five or ten minutes before he eased his way inside.

"You feel good as fuck, shorty, got-damn," he panted in my ear, gripping my thighs in his hands. "I got you, Ne'Vaeh. I'm not goin' anywhere."

That boy had me crying and squealing his name just about every morning. He had rejuvenated my heart. I tried to fight my feelings for him, but my heart embraced each and every moment with him.

That afternoon, Jamie asked me to meet him back at his place to help him set up the pre-Thanksgiving Dinner. Just a few friends would be there. I invited Alisha, Kelissa, and Renée over. A few of Jamie's friends came over around 7:30. Jamie was nowhere in sight, though. He wasn't answering his phone. My girls and I had done most of the setting up ourselves. Jamie's cooks were off that day, but Plata, the eldest Jamaican cook, helped start the turkey early that morning. Kelissa and Alisha helped entertain the guests in the party room. Renée tried to comfort me in the kitchen.

I tossed my phone on the kitchen counter after calling Jamie the tenth time. The last time I talked to him, he was on his way to his sister's house. "Where the fuck is he?" I exclaimed.

Renée sighed, shrugging. "Girl, he's probably with his agent, Rodney. You know that dude is always dragging him off to some event at the last minute. You know he doesn't care about Jamie's life outside of football."

Kelissa walked into the kitchen. She was dressed in a sexy navy-blue lace gown with a belt by Nicole Bakti. She always knew how to dress for the occasion. Her boyfriend kept her in expensive clothes. That girl didn't want for anything. "Still no Jamie, huh?" Kelissa came over and sat down on the stool at the granite-top island in the middle of the kitchen.

I sighed. "No. Where the hell is he? Has anyone seen him today?"

Kelissa looked at me. She hesitated. "Well, the last time I saw him was at the Gaylord at the National Harbor."

I looked at her, heart pounding in my chest. He promised me that he wouldn't cheat on me. I trusted him. But what was he doing there? "The Gaylord? The fuck he doin' at the Gaylord?"

Kelissa sighed. "Girl, don't trip. You remember Charlie's engagement party is tomorrow?"

I gave out a sigh of relief. "Okay, yeah, I remember her party is tomorrow. What was he doing there today, though?"

"He dropped his sister off to help with the setup. I was glad too, because I was ready to get the fuck outta there. Charlie's got everyone waiting on her hand and fuckin' foot. She needs to hurry up and have this baby because her emotions are driving me up the wall," Kelissa exclaimed, smoothing her edges down.

Renée laughed a little. "Yeah, being pregnant will have you driving everybody around you crazy, girl. My older sister had us all fuckin' trippin' when she was pregnant. I wonder how Aaron's doing. I don't think he's been with her to even one appointment. The last one he was supposed to go to with her was rescheduled. Didn't you go to that one with her, Kelissa?"

Kelissa quickly glanced at me. "Ummm, yeah. Never will I go with her again. I just don't agree with anything that she's doing, and I'll leave it at that. She's playing with fire."

I looked at her, sweeping my bangs from my face. "What do you mean?"

Kelissa shook her head, her eyes coated in tears. "Girl, I have so much I wanna say to you right now, but I just can't bring myself to say it. You need to talk to Charlie. I'll let her tell you."

"Tell me what?" I turned to Kelissa.

"It's about time y'all showed up." I heard one of Jamie's friends coming from the entertainment room.

I was too upset to move. I sat down at the stool next to Kelissa. Running late was not like Jamie. Something was going on. The way Kelissa rolled her eyes as soon as she heard Jamie's friend's voice let me know that whatever she had to say to me was serious.

I looked at Renée.

Renée had the same expression on her face that I probably had.

Jamie came into the kitchen, eyes low, looking like he'd been smokin' some loud. He was dressed in white Adidas from head to toe. He looked good in whatever he wore, whether it was sports apparel, urban wear, or an Italian tailor-made suit. It was so hard to be mad at him when he looked so good.

"Where the fuck have you been?" Kelissa hopped up from the stool, taking the words that should have been coming out of my mouth.

Jamie grinned at her. "What's up, ladies?" He looked at me, holding out his hand for me to come to him. "Shorty, can we talk for a minute?"

I looked at Renée and Kelissa, who both stood there with their arms folded. I looked back at Jamie, then hopped off the stool, going over to him as he took me by the hand.

We stood face-to-face in his bedroom. He just looked down at me, hands in his pockets.

I looked up at him. "So, where have you been, Jamie? We were supposed to be cooking together tonight. Everything is already done. My girls helped me cook. Even Plata helped out, and she's supposed to be off today." I stopped talking to look up at him.

He just stood there, not really sure what to say.

I held his face in my hands. "Baby, what's wrong? Where have you been?"

He hesitated. "I don't wanna hurt you, shorty. You're my best friend, my soul mate, my heart, my life, my air. Baby, I would do anything for you."

I just looked up at him, in shock, not really knowing what to do. It was hard seeing him so upset, especially when he barely showed any emotion about anything. If Jamie was speechless, it had to be something serious. My heart was pretty much prepared for anything. "Whatever it is, baby, just say it."

Jamie shook his head while biting his lip. "Nah."

I looked up at him, taking my hands from his face. "Are you leaving me again?"

He vigorously shook his head. "Nah, babe, I'm not leavin'."

"Did you cheat on me?" My eyes bore into his.

Jamie dried the tears that wouldn't seem to stop. "Nah, shorty, you know me better than that. When I'm with you, I'm with you."

"Then we're good, Jamie. No worries," I grinned, taking his hands in mine.

He put my hands to his lips, kissing both of them. "Shorty, I went to see your mother today." He hesitated.

Instantly, I slipped my hands from his. It was just a reflex to flinch every time I heard someone mention Juanita. Every time I heard anything about her, my little brother's face would flash before my eyes.

"Wha—" I couldn't even find the words to express how angry I was that he would go see her. My heart beat rapidly in my chest. I had to sit down. I sat down on his bed to catch my breath and gather my thoughts. "Why would you go to see her, Jamie?"

He exhaled deeply before explaining himself. "I got some news today that threw my entire life off track. I did something stupid as fuck, and who else better to talk to about making stupid, fucked-up decisions than your mother, shorty?"

I looked up at him, shaking my head. "There is no advice that she could give you that is worth a damn, Jamie, and you know it. The bitch is crazy. She killed my brother. She doesn't deserve for me or anyone in my life to visit her, Jamie. Why did you go to see her? What did you say to her?"

Jamie reached for my hand, but I pushed him away. He breathed heavily, sitting down next to me. "I fucked up, shorty. My life caught up with me, and I don't know what to do. All I want is to play football and be with you. My father told me to slow down, but I wouldn't listen."

I was confused. He wasn't making any sense. "Jamie, baby, I'm lost. If you're not ready to talk about it, it's cool. I haven't been back in your life long enough to sweat you about anything you did before we got back together. I love you, and it's cool. Now, I don't appreciate you going to see Juanita, but I'm not gonna pressure you about talking to me if you're not ready to talk."

Jamie looked at me. "She looked good for a change, shorty. She's not the fucked-up-in-the-head person she used to be. She has her mind right now. And I know what she did was fucked up, but that person wasn't your mother."

I cringed at the thought of Juanita. "Please, can we talk about something else?"

Jamie nodded. "I'm afraid of losing you, shorty. That's my biggest fear right now. I've been gone a long time. I can't even get you to spend the night with me. I'm lucky you even came by the crib today. Just stay long enough for me to give you a special gift, a'ight?" He got up from the bed and reached for me, pulling me up by the hand. He held my body up against his and gently kissed my lips. "I just have a lot on my mind. Give me some time, shorty, and I'll be ready to talk."

The evening went well. Everyone enjoyed the cooking and the drinking. Kelissa couldn't get this irritated glare off of her face every time she was in Jamie's presence. I sat with Alisha on the love seat in the entertainment room. That night, I caught her in the bathroom, kneeled over the toilet, throwing up, sounding like she was coughing up a lung. When I asked her what was wrong, she told me that the chemo always made her sick. It was the first time I had heard her mention chemotherapy. It was the first time I had heard her mention that she had cancer. She had a massive brain tumor that was inoperable. She was dying, but she seemed happy. She made everything that I was going through seem trivial. I sat next to her, talking to her on the couch, when Jamie sat down at his grand piano.

"Look at this fool." Alisha giggled, pointing over at him.

Renée clapped as soon as he sat down at the piano. "You go, boy," she cheered.

I laughed a little. I have to admit, it was a little hilarious to see dude sitting in front of a piano. I had never known Jamie to play anything but football and his PlayStation. But there he was, fingers stroking the ivory keys of his piano, and everyone was stunned, myself included.

I looked at Alisha, whose mouth dropped open.

Kelissa's glare changed to an awestricken grin. "Okay, Jamie." She was impressed.

Jamie smiled at me. "This song is for my baby, Ne'Vaeh Washington. It's called 'I Never Thought I'd Get Her Back.'" And then . . . He began to sing.

My heart nearly exploded, it was pounding so hard. I had never in my life heard Jamie sing. He never even mentioned that he could sing. Never gave the slightest interest to anything musical. The studio had only been used by people he knew who were putting down tracks for demos. You should have seen the looks on everyone's faces. Both his agent and his manager looked at each other like they both struck liquid gold.

There Jamie sat, singing his heart out to me, playing that got-damn piano like he was John Legend. Once my tears started flowing, I couldn't stop crying.

"You're my heart, you're my soul, the best part of my life. I'm not playin' no games, gonna make you my wife." Jamie's voice serenaded my heart and soul that night.

I held my hand over my heart, my face wet with tears.

Alisha held my hand tightly in hers, tears in her eyes as well. She looked upset by the lyrics in the song. I wasn't sure if she was angry that her life was ending, or angry that Jamie was trying to make a change in his. She excused herself in the middle of the song, hurrying off into the bathroom. Kelissa went after her. I stood from the chair as Jamie brought the hypnotizing song to a finish. The applause in the room was deafening.

He stood from the ebony piano bench as I walked into his arms. He squeezed me in his warm arms, kissing the tattoo on my neck. "I love you, Ne'Vaeh," he whispered in my ear.

"Well," Rodney spoke over the excitement, "if you ever get injured playin' football, we know what your fallback career is gonna be, dude. Why the fuck didn't you tell anybody that you could sing?"

Jamie let go of me. "It's not something I do often. I keep it to myself because I don't want muthafuckas thinkin' I wanna make a career out of this. I don't want people expecting me to sing every time they see me. Man, y'all know how it is. I just did this to surprise my girl, that's it, yo."

Jamie looked down at me, drying my face. "I did good, right?" he smiled, gently kissing my lips.

I smiled up at him, face full of tears. "Yeah, boo, you did good."

Jamie watched me slip back into my panties that night in his room. I ain't even going to lie, hearing him sing was a huge turn-on. I couldn't wait for everyone to leave so I could fuck the shit out of him.

I sat on the bed, placing my arms through the bra straps.

"So, you still not gonna stay over, huh?" Jamie laughed to himself. "After I opened up my heart to you and sung that song that I wrote just for you in front of everyone, you're not gonna stay over?"

I pulled my hair to the side, looking back at him as he hooked my bra for me. Shaking my head, I grinned a little. "No, Jamie, I am not."

He sighed, sitting up in the bed, reaching for his boxers. "Man, ain't this a bitch? You just gonna fuck the shit out of a nigga, then leave a nigga?"

I turned around facing him as he stood from the bed to put his boxers on. I knew he was getting tired of sleeping alone every night. Jamie craved my touch. He did any and everything he could just to get next to me. It had been that way since we were kids. I loved him more than anything, but I was tired of getting hurt. Of course, I wanted to spend the night with him, sleep with his dick inside of me, but my heart wasn't ready for that.

"Shorty, you're scared of me, and I don't know why. You've always been afraid of me. I'm your friend, shorty. Your best friend, your soul mate, your boo, your man, your partner. I have plans for us, and sometimes I don't know if your plans even include me." Jamie slid into his white ribbed tank top.

I looked up at him. "That song that you sang to me was amazing. It really pulled at not just my heartstrings but at everybody's, Jamie. You have been and probably will always be the most romantic guy that I have ever met, but your life-style is not only gonna haunt you, but it's gonna haunt me too. Now, I'm cool with your career, but I'm not cool with the women, Jamie. Damn right I'm afraid of you. Damn right I question your love for me. You left me here alone, and in the process, you began to live reckless. I feel it in my bones that your shit is gonna destroy us."

He just looked at me.

"Jamie, I never tried to change you. I have known you for a very long time, and I have always accepted you for who you are. When you know someone's ins and outs, nothing really surprises you. You haven't kept anything from me so far, and I plan to keep it that way. I like everything out there on the table so I won't pass the fuck out when the truth comes out." I stood from the bed, walking over to my black duffle bag that had a change of clothes in it.

Jamie hesitated. "Ne'Vaeh, I haven't told you everything."

I looked at him as I took a pair of smoky-gray sweatpants out of my bag. I slipped into the pants as he walked over to me. "Just say it, Jamie. You've been acting weird all day."

"Ummm . . ." he scratched his head. "A few months ago, I got this girl back in Mississippi pregnant. She waited until she had an abortion to tell me about it."

I placed my hand over my heart, laughing out loud. I think I laughed because I was in shock. "You're joking, right?"

He shook his head, eyes misty. "Nah, I'm not. Her name was Chantelle. I met her at a game down in Mississippi."

Unbelievable, I thought, then continued putting my clothes on. I was so angry with him. I thought the best thing to do was to be quiet before I said something out of line. I get it. He had a fucked-up childhood, a mother who didn't give a fuck about him, and no positive male role models to lead him in the right direction. But that was no excuse. He knew better. He always made the girls feel special, and then forget about them. True, he had no cut cards—he told every last one of them the deal from the start. But let's be honest, do we really listen to dudes?

Jamie often used women to fill the emptiness he felt inside from not having his mother in his life. I think Jamie needed the closeness that sex brought to him. But at the same time, he ran from anyone who caught any feelings for him. He craved women, because he needed to be loved, but at the same time, he hated women and wanted absolutely nothing to do with one. I didn't know how I had gotten so lucky with him.

Jamie looked downcast. He could tell that I was disappointed in him. "Shorty, please, say something."

I couldn't. My heart pounded in my chest. I sat down on his bed to slip into my socks. "No, Jamie. You really don't wanna hear what the fuck I have to say about you right now, trust me."

He nodded. "Yes, Ne'Vaeh, I do."

I looked up at him, "Okay. Do you know anything about this girl?"

He hesitated. "Nah, not really."

"So, what about her made you wanna have sex with her with no fuckin' condom, Jamie? Why couldn't you have been just a little more fuckin' careful? You couldn't have went to the got-damn corner store and got a box of condoms? As a matter of fact, doesn't a guy who gets as much pussy as you keep a condom or two in his wallet?" I slipped into my white and gray New Balances.

"Shorty, I was drunk as fuck. I couldn't drive. A friend of hers drove us over to her place. I don't even remember a lot from that night. All I know was the girl was calling me nonstop after that night, asking me to go out with her. I blew her off for the most part. I came to find out that she was a virgin." Jamie could tell by the look on my face that he needed to shut the hell up talking to me.

I stood from the bed, arms folded, looking up into his face. "This girl liked you, Jamie. This girl gave her body to you, and you blew her the fuck off? What the fuck did you think she was gonna do when she found out that she was pregnant? Tell you? For what? You didn't want shit to do with her, Jamie. She didn't want a baby that she knew you didn't want. I don't blame the girl for having an abortion. You have been talking that no-love-we-can-fuck-but-that's-it shit to these girls ever since middle school. I love you, but you are fucked up!"

Yeah, I knew the boy was feeling some type of way about his life, but he needed to hear what I had to say. I was so angry with him. A baby? By a woman who he didn't even know? And then have the audacity to try to throw the blame back on her by saying she had an abortion without telling him?

"So, you just gonna kick me when I'm down, huh?" Jamie said.

I shook my head. "Jamie, you should know me and my mouth by now. I love the fuck out of you; you know that, Jamie. So you already know that I'm pissed with you right about now. But what can I do? A beautiful baby was killed because two people who knew nothing about each other decided to have unprotected sex when there are all types of ways to prevent pregnancy these days." I grabbed my Old Navy T-shirt hoodie from a chair in the corner of his room. "You went to my mother with this shit, Jamie?"

Jamie looked at me. "Among other things, yeah. Her words stung just as bad as yours. Yeah, I know I was stupid as fuck. I'm human, shorty."

"I feel sorry for that girl." I zipped my jacket. "I know she was in love with you. Who doesn't fall in love with Jamie Green after having sex with him? You be havin' them girls sprung, and you don't even give a fuck. There's really no tellin' how many babies you have out there that you don't know about, Jamie." I went over and zipped up my duffle bag.

"Wow, shorty, you are really goin' in on me." Jamie laughed quietly. "I could only imagine what you would say or do if Chantelle was a close friend of yours."

I chuckled. "I would hope that none of my friends would sleep with you knowing the history that we have together. I seriously don't even wanna ask you if you have ever had sex with one of my friends. If you did, Jamie, please just keep the shit to yourself. I can't do anything about whatever you did when we weren't together. I couldn't even be mad at you, but her? I would really fuck her up because, as my friend, you just don't fuck with someone who you know I have a weak spot for. Oh my goodness, why am I even talking to you about this? You would never do that to me. You love me too much."

"Shorty, I have to—" His phone rang over on his nightstand. He looked at me.

I shrugged. "Answer your phone, Jamie. We just need to leave this subject alone. I don't wanna hear about anymore females that you fucked. I really shouldn't even be surprised after what I saw in that pool before your father passed away. Whatever happened before me, friend or not, is really none of my business. I blocked you out of my life when you left me, so that part of your life is off-limits to me. We're together now. You make me happy. You make me feel whole again. I love you, but I'm not ready to fully commit until everything feels right. So just answer your phone."

Jamie went over and picked up his phone.

I put my duffle bag over my shoulder, preparing to walk out the door. Sounded as if Jamie's agent wanted him to make another club appearance. It was already late, around 2:30 that morning. Rodney always made a lot of money off of Jamie. It was mostly the groupies who showed up to see Jamie, paying whatever just to get his autograph or to take a picture with him.

Jamie sighed as he hung up his phone. He looked at me.

I shook my head, already knowing by the do-you-think-you-can look on his face what he was about to ask me. "Jamie, I already know what you're about to say, and the answer is no."

He laughed a little. "C'mon, shorty. You know I hate goin' anywhere without you."

"Jamie, it's fuckin' 2:30 in the morning. I can't look like shit at Charlie's engagement party tomorrow, a party that I really don't feel like going to in the first place. And I don't wanna be tiptoeing in Renée's apartment at fuckin' 5:00 in the morning. Last time I came in late, her man was fuckin' butt-naked with socks on, sitting on the couch playin' his X-box, smokin' a blunt. I'm not tryin' to go through that again." I rolled my eyes.

Jamie held my hand, pulling me closer to him. "Just stay with me tonight. Don't go back home. You have clothes here in my closet, shorty."

I hesitated. I was more upset with him than I allowed myself to show. "Jamie, I can't tonight. I'm so not in the mood to deal with all of your groupies. I swear when I see that Puerto Rican chic again, I'm gonna snatch her ass bald."

Jamie promised, "I swear, you're not gonna have to deal with that shit tonight. It's just some of Rodney's people coming out to the club to celebrate. We just signed a contract with Nike to start my own urban clothing line. Shit's gonna hit the market in about three months, shorty. C'mon, come celebrate with us."

I just looked at him. "Jamie, I'm so mad at you right now." I looked up into his face. It was so hard to be mad at a man with a face like his.

"Please, don't be mad at me." Jamie gently kissed my lips, sucking on my bottom lip a little.

I just looked up in his face, butterflies flapping hysterically in my stomach. "You get on my nerves, Jamie, with all of this sexy shit . . ."

Chapter 7

The Breakup

Ne'Vaeh

"Girl, you need to do something with this voice that you have," my classmate Laysha said to me on December 24, that afternoon in choir practice. We were practicing for this huge holiday event that was going on at Howard on New Year's Eve.

I rolled my eyes, zipping up my sweater. "Girl, I already told everyone, I just do this for fun."

"Girl, whatever." Laysha rolled her brown eyes back at me. "Your cousin and his wife are supposed to be at the event too. I heard that they were thinkin' of adding some Gospel artists to their recording label. That would be awesome."

I smiled at her. Laysha was a big, beautiful, full-sized woman with smooth chocolate skin, long dark hair, a beautiful smile, and the strongest most amazing voice. That girl loved to sing. I admit, our voices did harmonize angelically together, but I liked my feet planted on solid ground. I really didn't have much hope in dreams. Yeah, I knew Darryl could take me places that I had never been, but I didn't want to leave Jamie.

Things were already a little shaky between us since the day before Thanksgiving. Don't even get me started on what happened the night we bumped into Aaron at the club. I was standing outside of the club with a few of the Morgan Girls. Aaron walked by with a few of his teammates. Aaron's friends stopped to chat with us. I stood there, quiet, not saying a word. Aaron looked right at me, asking me for a lighter. The funny thing is, I had Jamie's lighter in my purse. And just when I handed him the lighter, Jamie walks out of the club with his friends. And all hell breaks loose. I had been dealing with bitches in my face all month at school, calling me names, talking about me behind my back, telling me that they fucked Jamie, and I didn't once confront Jamie about any of it. I kept it to myself. But as soon as Jamie saw Aaron in my vicinity, he accused me of still being in love with Aaron.

My blood pressure dropped one day after a long day at the gym. I spent a night in the hospital. Choir practice was my first night out of the house in a week. Renée was upset about my hospital stay because I couldn't do any last-minute Christmas shopping with her. I did all of my shopping online two weeks earlier. I had my gifts already wrapped and hidden under my bed at Renée's apartment. Though my relationship with Jamie was still on edge, he would still pick up my prescriptions from the hospital. The thought of losing me seemed to run wild in that boy's mind.

Any time Jamie saw a male talking to me, I think the dude saw bright red. Earlier that month, I asked him to meet me in front of my dorm to take me out to lunch in the city. I was standing outside of my dorm, talking to the damn choir director about my solo for the holiday concert. Jamie caught sight of us laughing together and went flying straight at the man, no questions asked, pinning him up against the wall of the building. I had to pry Jamie's hands from around Kevin Patterson's neck that day. Luckily, Kevin Patterson was a fan. He was shook, but he was a fan, so he let it go. Jamie has issues that go far beyond me.

"I heard Jamie's radio interview this morning," Laysha teased.

I looked at her. I had been hearing about his interview all month. I had yet to hear it. The few people who did like me couldn't stop telling me how Jamie couldn't stop talking about me during the interview. I knew it had to be something special when the groupies started approaching me at school or leaving panties on my desk in class, or sending a nude pix to Jamie's e-mail, and then cc'ing me so that I could see the pictures too.

"That boy loves him some Ne'Vaeh, girl." She nudged me. "He made you sound like you were a piece of heaven on earth. Got all these dudes wanting a girl like you. Y'all seem to have a beautiful relationship."

I smiled a little. "I don't know, girl. I'm not so sure about us these days."

"Girl, please." Laysha rolled her eyes. "They say if you love something, let it go, and if it comes back to you, that's how you know it's a sure thing. You said yourself that dude left you four years ago, right?" Laysha asked.

I shrugged. "Yeah, but—"

"And he came back to you, right?" she grinned.

I rolled my eyes. "Yeah, but—"

"Then it's meant to be, Ne'Vaeh. He could have any girl that he chooses, yet he chose you. I know you're scared because you have been through a lot in life, but you gotta let that go. You're in love, and it's okay." Laysha looked deep in my eyes. "It's really okay. I'm pretty sure there are some things that Jamie is afraid to talk to you about. Probably some things that you may not wanna hear. I don't know what it is, but what I do know is that boy loves you. And for a man like that, love don't come easy." Laysha put her purse over her shoulder as we walked down the aisle and out of the auditorium.

I said, "He's keeping something from me. Something big, Laysha; I can just feel it. I don't wanna pressure him because I don't wanna push him away, but I know that whatever it is that he has to tell me has him thinking I'm gonna leave him when I find out."

It was 6:30 that evening. Jamie and I were supposed to be going to his aunt Bethany's Christmas Eve party. Christmas was her favorite holiday. She always went all-out on Christmas. Even when we were kids, his aunt would let us all roast marshmallows on Christmas Eve in her fireplace. And she would always let us open the smallest gift from under the tree. That year, she'd invited just about every one of Jamie's friends she could find to her house. Jamie seemed to be out of his element lately. Ever since I've known him, he would spend hours in the gym working out or running between three and five miles a day. Ever since the day before Thanksgiving, Jamie lost focus. He stopped coming over my apartment at 7:00 in the morning regularly. It wasn't purposely. It was like he would drink or smoke himself to sleep, and then wake up around 2:00 in the afternoon. His manager was worried about him. His agent was worried about him. I was worried about him.

When Jamie didn't show up on time to pick me up at Renée's apartment that night, I was a little worried. I sat at the vanity mirror in Renée's bathroom applying lipstick. Sighing, I kept looking at the time on my iPhone. Jamie was supposed to pick me up at 5:45, and he was almost an hour late. I called him about five times that night and received no answer.

"Knock, knock," Renée spoke and knocked softly as she entered the bathroom, dressed in a tight white silk blouse and high-waisted tight black pants. Her Poetic Justice braids were pulled up into a bun. She looked wonderful.

I smiled up at her a little. "You look amazing, cuz."

Renée grinned. "Girl, bye. Look at you. Lookin' like a boss chick. Jamie keeps you lookin' like you just got paid." She looked down at her watch. "What time were we supposed to be at Jamie's aunt Bethany's party? Isn't she like a stickler for people showing up on time?"

I exhaled loudly. "I think we're supposed to be there at 7:30. Jamie was supposed to meet us here at 5:45. I don't know what's up with him lately, girl, but he's really got me goin' crazy."

Renée looked into my face as she sat down at the vanity mirror beside me on the bench. "Look, cuz, I have to tell you something. I saw Jamie this morning at the hospital. He was standing outside of the main entrance smoking a cigarette."

I looked at her. "So? He was at the hospital picking up my meds, I know, sweetie."

Renée nodded. "Yeah, I saw the bag in his hand, but before I could walk down the sidewalk over to him, here comes Charlie's pregnant ass walking out of the main entrance. They were outside of the hospital crying, yelling, and screaming at each other."

My heart pounded in my chest. Something was telling me that I didn't even want to know what the two were arguing about.

"I couldn't really hear what they were sayin'. All I know was that Charlie did some shit that Jamie apparently didn't like. Regardless, it didn't look like a conversation that either of them wanted to have with each other." Renée watched the tears form in my eyes. "Look, Ne'Vaeh, it's probably nothing."

"Then why would you tell me if you thought it was nothing, Renée?" I stood from the bench, just when the doorbell rang.

Renée held my face in her hands, drying my tears. "Calm down. Don't go off on dude as soon as he walks through this door. Give him a chance to explain himself."

She walked out of the bathroom to answer the door.

I took a deep breath, then followed her. My stomach was doing all sorts of flips and twists and turns. My heart felt like it was going to explode.

"Hi, Jamie." Renée greeted him as he walked through the door.

"What's up?" Jamie said, lookin' real good, semicasual, dressed in black and white. He looked at me as I approached him, eyes tracing my entire body. Then he looked back into my face, "Hey, Shorty."

My lips trembled. I didn't even know what to say to him. I wanted to ask about Charlie, but at the same time, I was afraid to know.

"Dude, my cousin wants to know why you're late." I could always count on Renée to get straight to the point. "You must have been contemplating about what you were gonna tell her about the conversation that you were having outside of the hospital with Charlie earlier."

Jamie looked at Renée. "Not tonight, Renée. You always in somebody's mix, and you always got somethin' to say. You need to chill with all that shit. Damn." He looked at me, eyes watering. "Yo, we're already late, shorty. Can we talk about this later?"

Renée folded her arms. "No, nigga, she doesn't wanna talk about this shit later. What were you doin' talkin' to that girl—no, cursing at the girl in front of the hospital? Are you fuckin' that girl?" Renée had no filter. So much for not going off on Jamie. I had to get her to leave before she said some shit to Jamie that would get her ass slapped.

"Renée," I exclaimed. "Please, stop. Not tonight, okay? I really can handle my own business without your help. Can you just go to Aunt Bethany's house and wait for us there?"

Renée shook her head. "Nah. I'ma be outside in case you need me. I'm not goin' to this party without you, sweetie." Renée grabbed her purse and coat and left the apartment.

I turned to Jamie, who stood there biting his lip, trying not to cry. I looked up into his gorgeous face. "Jamie, I love you," I whispered.

He held my hands in his, trying to pull himself together. "Shorty, you are the most amazing woman I have ever met." He choked. "I love everything about you. You don't even know how much you mean to me. I would be totally lost without you. You are my best friend, and the only person I trust with my heart. I let you down, shorty. You're gonna hate me when I say this."

I shook my head. "No, Jamie, I could never hate you. Just tell me. Just say it."

He looked down into my face. "Shorty, I'm probably making the biggest mistake of my life, but we have to end this."

I just looked at him. My mind hadn't processed what he was saying. I had a blank look on my face. I wasn't sure how to respond. "End what, Jamie? You don't wanna go to your aunt's party?" I laughed a little. "Aunt Bethany would be pissed if her favorite nephew didn't show up. Come on, Jamie, stop playing; we're already running late. Let me get my purse."

I turned to walk away, but he grabbed my hand, pulling me back to him.

I looked at him as he held my hand in his.

Jamie just shook his head, holding my hand in his. "Nah, shorty, it's over. We're over."

My lips were trembling, heart pounding. "What? What are you talking about?" I was lost, I was confused, I was hurt. "What did I do? Is it because I won't move in with you? Okay, I will. Just give me a chance to tell Renée that I'm leaving so she can help me pack up my stuff." I slipped my hand from his, walking past him to the front door. But Jamie grabbed my arm, pulling me back to him. I pulled away from him.

Sadly, Jamie said, "This has nothing to do with that."

I pushed him in his chest. I was growing angrier by the second. "Then what does this have to do with, Jamie? Is it Aaron? Are you still mad at me for what happened between us? Are you still trippin' over that night at the club? There is nothing going on with Aaron. I promise. I swear."

Jamie's eyes searched mine. "Baby, I love you. I just—I made some stupid decisions, and for that reason, I have to put our relationship on hold. You were right—my past came back to haunt me."

"What is it, Jamie?" I cried. "Whatever it is, we can fix it. You don't have to leave me. I just got you back, and you wanna dump me?" I pushed him again.

"Nah, I don't wanna leave you, Ne'Vaeh. I love the fuck out of you. I have some shit that I need to take care of. You don't need to be caught up in my mistakes. You don't deserve any of this shit, so I gotta let you go."

I sat down on the arm of the couch, catching my breath, drying my tears. I looked up at him. "Does it have to do with another woman, Jamie?"

He hesitated. "Yes."

I knew it. "Is she pregnant?" I whispered.

He nodded, biting his lip. "Yes."

I sighed, shaking my head. "Is she keeping the baby?"

Jamie rubbed his head anxiously. "Shorty, I really don't wanna talk about this. I don't want to have a baby with this girl. I don't love her, I don't like her, I don't wanna be with her, and I should have never slept with her. I didn't mean for any of this to happen. She's four months pregnant, and she's having a boy, my boy. My firstborn son is gonna be with a woman who I don't plan on spending the rest of my life with. I wanted my firstborn son to be with you, with the woman who I wanna be with forever. Ne'Vaeh, I love you, and I didn't wanna tell you like this."

I wanted to be angry with him, but I couldn't. He had slept with the girl before we even started dating, before I knew he was even coming back to Maryland, before the thought of us getting back together crossed either one of our minds. Jamie was devastated. I would have stayed with him and worked through it with him. I would have tried my best to get along with whichever groupie or classmate he was having the baby with.

"So, you don't think I'll accept your baby in my life? Is this why you're breaking up with me, Jamie?" I whispered.

Jamie shook his head. "I can't do this to you, shorty. You don't deserve this. When I slept with this girl, I had no idea that me and you would end up back together. I didn't sleep with this girl to hurt you, to disrespect you, or to get over you. I'm young, I'm dumb, and I do stupid shit from time to time. I'm cleaning up my life. And just when I get you back, this girl drops this news on me. I can't be with you knowing I did this fucked-up shit to you."

I was prepared for the worst. I had my guard up our entire relationship because something told me that some stupid shit was going to happen to pull us apart. "So, are you leaving me and Maryland? You gonna give up everything that you worked for just because you're having a baby, Jamie?" I looked up into his face.

Upset, he said, "Nah, I'm not leaving. I know I'm fuckin' up, Ne'Vaeh, but I gotta get my shit together. If you wanna go to my aunt's party, you can, but I'm—I'm just gonna go home, shorty."

I gazed into his face, tears dangling from my eyelashes. He was really ending it with me. He was really angry with himself. And I was starting to think that it had more of who the woman he had the baby with was than the fact that he was having a baby with someone else. "Who is she, Jamie? Or do I even wanna know?"

"Nah, I can't tell you," he said adamantly.

I stood up. "So, you're leaving me because you're not man enough to tell me who you're having a baby with?"

"Nah, shorty, I'm leaving this relationship because I wasn't man enough to walk away from a woman who I never should have involved myself with in the first place. It's bad enough that I'm breaking up with you on Christmas Eve, shorty. C'mon, please don't make this more difficult than it already is. I'm angry with myself right now. I hate myself right now for leaving you, but I can't stay with you knowing what I did to you."

I looked at him. "So, what now, Jamie? What do you expect from me? To sit and wait for you again? You're leaving me again for a reason that you don't wanna tell me, and you expect me to wait for you again?"

Jamie shook his head, eyes misty. "No, I don't. I don't deserve for you to wait for me. All I'm asking you is if we can still be friends. If you'll still be my shoulder to cry on, be my ear to listen, and let me hold you from time to time. I still love you, Ne'Vaeh." He reached for me, but I pulled away. "Shorty, it wasn't easy telling you this. I have been holding it in for a month because I didn't want you to leave me. I couldn't hold it in anymore."

Tears stung my cheeks. "I love you, Jamie Green, but you need to get your shit together," I sighed, shaking my head. "You know I'm not goin' anywhere, but I won't let anyone make a fool out of me."

He nodded, looking down into my wet face.

I laughed to myself, shaking my head, wondering how I could let myself fall back in love with a man who had issues as deep as his were. "I just can't believe I let myself fall for you again. I knew you would find a way to hurt me once more, some way or another. You don't know how to love anything but sports, Jamie. I've known that about you all my life."

He disagreed. "That's not true, Ne'Vaeh—I do know how to love. Shorty, if I would have known about this before we got back together, I swear, I would have told you. You know I wouldn't keep some shit like this from you, Ne'Vaeh."

I waved him off, because I had heard enough of his lines. "Let's just change this subject. Are you still coming to my holiday event on New Year's Eve? I know we gotta be at Charlie's wedding the next morning, but I would really appreciate it if you came. No one else in my family is gonna be able to attend because most of them have to work that night, and you're family so I need you to be there . . . please."

Jamie nodded. "A'ight, I'll be there. I'll—I'll holla at you tomorrow, shorty." He turned to walk away, but I grabbed his arm, pulling him back to me.

I threw my arms around him, holding him tight, crying, burying my face in his chest.

Jamie surrounded me in his arms, kissing the "J" on the back of my neck. "See you tomorrow night at the club, shorty." He let go of me, then walked out the door.

Renée must have been listening right outside of the door because as soon as Jamie walked out, she walked in. "Ne'Vaeh," she exclaimed as she saw me sitting down on the couch, face drenched in tears, makeup probably smeared-to-be-damned. "What just happened? Don't tell me the nigga broke up with you the night before Christmas."

I looked up at her, lips trembling. I couldn't even speak. The expression on my face spoke for itself. "He dumped me. Renée, Jamie, left me again," I cried out loud.

She threw her purse and jacket down on the recliner, then raced to my side. "Oh, poor baby. I'm so sorry." She cried with me, surrounding me in her arms.

Christmas really didn't feel right without Jamie. I didn't get any sleep the night before. I stayed up the entire night, crying, pissed, angry as a muthafucka. I finally had Jamie back, and just when I felt comfortable allowing him to hold me in his arms, he breaks up with me. Sometimes I wished Jamie wasn't so fuckin' honest. Why couldn't he lie to me like a normal guy? Keep the pregnancy from me? Deny the baby was his? Why did he have to have a conscience? I needed that man. I loved him. It felt good to be with him again. Jamie was ashamed of what he'd done, and he didn't think that he deserved me. We had all made mistakes. None of us were in the clear.

Renée brought me milk and warm cookies that night to my room. We opened our gifts around 3:00 that morning. I bought her the Coach bag that she wanted, and she bought me the Red Bottom black heels and tight black dress that she saw me eyeing in a Vogue magazine a few weeks earlier. Renée always bought the best gifts. When you think she's not watching your expression on your face when you like something, she is, and she'll do whatever it is to help you get it. I loved her. She was the mother that I never had. The mother that I needed. She had a way of cheering me up when she knew I felt like shit.

Renée begged me that afternoon to go with her to Ms. Theresa's house. I wasn't in the mood. I had to prepare my heart for seeing Jamie that night at the Christmas party. It took everything I had not to drink myself to death the night before. I knew that was the only reason Renée stayed with me that night. She knew I was tired of being disappointed. She knew I was hurt to my soul. Though I had my guard up that short while that Jamie and I were together, I wasn't prepared for him to end things with me. I bought Jamie a casual Better Menswear shirt, jeans, and jacket—something I knew he would look good in. I wasn't sure when or where I was going to give them to him. Any and everybody was going to be at the Q-Club for the Christmas party that night. People were always sticking their noses in my business, and there was no telling how many people already knew about my breakup with him.

My cousin Jennel brushed my hair up into a bun that night, while Renée sat facing me, smoothing foundation over my face. My tears were making it hard as hell for her to do my makeup.

"C'mon, sweetie, you have to stop crying." Renée dried my tears. "Oh my goodness, please stop. How am I gonna get you all dolled-up if you're crying?"

Sadly, I shook my head. "I'm sorry, Renée. Maybe I shouldn't go. I don't wanna ruin anyone's night."

"What?" Jennel exclaimed. "No, you are going to this party. Everyone is gonna be there. There will be so many people there, you probably won't even run into Jamie."

Renée threw a makeup sponge at Jennel. "Jennel, got-damn, you never know when to shut up."

Jennel shrugged. "What? You know that's the reason why she doesn't wanna go to this Christmas party. Fuck Jamie, okay? And fuck whatever he did with whoever he did it with. You're beautiful, you're smart, you're talented, you can sing your muthafuckin' ass off, and you don't need him. You went four years without him. Just pretend like the muthafucka never came back."

I shook my head. It wasn't going to be that easy. I had known Jamie my entire life. He was my first. You never forget your first no matter how much you may want to. I was in love with Jamie way before we started dating. He loved me through every phase of puberty. He loved me when I was a nerd, he loved me when I was a tomboy, he loved me when I was a girly-girl, he loved me when I was depressed, he loved me when I was a bitch. He had taught me everything about life. And at that moment, he was teaching me the hardest lesson learned—heartbreak is a muthafucka.

"I don't want to go back to that life. I was so lonely then that I let myself fall for my best friend's boyfriend, y'all. I'm nothing without Jamie," I cried. "Nothing and nobody can replace him. I tried. Whatever he did with whoever he did it with, I don't care. I just want him back. We can work through it. I don't care who she is, y'all. We can work through it."

Renée shook her head at me and sighed, "Sweetie, there are some things that you need to talk to Charlie about that really don't need to wait. I thought you should know that I talked to your mother a few weeks ago."

I looked up into her face. Why was everyone talking to my fuckin' mother about me? She dabbed my face with some tissue. I pushed her hands away. "What is it with y'all going to see my mother behind my back?" I exclaimed. "First, Jamie, and now you too?"

Renée's eyes glistened. "Sweetie, she was my aunt just like she was your mother."

"She's a fuckin' murderer. She doesn't deserve any love from you at all, Renée," I cried.

"Can you just listen before you go off on the girl?" Jennel smoothed the edges of my hair down.

I looked at Renée.

Renée took a deep breath. "I didn't wanna tell you what she talked to me about because it's for her to tell you, not me. Your mother has gotten a lot of help with her addictions and depression while she's been in prison, Ne'Vaeh. She doesn't hate you. You know she was on all types of drugs when she killed your brother. You know she was hallucinating. You know she didn't mean to kill him or make your sister run away."

Disgusted, I stood from the vanity stool in Renée's bathroom. "So, what about selling my sister for drugs, huh? What about leaving us in the house hungry for months? What about letting her boyfriends rape my sister? What about beating the shit out of all of us for years? What about being so high she gave us bleach to drink instead of water?"

"There's nothing that anyone can do or say to take back the pain that she caused, honey. I get that. But you have to put the past behind you and move on. Holding onto this pain is what has your heart confused, Ne'Vaeh." Renée grabbed my arm before I could walk out of the bathroom.

I pulled from her. "I don't wanna hear the shit you're talking about, Renée."

"Aunt 'Nita said she had been trying to get in touch with your sisters. Your older sister got in touch with her two weeks ago," Renée exclaimed as fast as she could because she knew I was seconds away from walking out of the bathroom, screaming "fuck her and everyone else too."

I looked at her, lips trembling. "W-What? Autumn got in contact with her?"

Jennel looked at me. "Sweetie, she said sisters, with an 's' at the end. Plural, honey."

I looked at Renée, "What do you mean?"

Renée gulped. "Yes, sweetie, your mother said that Autumn got in touch with her, and she gave me her address. She was living in California. I invited her to the Christmas party tonight. I wanted to surprise you tonight, but this seems to be the only way to get you to come to the club."

Shocked, I shook my head. I thought Autumn was dead because I hadn't heard from her. She never got in touch with me. She abandoned me once our brother was murdered. I hadn't heard from her in six fuckin' years. I already had enough jagged pills to swallow. I couldn't handle any more heartbreak, but it seemed that once my mother started it, the ball just kept rollin'.

I looked at Renée, "Sisters, Renée? You said sisters?"

Renée looked at Jennel, and then back at me. "Well, have you ever wondered why your mother and Charlie's mother don't get along?"

I shrugged. "I don't know. Theresa didn't think Juanita was a good influence. You know my mama had all types of dudes running in and out of our house. Theresa wasn't going to let Charlie's fast ass around all that shit."

Renée shook her head. "Sweetie, your mother and Theresa grew up together. Used to be best friends. That was until your mother started sleeping with Theresa's boyfriend. Your mother ended up pregnant by Theresa's boyfriend when

Theresa was just a few months' pregnant herself."

I stared at her. I was confused. "Okay, so, my mother and Theresa were pregnant at the same time? What happened to the baby? Did my mother give the baby up for adoption or have an abortion?"

Renée hesitated. "No, the baby is you, sweetie. Theresa's husband is your father. Was your father, rest his soul."

I held my hand over my heart, feeling my heart pumping a million miles per hour. My head felt like it was spinning. Jennel caught me before I stumbled over her. She sat me down on the vanity stool as I struggled to catch my breath.

Renée placed a bag over my mouth, as I covered her hands with mine, breathing in and out of the bag. "Where is the inhaler that the doctors gave you?" she panicked.

I waved my hand, letting her know that I was going to be okay. I took the bag from my face, tears coating my lashes. "I'm-I'm okay." I struggled to breathe at first. "I'm okay." I looked at Renée, who stood there, looking like she was having a hard time breathing as well. "So, Charlie is my sister? Is that what you're telling me?"

Renée hesitated to nod. "Yes, sweetie. I sent her to visit your mom today so she knows too.

She's just as much in the dark as you are, sweetie. Her mother didn't tell her shit either. Theresa hates your mother, but she loves you, probably because you're the part of her husband that she never really got to know."

I just sat there, clinching the cushion of the vanity seat in my hands. Yeah, Charlie was definitely going to pay me back for sleeping with Aaron. I had slept with my own sister's boyfriend. I had betrayed my own flesh and blood over a man who should have went for what he wanted in the first place.

I looked at Renée, tears sliding down my face. "So, I slept with my own sister's boyfriend? Oh my goodness, I am such a fuckin' ho. I deserved for Jamie to leave me."

Jennel shook her head at me. "No, no, Ne'Vaeh, I am not going to allow you to do this to yourself. Not on Christmas."

Renée nodded in agreement. "We need to just go to this party, have a good time, and if your sister Autumn shows up tonight, you get to reunite with her. Don't try to create drama in your head that might not even happen. Please, let's go and have a good time. Your sister's comin' with some of her crew from L.A. I heard she was a damn famous Sioux Chef."

I looked at Renée, then back at Jennel.

Jennel shrugged. She had no idea about which way the evening was going to turn out either. "Look, I don't know what else to tell you except try to have a good time tonight. And don't sit here and feel bad about what you did, because trust me, from what I heard, you are not in the wrong on your own."

Renée glanced at Jennel, and then back at me. She swallowed hard because she knew I was going to ask questions about the comment that Jennel just made.

"What do you mean? The worst thing that Charlie has done to me is call me a fuckin' groupie. True, that was fucked up, but she was mad at the time. I don't blame her for what she said. I would have cursed a bitch out too, if she slept with my man and tried to deny the shit in my face."

Jennel looked at me. "All I'm saying is I heard that Charlie's not even pregnant by Aaron."

Renée's eyes grew wider. She looked at Jennel, and then back at me.

"Wha-What do you mean?" I stuttered.

Jennel laughed out loud. "Girl, rumors have been floating around town for months now about the Morgan Girls' trip to Miami. I didn't hear who the dude was that she was supposedly messing around with down there, but I did hear that she was fuckin' somebody in Miami in August. Not sure if there is any truth to it, sweetie, but it's what I heard. I heard it from my husband's cousin who works at the abortion clinic. Yeah, she was down at the clinic trying to get rid of the baby. Now who do you know that would kill a baby when they are as well off as Charlie and Aaron are? Even your girl Alisha said that she caught Charlie cheating on Aaron these past few months. Kelissa said the same shit too. Why would these people say all this shit if it wasn't true? Girl, let me be quiet before I say too much."

I looked at Renée, who stood there, back against the wall, not sure what to say. It was all new information to me. Last I heard, Charlie was in love with Aaron. I shook my head at Jennel in shock, or maybe it was disbelief. "If what you're saying is true, why would Charlie get all in my face when she thought I was sleeping with Aaron? Why would she lie to the man telling him that she was having his baby? They're getting married in a week, Jennel."

Jennel shrugged. "Girl, don't get me to lyin'. I have no idea. Probably because she was trying to keep Aaron from you."

Renée nodded. "Now, I can agree to that."

I just sat there, my mind racing. My heart was pumping a million miles per hour. I felt a surge of guilt mixed with terror taking over my body. I didn't know who or what to believe. Charlie had been faithful to Aaron for years. I didn't know anything about their love life until Charlie told me that she was pregnant, though I questioned their relationship the day that Aaron confessed his feelings for me.

"Look, Ne'Vaeh, let's just go out, have a good time, mingle, drink—but not too much for you—and party until the sun comes up. Everybody who is anybody is gonna be in that bitch tonight. It's Christmas. We're supposed to be happy." Jennel shook my shoulders.

I looked at her. "Happy? Jamie dumped me last night. I just found out my sister who I haven't seen in six years may be showing up to a party I really don't feel like going to. I also just found out that my best friend is my own fuckin' sister who our parents neglected to tell both of us about. And now I'm finding out that Charlie may be forcing Aaron to marry her when she's pregnant by someone else? Happy? Girl, if this is happiness, what the fuck is sadness?"

Chapter 8

The Dance

Ne'Vaeh

Despite the fucked-up way that I felt, I was rocking the hell out of that tight, black dress and black Red Bottom five-inch heels. When we stepped outside of Renée's apartment that night, Jamie's driver was parked waiting in Jamie's 2015 Chevy Tahoe. I loved that truck. Outside, it was coated in grape jelly candy paint. Inside, the leather looked like it was drenched in peanut butter. Jamie and I had made love about three times that week in the car. I started to turn back around and walk back in the apartment, when Jennel's and Renée's happy asses pulled me toward the car with them. Jamie really made me sick. I really hated how much I loved that boy.

Jamie's driver dropped us off in front of the club. The club parking lot was packed that night, and the line to get in was wrapped all the way around the building. As usual, we didn't have to wait to get in. The Morgan Girls were waiting at the entrance to let us in. Kelissa greeted me with open arms, dressed in all white. She escorted us to the booths where the other girls were sitting, drinking, exchanging gifts, having a good ol' time. Alisha wasn't with them, which was surprising.

It seemed like every one of Jamie's groupies—the ones that I knew of anyway—were at the club that night. I caught sight of Charlie sitting at the bar, laughing with a few of her family members. She didn't see me, and I was glad. I really didn't feel like talking to her. I wasn't feeling any type of sisterly love at all, and I dreaded the thought of seeing Autumn.

We all sat at our booths, getting drunk. I was on my second (or maybe it was my third) Strawberry Daiquiri, when Danita decided she wanted to get on the subject of my breakup with Jamie.

"So," Danita sipped Rosé from her glass, "I heard from one of them groupies at the bar that you and Jamie broke up last night."

Everyone who had no idea that we had broken up looked at me for a reaction.

Renée rolled her eyes. "You bitches are so messy. Why are you bringing that shit up? We came here to have a good time, not for y'all hoes to go digging up dirt. How the fuck would you feel if you just broke up with someone? Would you want bitches bringin' that shit up to you on Christmas?"

"I'm just saying that now that you two aren't together anymore, I wanted to tell you some information that I heard about Jamie. I heard he was sleeping with one of your friends, sweetie." Danita's brown eyes examined my face.

I sat there sipping from my glass. I wasn't in the mood. I had enough on my mind. "You know what? I don't give a fuck which one of y'all hoes was fuckin' Jamie as long as it didn't happen while we were together. Was it you, Danita, since you wanna bring the shit up?"

Danita's eyes widened. "Me? You think I would sleep with Jamie? I mean, he's fine as a muthafucka, but I already know where his heart belongs. I'm just sayin' there's some hoes in this house who want your boo. I'll point 'em out if you need me to."

I wasn't in the mood for her shit. "Danita, I didn't come here for this. I wasn't even gonna come to this party because I knew some shit was gonna get thrown up in my face. As long as I don't know who the bitch is, I'm cool. Trust me, the way that I'm feeling right now, y'all really don't want none of me. Let's just change the subject."

"Please do." Kelissa said, "I'm not about to sit here with y'all, all depressed, drunk, and shit. I'm about to go dancing. C'mon, Ne'Vaeh, let's hit the floor." Kelissa grabbed my arm.

I grinned a little, standing up from the table when I spotted Alisha sitting by herself at the bar. She didn't look happy. She didn't look like her usual self. She looked depressed, like she didn't feel like being bothered with anyone. She looked the way that I felt on the inside. "I'll be right back." I walked through the tables, across the dance floor, making my way over to her.

Her face lit up a little when she saw me walking toward her. She clapped as I approached her. "Yes, work it, girl." She laughed out loud. "Look at you, sexy mama."

I smiled, hopping up on the stool next to her. We gave each other a snug hug, then let each other go. I smiled at her, looking into those sad eyes of her. "What are you doing over here, sitting all by yourself? Why aren't you over there with the girls, trippin' and gettin' drunk?" I exclaimed.

Alisha rolled her eyes, sipping from her glass. "Girl, please, them bitches been startin' drama all night. The only one I'm really cool with right now is Kelissa. She's the only one not with the drama. Miserable bitches love them some company, you remember that shit." Alisha coughed, chest sounding really congested.

I looked at her, worried out of my mind. I'd known Alisha a long time. She was the gossip queen, but she was my friend. She never had anything negative to say about me. She always stuck up for me. She never steered me wrong, and her advice was always for the best. There were times that I wish I would have listened to her, and I didn't. I prayed that the doctors were wrong when they said the treatments had stopped working. I couldn't imagine a world without Alisha in it, and I didn't want to.

"Well, I couldn't even get two drinks up in me before they started talking about Jamie." I sighed, signaling the bartender to come over.

Alisha looked at me. "Yeah, I heard about the breakup. There are a lot of hot, horny bitches in here tonight, happy as hell to hear that shit. You should have heard them bitches talkin' shit when they heard Jamie's radio interview."

I looked at her as the bartender slid me another Strawberry Daiquiri. "You weren't talkin' shit with them, Alisha?"

She laughed a little. "What? Me? Whatever do you mean?"

"Yes, you, bitch. You're like anti-Jamie 100 percent." I watched as Alisha threw her head back in laughter.

"Girl, I don't hate Jamie, I just can't stand that conceited, sexy muthafucka." She shook her head, eyes shimmering. "I know you love that boy, but he fucked with the wrong bitch. And by that I mean, he hurt you, and he got involved with someone he had no business getting involved with. I really wanna tell you, but I think that bitch should tell you herself. She at least owes you that much." Alisha looked over my shoulder, her brown eyes growing wider. She looked back at me as I felt a tap on my shoulder.

I turned around to face Autumn Washington, the sister I haven't seen in six years. I stood from the stool, facing her. She looked like she came straight out of a fashion magazine. She had long, bone-straight, dark hair that grazed against her hips. Her makeup was flawless. Tattoos painted her shoulders. I couldn't help but notice the Marilyn Monroe piercing above the right side of her lip. She looked amazing. She still looked like a bottle of honey mustard, with that golden complexion of hers. I was in shock as she pulled me closer to her to hug me. She was so excited to see me, in tears as she cried on my shoulder. Alisha stood from her seat, about to walk away from us when I grabbed her arm, as I let go of my sister. I shook my head at Alisha. I didn't want to be alone with her just yet.

I looked into my sister's face.

"Ne'Vaeh, oh my God, you look amazing," she squealed, hands covering her mouth. "My little sister is all grown up."

I nodded, still a little in shock. "You look great too, Autumn. Ummm," I cleared my throat. "How have you been? Where have you been?"

Alisha grabbed my hand, holding it tightly in hers, slightly pulling me away from Autumn. Alisha knew that I was upset. Everyone who had left me all of a sudden started appearing back in my life whenever it was convenient for them. Jamie included. He came back in my life when I least expected it, and just when I was getting comfortable having him around again, he pulled a fast one on me. I wasn't going to let Autumn do the same.

"I've been in Hollywood, girl. Engaged." She flashed her ring at me. "I'm getting married Valentine's Day."

Yes, I cried. I'm emotional. How would you feel if the sister that you thought was dead showed up on the day after your boyfriend dumped you? The tears that I fought so hard not to show that night came pouring down my cheeks like rain. "Why are you here, Autumn? After all of these years? You never once called or came to check on me. You didn't even know whether I was alive. You just up and ran the fuck away, not even looking back. Yeah, I know you wanted to leave behind all of these awful memories, but you left me behind too, Autumn. Was I a memory that you wanted to erase too?"

Autumn's light eyes searched my face. "No, of course not. Ne'Vaeh, you know what happened to me. I had to get away from here. I loved you so much. I knew you would be okay with Mrs. Theresa. She loved you like her own daughter. I knew for years that Charlie was your sister. I found your original birth certificate with Charlie's father's name on it."

Alisha interrupted. "Hold up, hold up, hold up. You're telling me that Charlie is Ne'Vaeh's sister? As in they have the same father?"

I sighed. "Yeah, I found out tonight. Renée told me."

Alisha shook her head, dumbfounded. "Cutie, I had no idea. Shit is about to get real. I really can't deal with this tonight, girl. I'm out." Alisha let go of my hand, starting to walk away from me, shaking her head to herself.

I grabbed her arm. "Wait! What's wrong, Alisha?"

Alisha's eyes swelled up with tears. "Girl, your heart is going to break when the truth comes out. I can't be the one to do it to you. Spend some time with your real sister. Autumn cares about you, wants what's best for you. I'm sure she never meant to leave you. Fuck Charlie and her got-damn feelings. Spend time with Autumn, get to know her, start over." She dried my tears, kissed me on the cheek, then walked away.

Autumn looked at me, her light eyes sparkling under the club lights. "Sounds like you have a lot going on, sis."

I nodded. "Yes, I do, and you coming here doesn't make my situation any better. I don't know what makes you think that you can just pop back up in my life whenever the fuck you feel like it."

"I never meant to leave you, Ne'Vaeh," she cried. "I've been through too much with Ma and her lifestyle. When our little brother was killed, I couldn't deal with it. I had been molested, kidnapped, raped, traded for drugs, beaten, abused, addicted to drugs myself. I had to get out of here. Do you think I didn't wanna take my little sister—my best friend—with me? I couldn't take you from Jamie, and I wasn't about to make you choose between me and him."

"Well," I dried my tears, "just like you, he ended up leaving me too, Autumn. I just got him back. It hasn't even been two months, and the muthafucka has left me again. I love him, and he knows I can't live, breathe, or think without him. You know what? I really don't wanna talk about this. I'm not drunk enough to talk about this."

Autumn laughed a little, still in shock at seeing that her little sister was not so little anymore. "Oh my goodness, I just can't get over how much you've grown up. You're in college. I even heard that you were in a gospel choir. I found out from Renée that we're related to Darryl Allan, the producer-filmmaker-entrepreneur. I talked with him a few days ago, and he told me that you turned down a chance to sing with his wife."

I shrugged. "Girl, I'm not about that life. I just sing to free my mind. I don't wanna get mixed up in that lifestyle, Autumn, I just wanna go to school, start my career in law, and be loved by someone."

"We have so much to catch up on." Autumn smiled, dimples piercing her cheeks.

I nodded, dabbing my eyes with a napkin from the bar. "We do, girl, we really do."

"I know you're mad at me, but you have to give me a chance to make it up to you," Autumn cried.

"I'll try." I cried with her.

"So, how has your heart been doing?" She hesitated to ask.

I shook my head, lips trembling. "Broken."

Autumn pulled me closer, surrounding me in her arms. "Oh, I have missed you so much."

Autumn and a few of her friends hung out in VIP that night. I tried inviting Renée, but she thought it was best that I spend time alone with my sister. Autumn was still that same sexy, fun-loving girl that everyone loved to be around. She introduced me to her fiancé who was an up-and-coming fashion designer from Paris named Mark Antonio. My sister had twins. Eighteen-month-old girls named Alejandria and Alayna. She and Mark had been dating for three years when Mark popped the question. She said he proposed to her the day of the grand opening of Autumn's restaurant, Autumn Breeze. The couple looked so happy. You should have seen the way they were talking about their children, showing me photos of their beautiful babies who were being taken care of by Mark's nanny while they were on vacation for the week. She received the worst end of my mother's abuse. By looking at my sister, you couldn't tell that her heart wore scars. You couldn't tell that she was hurting. She deserved a good life after all that she had been through. I was so happy for her. I just wished that I could have felt the way that she was feeling.

When Charlie and a few of her friends entered VIP that night, I had to make an exit. I wasn't ready to face that reality just yet. She glanced at me as I made my exit. She knew that I wasn't even ready to be in the same room as her.

I made my way back to Renée and her friends. They were drunk as hell. Jamie's driver and the other limos that were parked outside were going to make a killing that night. It had hit midnight, and there had been no fights so far, but everyone was drunk and high as hell.

I leaned over the railing outside of the club that night, sipping on a Long Island Iced Tea. It's funny because instead of snowing that Christmas Day, it rained so it was feeling really nice outside. I needed air once Jamie and his entourage made their entrance around 11:30. As soon as they came through the doors, it seemed like even more ladies showed up.

"Whatcha doing out here alone, Heaven?" I heard a serenading voice that I hadn't heard in a while.

I looked over my shoulder to see Aaron walking toward me. I turned back around, sipping my drink. "Oh my goodness." I mumbled to myself. "Just my luck."

Aaron approached my side, leaning over the railing beside me. His eyes traced my profile as he took a pack of cigarettes out of his pocket. "What's good wit'cha?"

I just looked at him, lips trembling, I had no strength to talk to him about my situation. Instead, I took a sip from my glass.

Aaron put a cigarette to his lips, lighting it. "You know, it's not really over with you and Jamie, right?" he tried to assure me.

"Oh my God, we just broke up yesterday," I exclaimed. "How does everyone know about this already?"

Aaron chuckled. "Girl, you know news travels fast among your 'friends.' But I'm serious. You know y'all are gonna get back together. It's not over 'til it's over."

I shook my head in disagreement. "Well, it's over, Aaron," I whispered.

His eyes searched my face. "Real love doesn't ever end. I can feel your love for him, Heaven. Him being back did something to you. Something that I've never seen in you. He brings out the best in you. I can see it, and I know everyone else does too. I've seen you around. Whenever I see you two together, you're nothing but happy, smiling ear to ear. I've never seen you like that. It's beautiful; you're beautiful." He exhaled smoke from his nose.

I looked at him, drying the tears that refused to let me fight them back. It had been a minute since I really talked to him, up close and personal. He looked so good and smelled nice too. I'll admit, I did miss him. "How are things with preggo?" I asked.

Aaron snickered. "Rough, but we're making it work. She's got them 'Three As' that my aunt warned me about."

I made a what-the-hell-are-you-talking-about face. "What, Aaron?"

"You know, Attitude, Appetite, and Ass," he grinned.

I laughed a little. "You're a fool, Aaron."

He inhaled smoke from his cigarette, then slowly exhaled it from his nose again.

I sighed. "He sang to me," I whispered.

Aaron looked at me.

I nodded. "At our little pre-Thanksgiving get-together at his place, Jamie sang to me. I have known him all my life and never even knew he could sing. He wrote this beautiful song for me, and he sang it to me in front of like twenty people that night. It was the most beautiful song that I ever heard, and he sang it to me. Me, a person who wasn't even ready to make a full commitment to him. That's probably the real reason he broke up with me. He's been begging me to move in with him since his father's funeral."

Aaron's eyes searched my face. "I heard his interview on the radio yesterday." He nodded. "The nigga has got it bad. About as bad as I used to have it."

I looked at him, eyes growing misty again. "Used to, Aaron?"

He hesitated. "I'm not completely convinced that I'm over you, but I'm getting there. I really don't have a choice, do I? I'm getting married and Jamie's already claimed you, breakup or not. What about you? Seems like you didn't have any problems flushing me out of your system."

I shrugged. "It was a struggle, but Jamie has always had the key to my heart. You know that. You knew before we even had our first conversation that it was hard for me getting over him. Everyone in high school knew I was sprung. You even said so yourself."

"So, I was the rebound nigga."

I faced him. "That's not what I said, Aaron. I was torn that morning that we left the hotel. I had been infatuated with you for over two years. I felt ways about you that I made myself forget how to feel. When you dropped me off at my dorm after those days we spent together, I could still feel you all over my body for nearly a week. But when Jamie got a hold of me, every-thing changed. It took me four years to shake him from my system, Aaron. He moved back here, made me fall in love with him all over again, and just when I get used to having him around again—he dumps me. I'm telling you, I feel like a part of me is missing. It's like he is me, I am him, we are one. And without him, yes, I feel like I'm nothing because I have nothing if I don't have him." Tears slid down my face.

Aaron's eyes glistened. I know he hated to hear me talk about Jamie, but I had to tell some-body. "Why did y'all break up? Did he cheat on you? C'mon, baby, stop crying." Aaron held my face in his hands, drying my tears. Yes, his touch was still intoxicating, but my broken heart tried to fight back any feelings that might have still been there for him.

I took his hands from my face. "No, he did not cheat on me, Aaron. I don't even wanna talk about this."

"I hate to see you like this, Heaven. I like to see you happy, even if it's not with me. You have put up with so much shit that you didn't deserve, sweetheart, so you should have everything that you do deserve. I know I'm wrong for sayin' what I'm about to say to you, but you know I'm straight-up about the way how I feel, especially since I held it in for so long. I'm not gonna lie. I'm jealous as a muthafucka of the way that you feel about him. I waited too long to tell you, and I didn't approach you in high school because of the way everybody knew you felt about him. I'm working on getting over you, but it's not easy. I'm still very much in love with you."

I was speechless. I didn't even know what to say. Aaron was an amazing guy, true, but as amazing as he was, I was in love with Jamie, and I promised him I would never do anything to hurt him again. I felt guilty enough as it was involving myself with Aaron in the first place. I should have known better than to sleep with him. I didn't mean to confuse him or to lead him on. The way he felt about me was my fault. I'm not gonna lie, seeing Aaron still did something to my heart, but he was already taken, by my own sister, at that.

"I didn't fight for you," Aaron muttered under his breath, shaking his head shamefully to himself.

I looked at him. "What did you say?" I heard him; I just wanted to hear him say it again.

He looked at me. "I know you think I didn't fight for you hard enough."

I hesitated before answering him honestly. "No, I don't think you fought hard enough, but it's cool. It's all good."

Aaron laughed a little. "No, it's not 'all good.' I didn't fight for you because I couldn't make you happy. Jamie does that for you. Y'all have history. Y'all have chemistry. I'm not gonna pretend that this situation isn't painful because it is. I'm always gonna wonder 'what if,' ya know?"

"What if what?" I tried not to look at his lips, but I couldn't help it.

Aaron was looking at mine too. He licked his lips. "What if I would have stepped to you that day instead of her? The wedding, the engagement party, the baby—that could all be us. I fucked up; I fucked up bad. I let you fall back in love with dude because I couldn't disappoint my parents again. Shit ain't been the same since they sent me here to live with my aunt. Everything I do disappoints them. Marrying Charlie seems to be the only thing about me that makes my mother smile. You must think I'm a weak-ass nigga."

I shook my head. "No, I don't. I wish I had a mother to make proud. Or a father. It takes a very strong man to let another man have something that he wants. You love me, I know you do. I was a bitch to you that day at Jamie's father's funeral."

Aaron shook his head. "Nah. I knew better than to show up to the funeral. I was wrong for trying to put more pressure on you. For that, I apologize. I knew better."

I disagreed. "I didn't make the situation any better. We had something special, and I wasn't trying to acknowledge it because of the circumstances. And I didn't mean to diss you once I started seeing Jamie again. I was just tired of being—"

Aaron interrupted me, "No need to apologize. You should be happy. I waited too long, so I missed out. One thing I can say is at least I got to touch, kiss, hold, and make love to you. I have been wanting to do so much to you for so fuckin' long, Heaven."

My cheeks were burning red.

Aaron grinned a little. "I got to see what heaven was like, literally. I know there's no feeling like that, and I'm not even gonna go looking for it. You deserve a man who's gonna be with you and only you. A man who will treat you like you're the only woman on earth. What I know about Jamie, I don't like. I'm not saying that he's the type of man you need to be with, but if he's who you want, shorty, I wish you the best."

"Can we please change the subject?" I blushed, leaning over the railing again. "So, did you decide where you wanted to play ball?"

Aaron flicked his cigarette over into the parking lot. "France."

I grinned a little, until I thought about the way Charlie would feel about that. "Wait, what about Charlie? How does she feel about you going halfway around the world?"

Aaron shrugged, "I don't know, and to be honest, I don't really care. I just need a break from her and from you. I can't stand to see you in love with this dude. I'm sorry. And I can't stand Charlie's need for attention. I asked shorty to marry me, thinking she would be happy with just a small church wedding or even going to the courthouse like a lot of folks do. Nah. She's planning this this big, extravagant, Kim-Kanye-type wedding, yo. You saw the engagement party, right? You don't wanna know how much her parents spent on that, and you definitely don't wanna know what both of our parents decided to spend on our wedding. It's sickening, shorty. I'm not with this shit, for real for real."

I shook my head. He was marrying the wrong girl if he thought Charlie's high-maintenance ass was going to get married at a damn courthouse. He was talking about a girl who wore stilettos to take out the trash. I couldn't believe we were sisters. "Well, what about the baby, Aaron?" I asked.

Aaron looked at me, his eyes shimmering under the moonlight. "My agent says one of his colleagues is interested in helping Charlene jump-start a modeling career. While I'm overseas, they'll be working with her to build up a portfolio. She'll be too busy with photo shoots to even notice that I'm gone. She's got nannies, maids, her mama, and her sisters helping her with the baby. Not to mention my aunt and cousins. To tell you the truth, I thought about bringing the baby and a nanny to Paris with me. You know Charlie thought about having an abortion?"

I looked at Aaron, turning to him. I had to tell him what I heard about her. I sighed a long, weary sigh. "Aaron, I have to tell you something that I heard."

He just looked at me.

"I heard that Charlie cheated on you back in August and that the baby probably isn't even yours." I watched as he took the Long Island Iced Tea from my hand.

He drank the entire glass, then handed the empty glass back to me, drying my lips. "You know, as long as I've been seeing Charlie, I've been hearing rumors about her. I have heard 'em all, shorty, so nothing that anyone says bothers me anymore."

I shrugged, feeling stupid for even mentioning something that I should have known Aaron would have a hard time believing. No one wants to think that someone they are about to marry is pregnant by someone else. "I'm sorry for saying anything to you about it. I just couldn't watch you marry Charlie if the baby isn't yours, especially when the only reason why y'all are getting married in the first place is because she's supposed to be having your baby. That would be fucked up."

He looked at me, "Yeah, it would be fucked up. So, which one of your cousins told you this?"

I folded my arms. "Why do you assume it was one of my cousins who told me? What the fuck you tryin' to say, Aaron?"

He smirked. "C'mon, Heaven, when are your cousins not sticking their nose in other people's shit? Your cousins are the main bitches talkin' shit about someone when they got their own fucked-up situations goin' on. I hope it wasn't Renée, Wanda, Janice, Kendel, or Jennel's ass who told you this shit, because they all live in fuckin' glass houses."

I sighed. "Okay, it was Jennel, but—"

Aaron laughed out loud, cutting me off. "Shorty, please, okay? She's the main one who shouldn't talk shit about anybody. Your cousin Jennel, who just got married in June, has been sleepin' with Ashton's cousin, Lauryn, for the past six months. So she really needs to shut her damn mouth. I don't know who your cousins think they are, man, talkin' shit when I know all the dirt on their asses. Niggas talk in that locker room, shorty. There are no secrets that your girls can keep that these niggas don't already know about." Aaron laughed to himself. "I'm the one who fucked up when Charlie was trying her best to get me to love her. Yeah, she was always busy, but when we did spend time together, I'm the one who shut her out because of the rumors that I heard about her. I should have went to her and talked to her, instead of judging her for her past. I'm through with the rumors, okay? I love you so much, and I'm wrong for that shit, but I'm not gonna hurt that girl again by listening to rumors. I'm not even gonna confront her about it. She's hurt enough, ya know?"

"Well, on top of everything that I've been through these past few weeks," my lips trembled, "I found out today that me and your girl, Charlie, are sisters."

Aaron just looked at me with a blank stare on his face. "Sisters? Literally or figuratively speaking?"

"We have the same father. Juanita was fuckin' Theresa's boyfriend, and they were pregnant at the same time, just a few months apart." I couldn't hold back the tears anymore.

Aaron shook his head, not really sure what to say. "Damn," he whispered, watching the tears slide down my cheeks. He pulled me closer to him by my hips, and then gently dried my face. "I'm sorry."

I pushed his hands away. "There's nothing to be sorry about, Aaron. I didn't know, Charlie didn't know, and both of our mothers knew this shit but decided it was best to keep the truth from us. And history repeated itself. Our parents aren't friends anymore over some man who couldn't keep his dick in his pants, which is the same reason why me and Charlie aren't really on speaking terms. This shit is fucked up. I have lost everything in my life. My parents, my siblings, my best friends, my boyfriend. I'm tired, Aaron. Tired of hurting." I felt like drinking myself to death that night.

And Aaron knew it too. He shook his head. "Heaven, I can't stand to see you like this. You want me to help you get Jamie back?"

I looked at him, drying my face. "What?"

He grinned. "Do you want me to help you get your nigga back? You heard what I said."

My lips trembled. "Aaron, why would you help me?"

His eyes searched my face. "I just wanna see you happy, Heaven. I already told you that I wanna see you smiling, even if it's not because of me."

I sighed. He really did care about me. Why, I wasn't sure, but I was glad that someone thought of my feelings for once instead of their own. "How are we supposed to do this, Aaron?"

He took me by the hand. "I'll show you. You just have to trust me."

We walked back into the club. The dance floor was covered. Lovers held each other so close it was hard to tell where he started and she began. I stood alongside the dance floor, facing Aaron as he stood there, surveying the room, looking cool as hell.

"What are we doing?" I spoke over the music.

Aaron grinned when he saw whatever it was that he was looking for. He looked back at me, as one of my favorite love songs, "New Flame," flowed through the speakers. "C'mon." He held my hand, leading me out onto the dance floor.

My heart pounded in my chest. I could feel all eyes on us. Everyone there knew us. His friends were there. My friends and family were there. Shit, Charlie and Jamie were there. We were about to piss a few people off, and I knew that was Aaron's crazy-ass intention.

Aaron stopped when he got in the middle of the dance floor, pulled me closer to him by my hand, and started dancing. Slowly, I started dancing with him.

Aaron grinned.

I was in tears.

Aaron leaned forward, whispering in my ear. "C'mon, babe, stop crying and dance with me. Look happy. Just trust me, Heaven. He's watching."

I dried my face and tried to put on a smile as I danced with him, swaying my hips.

It wasn't long before Renée, Kelissa, Jennel, Dana, Danita, and the rest of the gossipers danced their way closer to us. They weren't too close, but they were in view.

When Renée saw that she'd caught my eye, she mouthed, with eyes as big as saucers, "Bish, what the fuck are you doing? Jamie is gonna straight kill him."

I shrugged as Aaron pulled me closer to him by my hips. We were so close that I could feel his heart beating and feel his eyelashes brushing against the side of my face. Yeah, Jamie was going to try to knock his head off. And just when I looked over Aaron's shoulder, I see Charlie storming toward us. I stopped dancing with him just when Charlie reached him, snatching him away from me by his arm.

"What the fuck, Aaron?" she yelled at him, getting in his face. "Y'all muthafuckas back at it again?"

I'm not even sure if the music stopped, but at that moment, all I could hear was my heart beating and Charlie cursing Aaron out.

"Charlie, calm the fuck down. It's not even what you think." Aaron pried her hand from his arm. "Shorty, chill."

Charlie stepped in front of Aaron, getting a little too close to my face, as if I was just going to let her hit me. "So, you didn't hear me the first time when I told you to stay the fuck away from him, huh? What—you thought I was playin' or some shit, Ne'Vaeh?"

I sighed. "Charlie, you really need to chill the fuck out. I don't want your man, and your man doesn't want me. We were just dancing, that's it."

Charlie shook her head, really ready to fight me. "Nah, I think you want your ass whupped." She started kicking off her heels, taking off her earrings and shit. Kelissa and Danita pulled her away from me, kicking and fuckin' screaming. She really wanted to get a hold of me, but they wouldn't let her.

"So, we break up, and you're back up in this nigga's face the next day, shorty?" I heard Jamie's voice over my shoulder.

I turned around, heart racing, prepared to stop Jamie from charging straight at Aaron. Ashton was already prepared to throw down for his boy. Aaron just stood there, hands in his pockets, a slight grin across his face. He winked at me, as I struggled to pull Jamie back. I was the only one stupid enough to try to stop Jamie from fighting. Everyone knew that there was no stopping Jamie once he was in attack mode. He always had that protector mentality. He always felt the need to fight and protect what was his, even when a fight wasn't necessary because he had already won.

Jamie pulled from me, pushing me off of him. He got in Aaron's grill. "Didn't I tell you to stay the fuck away from her, nigga? You don't seem to know that I will kill a muthafucka over her."

Aaron laughed to himself. "Yo, I'm not trying to get with your girl. We were dancin', that's it. I'm gettin' married in a week, dude. You don't gotta fight me, Jamie, because you already won. But I can see why you would wanna fight for her. She loves you, dawg. Why would you break it off with someone like her, yo? Whatever you did to fuck it up, you need to fix that shit."

It didn't take Jamie long to go from zero to one hundred, but it took some convincing to get him to go from one hundred to zero. Jamie threatened Aaron. "Stay the fuck away from her, nigga. This is the last time I'm gonna tell your muthafuckin' ass. All these women in here, and you chose to dance with her? Muthafucka, don't fuck with her unless you ready to get fucked up."

"Okay, fellas, let's break this up." One of the bouncers in the club approached us, and didn't leave until the crowd dissipated.

I left the dance floor, Jamie following behind me. He snatched me toward him by my arm. "What the fuck were you doin' dancin' with that muthafucka? Why you tryin' to play me?" he yelled at me.

I pulled from him, pushing him. "Play you? Jamie, you're the one who broke up with me. You have no say-so about my life anymore. You dumped me, and you're mad at me just because you see me dancing with someone? Jamie, I love you, and you just left me like I wasn't shit."

Jamie's anger simmered down a little. Instead of one hundred, he was maybe around thirty by now. "Come take a walk with me real quick." He grabbed my hand, leading me out of the club.

We stood outside of the club that night, facing each other.

Jamie looked down at me, hands in his pockets. "Why you tryin' to hurt me, Ne'Vaeh? You know I can't stand to see you with dude—shit, any dude."

I looked up at him, heart sprinting. "Jamie, you broke it off with me, remember? I was just dancing with Aaron. That's it. He saw me outside, crying over you, and he said he knew what it would take to get your attention. That's why he took me out there on that dance floor. Everyone knows who I love. You're the only asshole who doesn't seem to know where my heart is." I pushed him in his chest. "Aaron is getting married in a few days. You were way out of line in there. You broke up with me last night, Jamie—why are we out here? What could you possibly have to say to me tonight? Haven't you ruined Christmas—our first Christmas around each other in four years—enough?"

He looked at me earnestly. "I just wanted to say Merry Christmas." He dug through his pants pocket, taking out a silver box from Tiffany's, about the size of a small index card. He handed it to me.

My lips trembled as I took the box in my hand. "Wh- what's this?"

Jamie grinned, taking the top off of the box for me.

I looked down into the box. There it was—the most beautiful necklace I had ever seen. It was a beautiful platinum necklace that had a platinum key speckled in diamonds hanging from it. I cried as Jamie turned the key over, revealing the inscription on the back: *Only Ne'Vaeh holds the key to Jamie's Heart.*

I was bawling, face soaked, snot dripping. Jamie laughed a little as he took the necklace from the box and hooked it around my neck. I looked into his face as he straightened the necklace out. The cold platinum and diamond-coated key hung between my breasts.

"This necklace symbolizes my eternal love for you," he whispered. "I know I'm jerk, I know I'm an asshole, and I know I fucked up, but I do and always will love you with all of my heart. I don't deserve to be with you. I'll always be your friend. I'll always be here for you. But I can't be your man knowing that I did something unforgivable to you."

"So, you don't wanna be together, but you don't want anyone else to be with me either? How is that gonna work out, Jamie?" I just looked into his face.

He shrugged. "I don't know, shorty. I just can't see you with anyone but me. I fucked up, and I need to see how things work out with this chick before I go involving you in my drama. I don't want you to have to go through that. You don't deserve to go through that."

Really, as crazy as it sounds, I didn't give a fuck what Jamie did or who he did it with. I just wanted him to hold me, to take me home, to make love to me, to run his fingers through my hair, to kiss me, to touch me, to lie facing me in his bed. You have to understand, I hadn't seen my baby in four years. I had just got him back and was nowhere near letting him go.

"Anyway, thank you, Jamie." I dried my face. "Renée made me put your present in the backseat of your Tahoe."

He nodded, eyes sparkling. "A'ight."

I looked up into his face. "You goin' back inside?"

He shook his head. "Nah, I'm headed to another party with my crew in a few minutes."

I nodded. "Okay. Well, when you get home or you get situated, just give me a call. Renée and her girls are partying all night. I don't have anything to do tonight, so if you want me to come over and chill, just call me."

Jamie hesitated. "Y-you wanna come by crib tonight? Kick it, like really kick it? As in spend the night with me?"

I shrugged. "I mean, you bought me this beautiful gift, Jamie. You didn't have to. I'm not gonna sit here and pretend that I can just be your friend, because I can't. If you wanna do this without labels for now, we can. I just wanna be in your life. I don't give a fuck who your baby's mama is, Jamie. I just wanna be with you. I can't just be your friend."

Jamie shook his head, misty-eyed. "Shorty, I don't know how this is gonna work out. I'm not gonna sit here and act like this girl is not gonna make my life and yours a living hell. The last thing that I wanna do is hurt you. I've taken you through enough as it is. You didn't have to take me back, but you did. You didn't have to love me, but you did. Dude in that club is in love with you, shorty. You could have got with dude, but didn't. He doesn't love Charlie, you know he doesn't. You know he wants you, but you want me, and I fucked up."

I held his hand, pulling him to me. "Jamie, please, just tell me what time to meet you at your place, and I'll be there. I just want you to hold me, if nothing else. I don't wanna be alone on Christmas. I'm always alone, and I'm sick of it."

Jamie nodded. "Fuck that party, yo. I'm ready to go to the crib now if you want."

I lay wide awake in Jamie's bed that night, in his arms, naked, wearing nothing but the necklace that he gave me. My sister, Autumn, had been blowing up my phone the entire night that I was at Jamie's. She sent me a text, saying that she was in town for a week and she would try to get up with me before Charlie's wedding so that we could go "dress shopping" together. Charlie sent me a text message saying that we needed to meet the next day to talk. I really didn't feel like talking to anyone other than Jamie, but I felt like he was holding back from me. We talked about everything that night except what was on our minds. I didn't even tell him that I found out that Charlie was my sister. That was a situation that I didn't even want to be in, let alone talk about.

Jamie and I didn't even make love that night. We showered, we kissed, we cried, we held each other; then he fell asleep embracing me in his arms. He was hurting on the inside. The more he tried to run from me, the more I forced him to stay. I just couldn't handle him leaving me again after missing him for so long. I was even willing to accept him having a baby with another woman just so he would stay in my life. I had no idea what was in store for me, but whatever it was, as long as Jamie was still in my life, it didn't even matter . . . so I thought.

Chapter 9

No Him without Her

Charlene

"So, you're really gonna sit there and act like nothing happened tonight, Aaron?" I watched Aaron stumble into my apartment, tossing his keys on the coffee table, then plopping his drunk ass down on the sofa.

He looked up at me, eyes damn near blood-shot red. "Charlene, we're not gonna keep goin' in circles. I don't know what the fuck else you want me to say. I can't even be in the same room with the girl without you thinkin' that I'm fuckin' her."

Oh, I wanted to throw my clutch purse upside his fuckin' head. "Aaron, you weren't just in the same room with the girl, you were damn near fuckin' humpin' her on the dance floor."

Aaron laughed out loud. "What? Man, them hormones got your ass straight trippin'. I'm marrying you in a few days, not her, Charlene. The girl was outside, heartbroken as a mutha-fucka because Jamie's ass dumped her yesterday, yo. She was crying over dude, talkin' about she was nothin' without him. I hated seeing her like that. I danced with Ne'Vaeh to get the dude's attention, just to show the girl that he was still in love with her. You said so yourself that she needed love. I was just trying to help her get it back. She doesn't deserve the shit that she's been through; you know that."

I sighed, going over to sit beside Aaron on the couch. When I saw Ne'Vaeh dancing with Aaron that night, I saw red. I was pissed. She always got everything that she wanted, regardless of whether she knew it. She wanted love, and everybody loved her. Aaron loved her, Jamie loved her—my family loved her. I still couldn't fathom the thought of being her sister. It still hadn't fully registered itself in my mind. I cared about Aaron, I loved Aaron, and I adored Aaron. But I was in love with Jamie, my sister's Jamie. I had no idea how my situation was going to turn out, but I knew that I was in for a hell of a ride if I planned on having Jamie in my life in any kind of way.

I looked at Aaron. He was in love with the girl; I knew he was. Everyone knew he was. It would have hurt more than it did if I didn't feel the way that I did about Jamie. Jamie could care less about me. He had broken up with Ne'Vaeh to save her from heartbreak when the truth came out about us. But as soon as he saw her just dancing with another man, he was ready to fight to get her back. I knew Jamie and I would never be together, but I was determined to keep him from Ne'Vaeh. I had it set in my mind that if I couldn't have him, she sure as hell wasn't getting him. And if letting the truth out about us was going to tear them apart, well, damn it, I was going to do what I had to do.

Yeah, you can say that it was a cruel thing to do to my own sister, but you have to understand where I was coming from. My heart was broken when I went to Miami. I went there to escape life at home. My career goals were a joke to my family. They were obsessed with me being with Aaron. My mother had it in her mind that Aaron was going to be a star and I was just going to be his trophy wife. She hated my independence. She thought that a man was supposed to take care of a woman, and the woman was supposed to take care of home. I supported Aaron all of the way; shit, I played a huge part in helping him get to where he was. But I had my own dreams of being a model and ripping the runway, or being a dancer. My mother had other plans for me. My mom was determined to get me down the aisle to meet Aaron at the other end. She was furious when she heard the rumors about me from other mothers in the neighborhood. Nude photos of me with various men were all over Facebook and Instagram. Aaron hadn't looked at me the same since he saw the picture of me with one dick in my mouth and the other in my ass. There was no way I was getting a real job with photos like that floating around.

When I ran into Jamie in Miami, he made me forget about my problems at home. He spent time with me, he touched me, he kissed me, he talked to me, he laughed with me, he held me close, he ran his fingers through my hair, he told me that I was pretty, he flirted with me, he spent time with me, and he wasn't ashamed of me. The truth about me didn't scare him, and that was mainly because we had similar pasts. Ashton didn't lie about me when he called me out the day that he caught Jamie in my apartment. That wasn't his feelings talking—the truth spoke for itself.

"So, we cool, Charlie?" Aaron sat up in the chair, rubbing my belly.

I looked at him. I have to admit, it really hurt knowing that little August wasn't his. Though Aaron was in shock the day that I told him that I was pregnant, my pregnancy had started to grow on him. He was actually proud that I was carrying his baby. Had even ordered my son a bedroom set. He must have had twenty bags of baby clothes from Foot Locker, Baby Gap, and Children's Place, every place, at his apartment. We were two weeks away from closing on a house in Washington, D.C. Aaron planned for his baby's arrival better than I had. He was the one who registered little August at about five stores. When I checked the registries, everything had been bought. While Aaron was picking out bedding and wardrobe for my son, I was still stuck on the baby's last name.

I dried the tears that drizzled down my cheeks. "Yeah, we're cool, bae," I nodded.

Aaron looked at me, green eyes searching my face. "We got a lot to do in a week's time, Mama."

I nodded, not evening trying to think about all the shit I had to do. "Omg, I know, yo. I am just glad that everyone is already fitted for their clothes. They should have their clothes by the rehearsal dinner. Mama's already planned the bridal shower and baby shower that are on the same day, same time, by the way. And my cousins and girls from the squad are planning the bachelorette party. It's gonna be off the chain, yo—Anastasia 'Passion' Jones is flying in some of her girls from the club she used to work for in ATL. I can't wait."

Aaron laughed a little. "A'ight, shorty, don't twerk too hard. I know you're trying to avoid talking to your sister, but it's a conversation that you really need to have."

I rolled my eyes, taking his hands from my stomach. "Look, I will talk to Ne'Vaeh when I feel like talking to her, Aaron. The bitch got too close to you, just dancing, trying to get Jamie's attention or not. The bitch was grinding a little too hard on that dick, and I didn't appreciate it. Your hands were all over her. You can deny all you want to, but y'all look like y'all were having a little too much fun to me. I'm gonna let it go, though. I tried being civilized with her, but she's still pissed at me for calling her a groupie."

Aaron was stunned for a minute or two. He just looked at me like he didn't know what the fuck I was talking about. "What, shorty? I was talking about your little sister, Heather. You know she's gonna wanna bring that chick that she's dating to your wedding. Your mama and your from-the-old-school-where-they-don't-play-that-shit aunties ain't tryin' to see that girl-on-girl shit."

I sank back in my seat. I really didn't feel like discussing the fact that I'd found out Ne'Vaeh was my sister. I wasn't ready to accept the fact we shared the same blood or that we were following that same road that our mothers walked down nineteen years earlier. Dad had two chicks pregnant at the same time, and to throw more fuel on the fire, he tried to make my mother take the baby from her own best friend. I guess I was just like my father . . . too bold. There I was pregnant by my own sister's boyfriend, and lying to my own boyfriend telling him that it was his. History didn't repeat itself—it beat itself.

Aaron sat up in the couch, looking me in the face. "Charlie, when did you find out? Did Ne'Vaeh tell you this?"

I looked at him. "Ne'Vaeh?"

He sighed. "Outside of the club, she told me that Renée told her that y'all were sisters. She was feeling some type of way about that. I'm sure you are too."

I rolled my eyes, breathing heavily. "It really shouldn't even surprise me that she told you. I bet she hasn't even told Jamie yet. I really don't feel like discussing it. But to make a long-ass story short, Renée's ass was on me about going to visit Ne'Vaeh's mother in prison. Juanita told me that we were sisters. That the reason she

and my mother hated each other was because
of my father. The man who I looked up to and
respected. He was a family man. He went to
work every morning at 6:15 and was home
every night by 7:30. My parents had date night,
movie night, family night, prayer night, bowl-
ing night, double date night, and put-the-kids-
out-of-the-fuckin'-house-so-they-could-run-
around-the-house-butt-naked night. My dad
loved my mother more than anything, and
it's just hard to believe that he cheated on
my mother with Juanita, Mama's best friend.
Mama admitted the truth to me, said that
Juanita was a bad bitch back in her day. That
every nigga wanted her, including my dad. She
said she knew they were sleeping together, but
she ignored it. Said that she was trying to save
herself for marriage, and my father wasn't trying to hear that, especially when there were
girls like Juanita who were willing to do anything. Mama said she didn't want to taint the
image of my father. Said she didn't want to hurt
me or Ne'Vaeh by telling us the truth. She said
we were inseparable, sisters at heart anyway, so
she saw no need to tell us the truth."

Aaron shook his head, not sure what he could
say that would make the situation any better.
"Babe, I never meant to hurt you. I never meant

to hurt her. Please don't hate shorty because of me."

I quickly dried my face. I wasn't going to allow myself to cry over Ne'Vaeh. She had something that I wanted, and if I couldn't have it, she couldn't either. She stole Aaron's love from me, and it seemed like she was born to have Jamie's heart. I was really sick of it.

"Y'all need to talk, Charlie. Don't shake your head at me. She's your girl, your rider, your ace, your sister. If you wanna blame someone, if you wanna hate someone, put it all on me. It was my fault." Aaron looked at me beseechingly.

My lips trembled. "Aaron, I really don't wanna hear you taking up for her."

"I pursued her," he admitted. "Shorty cursed me the fuck out the day that I told her how I felt about her. Trust me, it wasn't easy doing what I did. She told me how fucked up that I was for even telling her how I felt, and that I should have kept the shit to myself. All she talked about was how you took her in when she had no place to go. She didn't wanna hurt you. I ignored her when she tried to run from me. I went after her even when she told me that we were wrong. She loves you, Charlie. So hate me, not her." Aaron's eyes glistened. "She told me to stop fuckin' with her heart, but I wouldn't listen, and

I'm sorry. I didn't mean to come between your friendship, your bond, your sisterhood. I was wrong, baby. Please forgive me. Please forgive her. You know she didn't mean it."

How could I forgive her? She had won over my family's affection. She'd won the heart of the man that I always wanted. Even when I knew she liked Aaron, and I basically stole him right from under her nose, she still managed to get his attention. She'd won from every angle of my life. No matter what I did to try to take either Jamie or Aaron from her, it really didn't matter. Jamie was in love with her. Aaron was infatuated with even the thought of her. At that point, there was nothing I could do but try to be in Jamie's life some way or another. I didn't want to hurt Aaron, and I didn't want to hurt Jamie. I'd gotten myself tangled in a web of lies that was going to be a muthafucka to escape from. Whatever decision I decided to make, everyone was going to end up hurt. However, as long as Ne'Vaeh was hurt in the process, I would at least have that satisfaction.

They (whoever "they" is) say you attract more bees with honey. I was never too keen on that phrase, but I was going to have to take the advice of the ones before and do what I had to do to get to Jamie's heart. I texted Ne'Vaeh that night, asking her if she could meet me the next morning to do a little day-after-Christmas shopping. She texted back, telling me to meet her at her choir rehearsal around 11:30 the next morning.

So, I showed up that morning in my cute Burberry jumper and stilettos. I walked into the auditorium at Howard University to see Ne'Vaeh on stage, singing her little ass off. For a girl as small as she was, she packed a powerful voice. Her voice always stunned you to complete silence. It was hard to jerk back the tears once Ne'Vaeh's voice infiltrated the air around you.

"It's about time someone shows up to support my little angel other than me." I heard Jamie's sensual, mesmerizing voice over my shoulder.

I turned around, facing Jamie as he walked down the aisle toward me. My heart vibrated in my chest as he approached me, dressed in all black from his head to his Jordans.

"What's good wit'cha, ma?" he asked, once we were standing face-to-face.

"I'm taking your girl shopping today. Hopefully, I can convince her to come to my baby slash bridal shower tomorrow. It's the least she can do since she turned down my invitation to be my maid of honor." I looked up into his face. Good God, my addiction to chocolate was getting stronger with each second that I was around that boy. Just his presence was intoxicating. His smooth chocolaty skin was flawless. Everything about the way he looked was perfect. I wanted to kiss his wet, silky lips. It took everything in me not to grab that boy by his collar and suck his fuckin' lips off.

Jamie looked up at Ne'Vaeh singing on stage. He looked at that bitch like she was the best got-damn thing in the world. Ugh. I rolled my eyes watching him watching her.

He smiled to himself. "Damn, my baby's got skills, shorty. Convincing her to do something with her voice is tougher than I thought, but I'm a fighter. You know I'm not one to give up. I'm gonna get shorty in that studio to record a demo if it's the last thing I do." Jamie looked at me. "You good? I mean, about last night?"

I rolled my eyes, "Boy, please. I had my talk with bae. It's all good. He knows how to press my buttons, that's for damn sure. What about you? I thought you and Ne'Vaeh broke up on Christmas Eve? Looks to me like y'all are back together. That was the quickest break-up-to-make-up in history."

Jamie laughed a little, watching Ne'Vaeh talking with the choir director.

"You just couldn't stand to see her with someone else, is that it?" I looked at his profile.

Jamie looked back at me. "Nah, I can't. I know I'm wrong for saying that, but I can't stand to see another dude touching her. It took everything in me not to knock you dude's head off of his shoulders last night. Dude was about to get fucked up. I don't play when it comes to shorty, yo, together or not. If shit doesn't work out with us, shit, I'ma have to relocate or some shit because I'm not gonna be able to see shorty with someone else, kissing on him and shit. The worst thing a nigga can do is let another nigga make his girl smile when he fucked up."

"I fucked up, Jamie." I had to tell him how I felt while I had the chance. "All jokes, smart comments, hard feelings, jealous feelings, hormones and all aside, I love you, Jamie."

He just looked at me.

I looked up at him. "I knew back in elementary and middle school that we'd never be together, so it doesn't surprise me now—even with my present situation—that you and I are never gonna happen. I get that. I'm dealing with that situation the best way that I know how. Aaron has been doing his best to work things out with me. He's a good man, Jamie, and I know that I don't deserve him."

Jamie looked at me and asked, "Why are you telling me this now, right here?"

"Because I have to be in your life some type of way, Jamie. I'm having your baby whether you wanna acknowledge the shit or not." I tried the best way that I could to keep my voice down.

Jamie tried to keep his composure the best way that he could. I'm pretty sure he was tired of me always causing a scene when I was near him. He looked around the room to make sure no one was listening before he dug in my ass the way he always did. "Charlie, I swear, you are the most selfish woman that I've ever met. You're only thinking about yourself. You're not in this fucked-up situation by yourself. You're about to marry this dude, knowing he's only marrying you because he thinks that you're having his baby. I tried to break it off with shorty, but she didn't even give a fuck that I have someone else pregnant. True, I may not have told her that you're the one who I got pregnant, but that's because I know that I won't be able to see the look on her face when your name comes out of my mouth. The only way that I'm gonna be in your life, Charlene, is if you manage to stay in Ne'Vaeh's life, and it's as simple as that, shorty."

I felt like slapping the shit out of him. "You're seriously saying that the only way to you is through her, and you're wondering why I'm fuckin' selfish. Why should I have to be alone when I wasn't at fault on my own? Aaron fucked up when he fucked with Ne'Vaeh, and, yeah, maybe I fucked up when I fucked with you. But I am not about to end up alone after everything that I've been through."

"This isn't about whose fault it is, Charlene. It's about doing the right thing," Jamie exclaimed. "And the right thing to do was to tell dude the truth from jump. Dude was leaving you because he wanted to be with her and you couldn't see that shit happening, so you lied to him. You're really gonna have this dude believing this baby is his? You both look damn near white. You never know with us black folk how our babies are gonna turn out. What if the baby comes out chocolate-coated like me? Or black as a muthafucka, because you know I got some crispy muthafuckas in my family, Charlene. How the fuck are you gonna explain that shit to him?"

I didn't know what to say. I just looked at him, at a loss for words. I hated when he was right about me being dead wrong.

"I'm sure you have him out there, buying all types of expensive shit for the baby. I'm sure his parents probably already know about the baby, huh? I heard his parents were some sort of heirs to some type of royalty. His parents probably already have a college fund set up for his ass. I'm sure little August Carter was added to grandpa's will. You're gonna crush this man's entire life. And I'll be damned if I let you get everything you want while you destroy mine. I know what I said to you at the hospital was fucked up, but I always come real with you, and you know it." Jamie watched the tears slide down my face. "Charlie, you're a gorgeous woman—sexy as a muthafucka. Just tell dude the truth. Trust me, you'll find someone else. It's never gonna happen with you and me, shorty, so face it. You're holding up this lie just so you can string along dude when you're not even sure you wanna be with him. You wanna be with me, and you know it's never gonna happen. Period. End of discussion."

Tears raced down my face, but I quickly dried them away as I heard the choir director bring rehearsal to a close.

"I'm man enough to tell Ne'Vaeh the truth when the time comes . . . even if that means losing her." Jamie fought back the tears. "I love her enough to let her go. Once I tell her, it'll be her choice whether she decides to be with me.

I can't force her. You're forcing Aaron into this, and it's not right. You know it, Charlie." Jamie watched as Ne'Vaeh walked off the stage steps. He looked back at me. "If you don't tell dude by rehearsal dinner, I'm gonna tell him. We have to face and own up to our mistakes, Charlene."

I was about to curse him the hell out when Ne'Vaeh hesitated down the aisle toward us. She slowly approached us, dressed in a cute, long-sleeved, knee-length dark denim jean dress that hugged her in all the right places. She could sense the tension between us.

"Is everything okay, J?" She eyed both of us, as Jamie gently kissed her on the forehead.

"Yeah, shorty, everythang is all good. Charlie here was just telling me she plans on inviting you to her baby & bridal shower." Jamie put his arm around her.

Ne'Vaeh looked at me and the way that I was watching Jamie. "You want me—the same girl whose ass you wanted to kick last night—to come to your baby shower?"

I laughed a little. "That was just me fighting for my man. I don't play when it comes to him. I'm sorry; I was wrong. But, yes, I'm here not only to take you shopping with me, but to also ask you to come to my party tomorrow afternoon. You already said no to being my maid of honor, Ne'Vaeh; I mean, it's the least that you can do."

Ne'Vaeh's eyes sparkled under the auditorium lights. She hesitated to nod. "Okay . . . I guess I'll come."

Ne'Vaeh and I sat across from each other that afternoon at Mission Barbeque. We'd shopped for a good three hours before my feet started to swell in my heels. She hadn't laughed or smiled; shit, she barely even looked at me. I knew Ne'Vaeh well enough to know that she was feeling ashamed for sleeping with Aaron. She always was her own worst critic.

"You know, I always sensed that we were sisters." I had to break the ice. "I always felt this sort of 'sibling rivalry' between us. We were always competing for shit. We fought over everything from clothes, to toys, to purses, to—"

Ne'Vaeh cut me off, eyes sparkling as she looked up from her plate, "to men."

I laughed a little to myself. "Yeah, I guess you can say our tastes are too similar."

"Yeah, I guess. Maybe a little." Ne'Vaeh finally flashed a slight grin. "Must run in the family."

"But all jokes aside, my father tried to move you into the house several times before he passed away. There were plenty of nights that my parents woke us all up, arguing over taking you from Juanita." My heart ached at the thought of losing my father. "He really loved you, and I should have put two and two together, but I was too jealous of how much my parents really cared about you. My mother took you in because my father—no, our father—asked her to look after you. It was his dying wish, Ne'Vaeh, to take you from her. According to Mama, everyone knew you were my father's baby. I was always jealous of you, Ne'Vaeh." I laughed a little to cover up my pain and frustration. "You were so got-damn cute, so adorable, so petite, so tiny, so loved, so heavenly without even trying to be."

Ne'Vaeh rolled her big, dampened eyes at me. "Girl, please, are you serious? With your young Mariah-Carey, Lauryn-London-lookin' ass? Jealous of me? Me? Who would want a cheeseburger when they could have fuckin' filet mignon? Who would want a girl with a mouth full of braces, a mouthful of breasts, and barely a handful of ass? You sittin' here with a titty explosion and an ass eruption, mermaid-down-to-your-ass hair, and legs for miles, but you're jealous of me? Women pay to look like you, Charlene. You always were an ungrateful somebody, never realizing your worth or how much better you have it than everybody else. Your parents felt sorry for me, but they didn't love me more than you. Everything to you is a fuckin' contest."

I ignored her. "I'm so attractive, so beautiful, so sexy, huh? Okay," I dried my tears, "well, what about Aaron? Between the two of us, who do you think he finds the most attractive? Who do you think he loves? I think he'd take the tiny, petite, brown Barbie doll over a light-skinned girl who looks like a fuckin' stripper. I mean, the muthafucka doesn't have any light-skinned, big booty models on the walls in the room at his apartment. All of the bitches on his wall look just like your ass. Ne'Vaeh, you know he's only marrying me because he waited too late to get to you. I'm not stupid. If I wasn't pregnant, he would have left me back in October, on your got-damn birthday. If his parents weren't so hung up on reputation, this ring would be on your finger, not mine."

Ne'Vaeh's lips trembled. "Charlie, I'm so sorry. I never should have slept with him. I know that no amount of apologies can make up for what I did with him, with my own sister's boyfriend." Her eyes watered.

I knew better. We were way past Aaron. He wasn't even the issue. I caused a scene the night before at the club just to try to deter my heart from Jamie. I actually think I was more hurt by the fact that Jamie was willing to fight for her than I was that Aaron was dancing with her. I wasn't sure what sort of inner conflict that Aaron was having with himself, but once Jamie was back in town, he knew he didn't stand a chance. If he even thought he had a chance at winning Ne'Vaeh, he would have never proposed, despite what his family's philosophies were.

"We're way past Aaron, sweetie, I assure you." I dried my face. "I know how he feels about you. It's my own fault that he even fell into your arms. I should've never lived the way that I did; then Aaron would have never have had to find out about me like he did. I can't keep blaming Alisha and her crew for my fallout with Aaron. I would have judged me too. Aaron has been nothing but wonderful these past few months. He genuinely loves this baby. I don't even know if I'm ready to be a mother. I'm so not prepared for this baby, but, Aaron, shit, he's already bought everything for this baby that I'll need to bring little August home from the hospital."

Ne'Vaeh sighed deeply. "Well, I'm sure you have heard by now why Jamie broke up with me. He came to me in November, upset because he got a girl pregnant, and she had an abortion before even telling him about the baby. I let him slide on that fuckery. But then, on Christmas Eve, right before we were supposed to be going to his aunt's Christmas party, he breaks up with me, afraid out of his fuckin' mind to tell me that he had got another bitch pregnant."

My heart thumped in my chest. The fool really did tell her. He really needed to learn how to lie to that girl.

"He broke up with me, Charlie, and I couldn't handle it. I'd just gotten him back. I hadn't seen, heard, touched, smelled, or kissed that boy in four fuckin' years. I was lost without him, so lost that I let my own best friend's—no—my sister's—boyfriend convince me that it was okay to have sex with him. I'm not myself without Jamie. I don't want to be without Jamie."

"You really love this dude?" I asked.

Ne'Vaeh looked at me. "When wasn't I in love with Jamie?"

I couldn't resist. "Hmmm, I don't know . . . maybe when you were fuckin' Aaron?"

I know, I went all the way left, but playing with her emotions was fun as hell.

Ne'Vaeh stopped midway through her chicken salad sandwich and set it back down on her plate. She felt a whole lot guiltier sleeping with Aaron than I did sleeping with Jamie, that's for damn sure.

"What made you sleep with Aaron when you knew he's my man?" I rolled my neck at her.

Ne'Vaeh sat quietly for a moment. She knew I'd show my true colors sooner or later. "I thought you just said we were way past Aaron?"

"I just wanna know what made you do this to me. Y'all muthafuckas waited until my uncle's funeral to act out this li'l fantasy. What did he say to you that night to get you to take the dick? How'd he get you to spend all those nights in that hotel?" I looked at her, watching the way her lips trembled. She was an emotional wreck, and I loved it.

"He-He called me Heaven," she admitted. "I always loved when he called me that."

Oh, I wanted to jump across the table at her. But then I remembered, yes, I remembered that revenge was mine. I rubbed my belly and grinned at her. "So, Jamie's having a baby with some THOT, huh?"

Ne'Vaeh looked relieved that I changed the subject. "I don't even care about all that anymore. Whatever happened with whoever happened way before we got back together. I just want to be with him. I know it doesn't make sense, but I'd rather deal with his baby's mama in his life than be without Jamie in mine."

I couldn't stop the words from coming out of my mouth. "No matter who the baby mama is?"

She hesitated, then shrugged. "He got the girl—whoever she may be—pregnant before we started seeing each other, so what can I do? As long as it's not that li'l Puerto Rican chick who keeps calling him, texting him, and showing up to all of his events asking about her got-damn panties, then it's all good. I'm surely gonna cut that bitch if she asks about them panties one more got-damn time." Ne'Vaeh laughed a little.

I was starting to rethink being so happy about getting revenge. Ne'Vaeh was holding in her anger a little too well. She was a ticking time bomb just waiting to pop off. It wouldn't be long until something sparked her short fuse.

Chapter 10

The Key to His Heart

Charlene

I sat crying alone in one of the bathrooms at Jamie's mansion the afternoon of my baby slash bridal shower. I just couldn't sit in the same room with Ne'Vaeh and not feel guilty about everything that I had done. Though I was guilty, I still felt some type of way about her and her relationship with Jamie. And I know the first thing in your mind is, why is this bitch at Jamie's house, huh?

My mother was the catalyst for the events that went down that day. At around 11:00 that morning, the pipes burst in the hotel where my mother planned on throwing my baby shower. She took it upon herself to confront Jamie. She argued with me all the way to Jamie's mansion around 12:30 that afternoon, after finding out that Ne'Vaeh was in Greenbelt getting her hair done. Mama let it be known to Jamie that she knew about us. That whether he wanted to or not, he was going to help provide for me and for his child.

I knew by the way Jamie looked at me while my mother was cursing him out that he was pissed off with me. Surprisingly, he kept his cool. "Mrs. Campbell, I never meant to hurt your daughter," Jamie's responded. He stood alongside the island in his enormous kitchen. He was dressed in a tank top and sweatpants, and looked high as hell. He'd probably just woken up. I was sure he didn't plan on being lectured by anyone's mother that morning. Even though my mother was totally, actually and factually, out of line, he listened to what her crazy ass had to say.

"I know you care about my daughter enough to support her through this pregnancy. This baby isn't Aaron's responsibility." My mother dried her tears. "Ready or not, here this baby comes, you two. How Charlene can go through with this marriage, knowing this baby isn't that boy's, I don't know—"

I sighed, rolling my eyes. "Oh my God, Mama, I—"

She cut me off. "I'm not fuckin' finished. I'm not sure how my daughter feels about Aaron, but you have grown up with Ne'Vaeh. You've both been through a lot together. You helped her through a lot, you watched her cry over a lot, and you've watched her lose a lot in her life. I don't know how my daughter feels about Aaron, but I know how you feel about Ne'Vaeh. You love her, don't you?"

I looked at my mother, then looked at Jamie.

He nodded without hesitation. "I don't think there's a person on earth who doesn't know I love that girl with every inch of me."

My mother folded her arms. "Okay, well, then, 'every inch of you' should have stayed out of my daughter."

"Okay, Mama, now you are out of line. You said what you had to say, now you can end this conversation." I pulled her arm, pulling her from him. My momma is one crazy white woman. She really didn't give a fuck. She approached a dude like a dude, when she scouldn't handle a dude approaching her like she was a dude.

Jamie shook his head, laughing to himself to keep from slapping my mama. "This is the way that you approach me in my house, Mrs. Campbell? The house that *I* fuckin' paid for with my got-damn money?"

Mama pulled from me. "I don't give a flying fuck whose house this is. This is my got-damn daughter you decided to have sex with without a condom. I know about you, Jamie—how many hoes have you had pregnant in your life time at the age of nineteen? Does Ne'Vaeh know about all the hood rats you screwed and got pregnant? Does she even know that her boyfriend is the father of her own nephew?"

Jamie looked at my mother, stunned for a few minutes. "Neph—"

Mama cut him off. "You got-damn right—your girl is Charlie's sister."

Jamie looked at me, not even sure what he could say.

I was upset at my mom's ignorance. It wasn't the time or the place to air out any more dirty laundry. "We just found out a few days ago, Jamie—it's not like she's keeping anything from you. She probably is just having just as much of a hard time accepting it as I am."

Jamie looked at my mother, "So, I'm still labeled the bad guy after all I did to prove myself to people? I don't know anybody who's perfect. Apparently, your life wasn't so perfect either if your man got another woman pregnant, Theresa."

There I was trying to pull my mama back again. "Keep my husband's name out of your fuckin' mouth, Jamie," she screamed.

He laughed at her hysterics. "Theresa, I don't even know your husband's name—I didn't even say his name, shorty. All I'm saying is you didn't know him, just like you don't know your damn daughter. Do you know what type of lifestyle that she lived for years? You wanna talk about somebody, you need to sit down and interview the niggas that she fucked, sucked, used, and dismissed. Your got-damn daughter is the one who waits until after I get back with Ne'Vaeh to tell me about the baby. She had damn near three months to tell me about the baby, yet she chose to keep it a secret. Shorty waited until the day before the engagement party to tell me about it. You wanna call me a coldhearted muthafucka, Theresa? You're the one who had the audacity to ask me to have your daughter's baby shower at my crib, when you know I haven't even told shorty about this shit. You don't care about Ne'Vaeh, and you can't care about your daughter all that much either if you're willing to put her in a situation where she could potentially get her ass kicked."

My lips trembled. Though what Jamie said hurt, it was the truth.

Mama opened her mouth to say something else ignorant when Jamie cut her off again.

"Now, y'all wanna have the baby shower here and your bridal shower here, that's cool. My girl's cool with it, so I'm cool with it. But I will be damned if you're gonna come up in my crib and try to make me look like the lyin', cheatin' muthafucka when the only one lying in this situation is your daughter, Theresa."

My mother should've known Jamie had no issues putting a mother in her place. Shit, he cursed his own mama out, so I don't know why Mama thought she was special. She put her hands up, surrendering, backing up just a little. "You're right, Jamie, and I apologize. I was out of line."

Jamie was pissed. She wasn't getting off that damn easy. "Nah, you're not gonna try to make me look like the asshole, Theresa. I don't have to live up to your expectations of me; shit, your own damn daughter right here probably hasn't even lived up to your expectations, ever. She came looking for some attention, and I gave it to her. I can't help that she fell in love. And it's the feeling that someone cared about her for just a split second that she fell in love with. Aaron didn't show her the attention that she needed at that time, and I did. Now she thinks I'm fuckin' superman, when I'm not. Your daughter is beautiful, sexy, and gorgeous. Her smile could bring even the strongest man to his knees. She's got that body and that walk that can drive a nigga crazy. But I told her before we even slept together that my heart was taken. I've been hollerin' 'I love Ne'Vaeh Washington' since like the third grade. I'm not the man for her, Theresa, and I told her that before we had sex."

Tears slid down my face. "Jamie, I just want you so bad," I whispered.

"Charlie, you got a man. You're about to marry that man. Charlie, I can't love you, you know that. I told you that before we even tried anything." Jamie's eyes screwed up. "We should have never slept together, and you know it. And you owe it to Aaron to let him know."

Mama turned to me, her blue eyes searching my face. She'd gotten what she wanted—for Jamie to give me a dose of reality. "Charlie, I am going to give the caterers the address and tell your friends to meet you here. I need you to pull yourself together. Jamie's right—you're either going to have to tell the truth or learn to live with a lie. Whether you want it this way or not, you created this problem, so deal with it." Mama grabbed her purse from the countertop, then left Jamie and I standing there in the kitchen.

"You good, shorty?" Jamie watched the tears trickle down my face. "I know what your mama just did was foul, but you gotta pull yourself together, Charlene. Shit is fucked up, yeah, but you gotta be strong enough to face it."

I bit my lip, fighting my emotions, trying not to cry out loud. I wasn't sure how I was going to make it through the day.

"Girl, Aaron is gonna bust a nut in his pants when he sees you in that," Danita exclaimed that afternoon in Jamie's living room.

I held up a pink, sheer, tiny dress and thongs in one hand and pink stilettos in the other. "Y'all know I can't fit my ass in this, pregnant or not. I don't know who y'all had in mind when y'all picked this out, but it wasn't my wide-hipped, big-booty, pregnant ass."

Tyra handed me another gift in a big blue box. "This one is from Ne'Vaeh."

I looked over at Ne'Vaeh, who sat at the edge of the sofa, waiting for me to open her gift. She grinned at me as I unwrapped. Inside the box was a big, fluffy, dark brown teddy bear. Around its neck was a gold chain with a "Little August" charm hanging from it. I hugged the teddy bear tightly in my arms. I had opened about eighty gifts at that point, and her gift was by far my favorite. There was something about that bear that was familiar.

"Ne'Vaeh, the necklace had to cost a grip, but a got-damn teddy bear? Really?" Danita joked. She always had it in for Ne'Vaeh.

The girls laughed with her.

I rolled my eyes. "Y'all are some gold-diggin' bitches, that's for damn sure. Ne'Vaeh, don't listen to these hoes. I love it—thank you."

Ne'Vaeh's eyes glistened. "That necklace cost about $400. The teddy bear might have been about thirty or forty. I didn't buy it. It belonged to my little brother."

The laugher subsided.

"Y'all know he is and will always be everything to me." Ne'Vaeh choked back tears. "That teddy bear got me through some long, sad, lonely nights. I held onto the thought of losing my little brother for years. I never forgave myself for not being able to protect him the night that Juanita—" Ne'Vaeh choked. Alisha hurried to her left side to comfort her, Renée at her right side. "It's all good, y'all. I'm okay." She laughed it off. "I'm giving you this teddy bear, Charlie, because although I lost my little man, I'll be gaining another one in my little nephew. I just know he's gonna be the cutest little boy with parents as gorgeous as you and Aaron. Congratulations on your wedding and the new addition to the Campbell/Whitehaven family."

Applause and whistling scattered throughout the house.

Kelissa, Tyra, Alisha, and Renée all shook their heads at me. Renée was no fool. I'm pretty sure she knew something strange was going on in my neighborhood.

Ne'Vaeh's speech is what had me in tears in the bathroom that afternoon. There was a gentle knock at the door. I quickly dried my face, dabbing it with aloe-scented tissue. "Come in."

Alisha, Tyra, and Kelissa made their way into the bathroom.

"Damn, this bathroom is about as big as that damn bathroom at the club." Kelissa was in awe, looking around one of the five bathrooms in Jamie's home. "What the fuck does a nigga need with all of this space? It's not like he's got any ki—" She stopped and looked at me, "Oops, spoke too soon."

I rolled my eyes. "Kelissa, you really need to shut up. I'm not in the mood for your shit today, okay? You're always trying to get some shit stirred up."

"Girl, please," She rolled her eyes, fluttering her thick, false lashes. "You're the one stirring the damn pot, not me, boo-boo."

"Man," I turned to Tyra, "what the fuck did y'all come in here for? Just to chastise me and crucify me?"

Tyra shook her head, light eyes searching my face. "No, just to see what had you sitting in the bathroom for damn near an hour at your own party. We didn't help set this shit up for you to lock yourself in the bathroom while them bitches out there eat all the fuckin' meatballs. You begged me to make that shit for you, and everybody else is out there eating it."

"Touching speech Ne'Vaeh gave, huh?" Kelissa smirked.

I looked at her. "Okay, bitch, keep pressing buttons."

"I'm just saying, the girl gave you her brother's teddy bear. She made a mistake by fuckin' Aaron, and you keep torturing her," Kelissa exclaimed. "And by the looks of things, Aaron is the last nigga on your mind anyway. You and your mama had the audacity to have the fuckin' baby shower here just to throw the shit in the girl's face. Whether she thinks you're pregnant by Aaron or Jamie, the shit is still fucked up. You know you're wrong."

"This is pretty bold, Charlene, I mean, even for you." Alisha leaned back against the countertop, facing me.

I looked at her. Alisha was holding herself together pretty well. Her brown skin was flawless without makeup. She wore a knit hat over her close-cut hair. She wasn't dressed in her usual sexy getup. She wore a long-sleeved fitted shirt and tight yoga pants. She was sexy effortlessly, sick or not. As much as she'd made my life hell over the past few years, I couldn't help but feel sorry for her. She was a lot stronger than I was. There she was, life on the line, holding it together. Meanwhile, my stupid ass couldn't even face the chaos that I created.

When Aaron tried to break up with me on Ne'Vaeh's birthday, I should have let him instead of trapping him with a baby that wasn't his. What I should have done was break up with Aaron as soon as he started acting cold toward me. Better yet, I should have never approached him that day, junior year in high school. I knew he was into Ne'Vaeh. Though she didn't notice, I saw the way he was looking at her. The muthafucka couldn't take his eyes off of her the entire class period.

"Look, I don't need none of y'all's shit today, okay? I have enough on my plate and don't have time to deal with y'all judging me for everything that I do," I exclaimed. "The last time I checked, y'all's 'list of fuckups' was just as long as mine."

Tyra said, "That girl out there really loves you, Charlie. That gift was from her heart, a heart that tends to get trampled on by the people who she loves the most."

Tears slid down my cheeks.

"You're really gonna go through with this wedding?" Kelissa exclaimed. "You can't possibly be that fuckin' selfish."

I dried my tears, laughing a little to myself. I was really getting tired of her mouth. "Kelissa, you're really working my got-damn nerves. Keep talkin' shit, you hear me? Keep talkin' shit." Alisha pulled me back, before I could get in Kelissa's face. I was two seconds away from snatching those three packs of five-dollar-ninety-nine-cent kanekalon tracks out her head. "Y'all betta get that ho before I snatch them damn cheap-ass tracks outta her head."

Kelissa just looked at me. "Look at the pot calling the kettle black. Ho? Are you serious? Girl, I'm gonna let you have that one, because apparently, you're a little slow and don't seem to know the definition of a ho. All I'm sayin' is you should've told Aaron the truth. He doesn't deserve this, and you know it. And poor Ne'Vaeh is out there hanging on by a thread. She waited four fuckin' years for Jamie to come back home, Charlene. Yeah, she went and fucked someone, but after four fuckin' years? Who do you know has waited four years to have sex? As soon as she gets that dude back, she finds out he's got a baby on the way. Little does she know, she's at his got-damn baby's baby shower." Kelissa laughed out loud.

Oh my goodness, that bitch had my blood boiling.

"You know you could have stopped your scheming, manipulating, think-she's-one-of-them-crazy-mamas-on-*Love-&-Hip-Hop* mama from having that baby shower here. You and your mama did that shit just to spite Ne'Vaeh, Jamie, and Aaron. You did this shit to get back at Aaron for fuckin' her. You did this shit to get back at Jamie for lovin' her. And you did this shit to get back at Ne'Vaeh because both men that you want want her. You deserved for her to sleep with Aaron when you were already fuckin' around on the man for months. Karma is a bitch, you stupid bitch. You deserve everything that's happening to your stupid ass, stupid ass," she yelled in my face. "I hope Ne'Vaeh stomps a hole in your face, bitch."

In an instant, my hands were around that bitch's neck. Don't ask me how we ended up on the floor, in the middle of the damn hallway. She got some good licks in, but she was going to need a lot of stitches. It took about four or five girls to get me off of her. I tried to rip that bitch's head from her body. She had talked her shit for the last time. I had been wanting to get my hands on her since the seventh grade, when she dropped me during cheerleading practice. Took Danita and Tyra a good five minutes to rip us apart.

"What the fuck is going on up in here?" Renée exclaimed, as she stood alongside Ne'Vaeh, between me and Kelissa.

Danita was holding me back, pressing me against the wall by my shoulders.

Tyra held Kelissa's bloody-lipped ass against the wall. She was fighting with all of her might to get back to me. Blood ran down the sides of face, from her nose, and down her chin.

"Charlie, you are pregnant. What the hell are you doing fighting? And why the fuck would you be fighting anybody at your own fuckin' party?" Aunt Stacen yelled, holding her fourth glass of wine in her hands.

"Tell them, Charlene." Kelissa's chest heaved in and out. "Tell her, bitch, or *I* will. I'll be damned if you get away with this shit. You're fuckin' evil."

"Kelissa," Alisha laughed to herself, "we already talked about this shit. I told you to let her hang herself. This isn't your problem so you need to back the fuck off, just like I did. Fighting this bitch isn't gonna make a difference. All it's gonna do is make you catch a case. She's pregnant, fool. But pregnant or not, obviously, her ass can fight. Look at you. Bloody as fuck, and for what? To prove the bitch wrong when she already knows what she's doing?"

"Ne'Vaeh doesn't deserve this shit, Alisha," Kelissa protested, pushing Tyra off of her. "I can't stand by and watch this circus anymore."

I looked at Ne'Vaeh, who stood there clueless about what was going on around her. Kelissa was right even when the bitch was dead wrong. I should've talked my mother out of guilt-tripping Jamie into letting us use the place for my baby slash bridal shower.

"Ne'Vaeh," Kelissa wiped her lip with her fingertips. Renée tried handing her a napkin, but she pushed her away. "You don't deserve what I'm about to say, but I can't stand by and watch you get played any longer."

I pushed Danita off of me in an effort to wring Kelissa's neck again. This time, my mother caught my arm. I looked at her, pulling from her. That was her plan all along—to force me to confront the truth. To put all of the cards on the table. She knew there was no way the people who knew my situation could hold it in any longer. She put us all together under the same roof, Jamie's roof. My mother set me the hell up, and I was pissed at her.

"Ne'Vaeh, c'mon, think, sweetie. Your man let your so-called best friend have her baby shower here. Why do you think that is? Why couldn't Aaron, her fuckin' fiancé, find a place to throw her a got-damn baby shower?" Kelissa attempted to straighten her hair.

I looked at the expression on Renée's face. I knew she had caught on. *Oh my goodness* was written all over her pretty face. She shook her head at me, and then at Kelissa. "Okay, y'all, let's just chill out. Your girl is pregnant, and I'm sure she already is under enough stress. Don't y'all think this is a private conversation that these people here have nothing to do with? Maybe you should excuse yourselves or ask Charlie's guests to leave."

Instead, everyone just stood there waiting for Kelissa to finish her statement.

"No, they all need to stay and hear this shit." Kelissa turned to Ne'Vaeh. "Jamie threw this party for her because" Kelissa stopped, watching the expression on Ne'Vaeh's face already beginning to change from confusion to disbelief.

Ne'Vaeh's lips began to tremble. "Kelissa, whatever you have to say, just say it. Whatever you had to say to Charlie must have been really serious for you to take an ass whuppin'. We're all grown here."

"Yeah, I got my ass whupped by this bitch, and I could really care less," Kelissa exclaimed. "You are my friend, and believe me, I'm not trying to hurt you. You need to know that Mrs. Campbell guilt-tripped Jamie into throwing this baby shower for Charlie here."

Ne'Vaeh laughed to herself, trying her best not to catch on. "And why would she do that, huh? Guilty about what?" Ne'Vaeh looked at me and my mother for answers.

"Ne'Vaeh, sweetie, I'm sorry." My mother stepped in front of me. "I love you, but this is my daughter, and I'm just trying to make sure that she's not alone, taking care of this baby that she didn't make alone."

Ne'Vaeh looked at Renée, and then back at me and my mother. "What the hell do you mean 'alone'? How the fuck is she alone when she has Aaron to help her? You're gonna have to explain yourself better than this and stop beating around the fuckin' bush, y'all."

Mama continued, "This baby isn't Aaron's responsibility."

Ne'Vaeh gasped, holding her chest. Renée quickly grabbed her cousin, but Ne'Vaeh pushed her away, tears already flowing. "Whose responsibility is it, ladies? It seems like everybody here already knows more than I do, so you all might as well just tell me." She looked all around the room at everyone who was standing there.

Everyone except for the ones who already knew looked just as devastated as she did.

Ne'Vaeh looked at me, nostrils flaring, fists started to clinch. "You slept with Jamie? This baby you're having is Jamie's?"

I opened my mouth to respond, but her aggressive voice just kept firing questions at me.

"I know this bitch didn't sleep with Jamie." Ne'Vaeh clapped her hands together with every syllable she uttered. "When did you sleep with Jamie, Charlene?" Ne'Vaeh demanded an answer.

"While we were on our squad trip in Miami, when the Memphis State dancers showed up the week of tryouts back in August, and the day after your got-damn birthday party." Kelissa counted the times on her fingers. "Shit, she stayed with dude the entire week they were in Miami. Alisha and I caught them fuckin' at the bathroom at the Q-Club the week of tryouts. And she went home with your dude the night of your birthday party. Shit, me, Tyra, and Ashton caught them fuckin' in her apartment the day after that."

The room was stunned to silence. All eyes were on Ne'Vaeh's reaction. You know a bitch is crazy when she's laughing her ass off when she's upset. Everyone began to back away from the scene. Some even went to grab their purse and coat and left the building. They already knew that Ne'Vaeh was about to snap, crackle, and pop on my ass.

"So, when you told Aaron you were pregnant, you already knew that you were pregnant by Jamie?" By now, tears coated Ne'Vaeh's face.

I sighed, my heart doing a high-speed chase in my chest. "Ne'Vaeh, I—"

She cut me off. "And when you confronted me about sleeping with Aaron, you had already been sleeping with Jamie for—let's see, the Miami trip was in August so . . . three months? You've been fuckin' Jamie for three months?" Ne'Vaeh started kicking off her heels, one by one.

Mama pulled me back, stepping in front me of. "Ne'Vaeh, you might as well just put your heels back on and calm down. You have a heart condition, and my daughter is pregnant. You're really gonna fight your sister over a man who's not even fuckin' worth the drama?"

"I need to calm down, Theresa? This isn't even about Jamie," Ne'Vaeh cried. "This is about your daughter's lack of respect for other people. She has a wonderful boyfriend who she chose to lie to about her past. Instead of confronting the problem dead in its face, she ran to another man for love. My got-damn man. Regardless of whether we were together back then, she knew what Jamie has always meant to me. Yes, I was wrong when I slept with Aaron. I admitted my wrong. But meanwhile, your bitch-ass daughter knew she was fuckin' Jamie for months. She had the nerve to call me a groupie. She never once admitted to sleeping with him. Instead of tellin' the truth about fuckin' him, she lied to me, and most importantly, she lied to Aaron. Tellin' Aaron the baby was his when she knew the baby wasn't, that's no way to pay him back for sleeping with me. Charlene, what you did was fucked up in every way possible."

Renée pulled Ne'Vaeh away from my mother because she knew that Ne'Vaeh was seconds away from pushing my mother out of the way to get to me. "Ne'Vaeh, this isn't all of her fault. Jamie played a role in this too. I mean, damn, did the nigga tell you that he even slept with the bitch?" Renée exclaimed.

Ne'Vaeh pulled from Renée, tears saturating her face. She removed her jewelry, tossing it on top of a table in the hallway. There must have been three bracelets, three necklaces, three sets of earrings, one Rolex, and six rings on the table. The only jewelry that she hung on to was the "Heaven" necklace that dangled from her neck. She was ready to pop off. "When did you tell

Jamie that the baby was his?" Ne'Vaeh's nostrils flared. She was waiting for me to say the wrong thing so she could sock me in the face.

"After she heard that y'all were back together again," Kelissa butted back into the conversation.

It took everything I had in me not to push everyone out of the way to get to her again. "Kelissa, I didn't bust your face wide open enough? You need to shut your fuckin' mouth."

"Nah, you should have shut your fuckin' legs; then maybe you wouldn't be in this fucked-up situation," Kelissa screamed back. "Look at your friend. No, excuse me. Your sister. Look what you did to her. How much more shit does this girl have to go through? She told you the truth about Aaron. She admitted her fault. You could have told her the truth months ago. This is your lie that had got out of control. Not anyone else's. Your whole family and Aaron's whole got-damn family are flying in tomorrow morning. Your rehearsal dinner is Tuesday night. You're getting married in four fuckin' days, and the man that you're about to marry doesn't even know that you're not even carrying his baby. You could fight me, you could fight Alisha, and you could fight the whole fuckin' squad. Shit, you can even get fucked up by Ne'Vaeh, but that's not gonna change the fact that you're in love with your best friend's man. You did this shit to hurt that girl, and you know that shit."

Ne'Vaeh looked at me, anger subsiding just enough to show how hurt she truly was. "You-You're in love with Jamie?" Her lips quivered.

I hesitated, looking around the room at everyone's eyes planted on my lips for a response. I sighed, trying to summon the correct response to that question. "Ne'Vaeh, when I was lost, confused, and needed someone to talk to, Jamie was there for me. He did everything to and for me that Aaron wouldn't or couldn't do for me anymore. Though he told me from the jump what the business was, my heart ignored it. You know how smooth Jamie is—you know he knows whatever language it is the heart speaks. After I found out about you and Aaron, yes, I was pissed. Aaron couldn't love me because of my past, yet as soon as I went to Texas to my uncle's funeral, Aaron runs to you? He couldn't wait to get to you because he had been waiting over two years to talk to the girl who everyone told him that he could never get with. Yes, I found out about a month after I left Miami that I was pregnant by Jamie. Yes, I had every chance in the world to tell him about the baby. When Aaron told me that he was breaking up with me, I had no idea that you and him had slept together. It wasn't until I saw y'all crying in each other's arms that night at your party and until I found that receipt to that fuckin' dress in Aaron's jacket pocket that I knew y'all were fuckin'. Yes, while you were out there fuckin' my man, I was out there fuckin' yours." I watched as my family members started to clean up the place, preparing to leave the house before all hell broke loose.

Ne'Vaeh dried her tears, trying her best to ignore my last comment. "I asked you if you were in love with Jamie. Answer the got-damn question, Charlene. Fuck all that other shit."

I looked at my mother, who stood there, arms folded. I was so pissed at her when I should have been pissed at myself. I should have told Jamie about the baby, and I should have let Aaron go when he tried breaking it off with me. Better yet, I should have stayed away from Jamie in Miami. Once he got a hold of me, going back to Aaron wasn't even an option. I tried not to love Jamie, but my heart craved his touch.

My lips quivered. I couldn't even let the words come out of my mouth. "I don't want to be in love with him, Ne'Vaeh; believe me, I don't."

Ne'Vaeh was furious, looking around at everyone who was invited to the baby shower. "I can't believe you bitches knew this shit the whole time and let me get back with that muthafucka. Why didn't any of you stop me? Why didn't anyone warn Aaron?" Ne'Vaeh yelled.

Alisha shook her head. "Cutie, I couldn't be the one to break your heart. I care about you. I didn't know how to break the news to you, but I threw subtle hints here and there, and you know it. There's really no need to even get mad at this bitch. She's gonna kick her own ass. Yes, boo, I know it hurts, but it won't last forever. Fuck Jamie, and fuck this bitch."

"Oh," I laughed a little, "she fucks Aaron, and it's cool, but I fuck Jamie and I'm the bad person? I'm the ho? What is the difference?"

"The difference is I didn't keep lying to you about it." Ne'Vaeh laughed, slipping her heels back on her feet. "You know, Charlie, you're really not even worth all of this. Before Jamie and I got involved with each other again, you could have told me this. I fucked up when I messed with Aaron. I was hurt and confused. My heart finally beat again after being frozen ice cold for so long. Jamie and Juanita did some serious damage to my heart. Juanita's abuse weakened my heart. And Jamie finished it off when he left me four years ago. I owned up to my mistake. I didn't tell lie after lie after fuckin' lie until everyone involved was damaged. Aaron cares about you, Charlie. If he didn't, he would have left you a long time ago, back when Alisha and her crew were airing your dirty laundry. This is gonna break his heart. And all you're worried about is saving your own. So you went to Miami, looking for someone to rescue your heart? Heal it from all of the pain that Aaron caused you? Pain?" Ne'Vaeh laughed and cried at the same time. "Bitch, you don't know what the fuck pain is. You told both of these dudes that you're having their baby. Where does that leave any of us?"

Ne'Vaeh was pissed that I had the nerve to cry about the situation. "Are you seriously crying about this? Charlie, you can stop crying because you've won," she exclaimed. "You stopped Aaron from leaving you, you stopped Jamie from being with me, and you made sure that I'd end up all alone. Aaron is a great guy who doesn't deserve this. Regardless of what you may think you're doing by marrying him, he still cares for me. You can't make someone not love someone any- more, Charlie. Your heart doesn't choose who it decides to give itself to. You're gonna ruin his life when all you had to do was tell the fuckin' truth. You're too selfish and stuck in your ways to see that there's more to life than you. I finally had Jamie back. I finally felt whole again. Jamie has been through so much this year. He just lost his father. I can understand why he was afraid to tell me about you. I get it—he had just gotten me back. I know he would have never tried to get back with me if he would have known about this baby. How could you do this to him?"

She'd struck the wrong nerve. "To Jamie? Ne'Vaeh, I didn't fuck myself. Your Jamie pursued me. I didn't go chasing after your so-called man."

Ne'Vaeh chuckled in shock that I would imply Jamie wasn't hers.

Renée and Alisha folded their arms, on standby, ready to jump to her defense when she needed them.

"So-called man?" Ne'Vaeh stepped forward, toward me, when Dana caught her arm. "Get your got-damn hands off of me." Ne'Vaeh pulled away from her.

"Yes, so-called man. You already know how the nigga is, Ne'Vaeh. Who in here hasn't fucked or doesn't want to fuck Jamie Green?" I dried my tears, through with the crying.

A few whispers scattered throughout the hallway and mansion corridor.

"Bitch, don't try to add us to your bullshit," Kelissa said angrily.

"All I'm saying is Jamie was not yours when I had sex with him," I exclaimed. "He hasn't been

for years. Yes, I love Aaron. He's the perfect
guy, but there has always been something about
Jamie. When he approached me in Miami, when
I was already hot, horny, lonely, and sexually
frustrated, hell, yeah, I jumped at the chance
to get on his dick. He invited me to his cousin's
place, and we made what felt like love on the
beach, beside the ocean, butt-fuckin'-naked on
the wet sand. He was amazing, made me feel
ways that I never knew I could. And, hell, yes,
we fucked the entire week that I was in Florida.
Your Jamie fucked me until my entire body went
numb."

Ne'Vaeh just laughed that "oh-I'ma-kill-this-
bitch-if-she-keeps-running-her-got-damn-mouth"
laugh.

Renée said, "Charlene, I'm telling you, I'm
warning you, you need to stop runnin' your
mouth." She warned me, but I wouldn't shut up.

Determined, I said, "Nah, I need to say this.
Yeah, they caught us fuckin' in the bathroom
at the Q-Club. He took me in the stall, damn
near suckin' my lips off of my face, holding
me up against the stall, stroking the shit outta
this pussy. Yes, the night of your birthday, he
asked me to take him home with me. I turned
him down, telling him to leave my apartment. I
waited on Aaron to come home, but he was out

there fuckin' your bony ass. I got tired of waiting on Aaron, so, yes, the night after your party, I called Jamie to come back over. He fucked me from the moment he came into my apartment until Aaron called me the next morning. Ne'Vaeh, you have taken everything from me. My family, my room, my style, my friends, Aaron, come to find out my father. But you won't take this from me." I rubbed my belly.

"Whoa," Jennel said, appalled, watching Ne'Vaeh come for me.

Dana tried to grab her, but Ne'Vaeh pushed her away.

Mama tried to block me, but I shoved her out of the way to face Ne'Vaeh on my own. "Yeah, Ne'Vaeh, you can't take this bond that I share with your man away. You may have Jamie's heart, you may even have Aaron's heart, but I have Jamie's baby. Now, have that, bitch."

Ne'Vaeh reached for the table where she had tossed her jewelry. She picked up a chain that had a key charm dangling from it. And in seconds, before I could defend myself or brace myself, she smacked me dead across the face, key in the palm of her hand. There are no words to describe the sting of that diamond-encrusted key scrapping against my skin. No one or nothing—except my face that was thrown back—moved. Everyone was in shock.

"You want Jamie, bitch? You can have him. You just remember that his heart belongs to me. You can borrow the key if you need it, though." And she tossed the necklace back onto the counter.

I held my throbbing face in my hand as Mom rushed to the kitchen. Tyra ran to my side, holding my face in her hands, putting a cloth over my face, putting pressure on my wound. I felt the warm blood sliding down my cheek.

"Ne'Vaeh, what the fuck are you thinking?" Tyra screamed. "Bitch, you're crazy."

"Nah, y'all haven't seen crazy. Y'all need to clean this shit up and get the fuck out of here," Ne'Vaeh screamed, turning around, walking down the hallway to grab her coat, purse, and car keys. "I tell you what, Charlie, you better call off this wedding before I do," Ne'Vaeh shouted as she stormed out of the house.

Everyone stood there looking at me as Ne'Vaeh left the house, cursing and screaming to herself.

Renée looked at me as she slid on her coat. "I would stay and help clean up, but I need to go after my cousin before she does something crazy. Come on, Jennel. Besides," Renée glanced at me, "this is you and your fuckin' mama's mess to clean up. Y'all had the audacity to have this got-damn baby shower at the man's house? After all this girl has been through, Charlie, you're gonna sit here and cry because some nigga doesn't love you? Bitch, please." Renée stormed out of the house, Jennel and their cousin, Tyreeka, following behind her.

"Oh my goodness, you're gonna need stitches. Look at all of this blood," Tyra exclaimed, applying pressure to my face. "Doesn't Jamie have a doctor he kept on call while his father was sick? Eh," Tyra signaled one of the maids, who stood by watching the entire argument, "call Jamie's doctor."

My adrenaline was pumping so hard at that moment that I couldn't even feel the pain anymore. "Okay, ladies," I laughed to myself as Mom came back to the hallway, dumping ice into a towel. Tyra moved so my mother could take over caring for my torn face.

"I'm the bad guy here. Y'all wanna blame me, then go ahead. Mama, this is what you wanted?" I pushed her away as she tried to soothe my face with the cold towel. "For Ne'Vaeh to bust my face open right before my wedding rehearsal? For her to find out the truth this way? For me to hurt her when I never intended for any of this to happen? I didn't mean to fall in love with the man she's waited four years to get back. Hurting her isn't going to get back at Juanita for hurting you, Mama."

Mama tossed the towel on a bookshelf. "Oh, so you're gonna put this all on me? You're upset with me? I wasn't the one who had sex with Jamie instead of talking to Aaron about the way that I felt. I wasn't the one trying to trap a man with a baby that I know isn't his. I wasn't the one who lied to everyone just to spite the girl who both men who I want are in love with. You wanna sit here and cry over the girl smacking you? You're lucky that's all she did. You should have told the truth when you had the chance, not after your child's father got into a relationship, and definitely not after your mother and fiancé's parents spent over $600,000 on your fuckin' wedding. You better find a way to fix this." Mom stormed out of the room.

Tears and blood slid down my cheek as I flopped down on a stool in the hallway. Seemed like there were four or five people doctoring my face in the hallway, trying to stop the bleeding.

"We have to get her to the hospital," my sister, Heather, exclaimed.

"No, y'all need to clean up first. I'll be fine. We need to get outta here. I don't even know what I was thinking, letting my mother talk me into coming here."

"Sweetie," Tyra handed a roll of bandage tape to Heather and a bottled water to me, "just sit here and relax. Jamie's doctor is on the way. We'll all clean up the house; just chill. As soon as we get this place cleaned up, one of us will take you to the hospital."

Chapter 11

Cheers

Charlene

Rocio, Jamie's maid, called the doctor for me. Unable to understand the doctor's instructions, Rocio handed the phone to Tyra. Since my face was still bleeding nonstop, Tyra was told to hold a wet towel on my face, applying a little pressure. You should have seen the "I told your ass to tell the truth months ago" look on her face. Jamie's doctor, Doctor Cole Parker, came in no time. But even by the time he'd gotten there, the hand towel Tyra was pressing against my face was soaked with blood. Tyra held my hand while the doctor stitched my face. I couldn't even feel the pain in my face. That pain was nothing compared to the pain in my chest.

"Okay, that should do it." Doctor Parker cut the end of the dissolvable stitch.

My face had begun to swell, almost sealing my eye shut.

"Do you want me to drive you to the hospital, Miss Campbell?" Doctor Parker was a little skeptical about my "fall."

"Okay, so tell me again how you fell and cut your face like this?"

"We're good, Doctor Parker, sir." Alisha cleared her throat. "We'll get her there. Thanks for your help."

It took a few hours to clean the house up. No one said a word to me that afternoon. And once my face stopped bleeding, no one was in that much of a hurry to get me to the hospital. My adrenaline was pumping when I should have fainted from the amount of blood that I'd lost. I sat there in the hallway in a daze as Alisha came over and flopped down next to me.

I looked at her, face swollen on one side.

Alisha looked at my swollen cheek. "Well," she pulled her CK knit hat down farther over her ears, "you sure took my mind off of cancer for a little while, I can say that much."

I shook my head. "Not now, Alisha, okay? Your timing is always whack as fuck."

"Well, when then? At the ER in about an hour? Tomorrow at your rehearsal dinner? You did add me to the bridal party, remember? I'm Ashton's date; we'll be walking arm in arm down that aisle, behind you. That dress fits perfect by the way. It arrived this morning." She grinned.

"I know I fucked up, but I don't wanna be alone, Alisha," I whispered, fighting back the tears. I could feel my heart beating in my cheeks. While I was being bandaged up earlier, I was staring at my face in the mirror. There was a key-shaped imprint on my face. It was going to leave an ugly scar. Ne'Vaeh made sure that I would remember never to disrespect her again. And she made sure that I would hate myself every time I looked at my reflection in the mirror.

"You won't always be, sweetie." Alisha patted my back. "Trust me, love will find you soon. In fact, I already know someone who has his eye on you. Has for a long time too, that muthafucka."

I looked at her.

Alisha just laughed to herself. "I never really liked you, Charlie, you know that. You've always been a stuck-up, trash-talkin', dick-suckin' bitch who thought you were better than any and everybody. We're two opposite ends of the color spectrum, and we've always been in competition. We were like oil and water, never quite mixing. You were light-skinned with light eyes and long brown hair. The only thing that got me noticed until high school was my long hair and fat ass. Shit, do you know how much it hurt to hear niggas say shit like 'you're sexy as hell for a dark-skinned girl'? The fuck is that shit supposed to mean?"

I felt sorry for her. "Girl, you know how stupid niggas are."

Alisha's eyes glinted. "I wanted so much to be like you growing up." She looked at me. "It took me a long time to come to terms with my skin and realize that I am beautiful. That my black is beautiful. Ashton helped me realize that, never letting me forget how beautiful he thought I was. He has always been and will always be my heart, but I've always known that he was in love with you. He was always playing Captain-Save-A-Ho, rescuing you from your fuckin' self. And that's why I hated you. The only thing that kept him from approaching you, asking you out, was when he found out that I had a brain tumor."

I looked at her. "What?"

She nodded, tears sliding down her face. "Yes, we were about to break up a few years ago, sophomore year, when he heard from one of my cousins about my test results. He loves me, but he is in love with you. I lost interest in everything but dancing. The medication I was on took my sex drive away altogether. Not to mention sex is painful because I have endometriosis. So I told him that he could have sex with anybody except for your ass."

Astounded, I looked at her.

She looked at me.

We both burst out laughing until we both started crying.

"I do know what pain feels like, Charlene." Tears wet her dark chocolate cheeks. "I know you love Jamie—there's no doubt in my mind that you do. But his heart belongs to Ne'Vaeh. And you were wrong for what you said to that girl about the baby. The only reason he didn't tell her about you is because he was afraid of losing her. He just got that girl back. You need to tell Aaron and your family the truth tomorrow at the rehearsal dinner. I mean, they're all gonna have questions when you show up, face all bandaged and shit. But, you're gonna be okay, Charlene."

"Yeah? How do you know that?" I dried my face.

Alisha shrugged. "Because when you stoop this low, the only way to go now is up."

***

I watched as Jamie's housekeepers and drivers loaded all of my gifts into my mother's Dodge truck, when Jamie's Challenger pulled up into the driveway.

I was just in the process of calling Aaron, whose phone had been off the entire day. I knew he was with his agent all day long, deciding on which team he was going to play for. He didn't think I knew, but I knew that he was considering playing overseas, possibly leaving me behind.

Jamie got out of his car, eyeing the cars that were leaving his house. He didn't look bothered or upset, so I assumed that he hadn't spoken to Ne'Vaeh or heard what happened at the party. It was going on 7:00 that night, and my mother was just deciding to take me to the emergency room. My face was on swollen, and once my emotions were stable, I started to feel the pain, and it hurt like hell to talk. I tried calling Ne'Vaeh a few times that evening myself, only to get a "Fuck you" recording on her voicemail. I knew Ne'Vaeh well enough to know she didn't take heartache well at all. There was no telling what she was going to try to do to herself after the pain that I'd caused.

Jamie approached me, eyes glued straight at my swollen cheek. He shook his head at me as we stood face-to-face. "What's up, shorty? I'd ask how the party was, but, uhhh, it looks to me like some shit went down."

It hurt to laugh at my own pain. "Dude, it's really not the right time to talk about this. I'm on my way to the hospital. And I've been trying to call Ne'Vaeh all afternoon."

His eyes searched. "What happened, Charlene?"

I reached into my jumper pocket and pulled out the necklace Ne'Vaeh smacked me in the face with. "Ne'Vaeh left all of her jewelry—except for the 'Heaven' necklace that was still on her neck—in your house."

He just looked at me as as I took his hand in mine, placing the necklace in his palm. His eyes traced my swollen cheek. I felt his pulse begin to quicken as he let go of my hand.

"She smacked me in the face with it, Jamie," I cried.

Jamie's eyes glistened. "Must have been something you said to her. You always did have a smart-ass mouth at the wrong got-damn time, shorty."

I pushed him in the chest. "Jamie, seriously? That's all you have to say? After my mama calmed down about what went down today, she told me that I should press charges."

Jamie laughed out loud. "Press charges for what? Smacking you in the face after you basically bragged about having my baby? After you told her that she'll never be able to break whatever 'bond' you believe we have just because we have a child together?"

I looked hard at him. That bastard. "You knew about this shit?"

He nodded. "Hell, yeah. Ne'Vaeh showed up to my got-damn agent's office with her cousins. She cursed me out in front of everyone about what I did with you. I was in a got-damn meeting with all types of important people when shorty popped off. She slapped the shit outta me in front of my manager, my agent, my new coach, radio deejays, magazine editors, my cousins, and my fuckin' aunt Bethany. It wasn't cool, shorty. I'm not sure what happens next, but shorty said she's fuckin' up your whole wedding if you even attempt to go through with this bullshit. Your cousin called a nigga too, saying you even invited me to your rehearsal dinner tomorrow."

I sighed. "Jamie, you both are part of the bridal party, remember? I told y'all that shit at my engagement party last month."

Sadly, Jamie looked at me and said, "Ne'Vaeh was the best thing in my life outside of football, and you took her from me. If you would have told me from jump about the baby, I would have been fine. I would have never hurt her. I wouldn't have to feel this way. She wouldn't have to feel this way." He fought back the tears.

"Jamie, I never intended—"

"Never intended what, Charlene?" he cut me off." To trap your nigga and me with a baby? If your ass was gonna live a lie with this nigga thinking that he was the father, then that's the way you should have kept it. You knew that once you told me, I wouldn't be able to live with that lie. You knew I wouldn't be able to stay with her, knowing we had a baby together. Yeah, I should have told her that we slept together—for that I was wrong. I'm serious, shorty—if Ne'Vaeh isn't in your life, I'm gone too . . ."

I looked up at him. "So you're telling me that you're leaving me alone with this baby?" I pushed him. "Jamie, you're seriously gonna leave your baby?"

"Are you seriously getting married this week? Doesn't dude think it's his baby? So how the fuck are you gonna be alone?" he exclaimed. "I deserve that girl, Charlie. You should have just kept this shit to yourself and let me have her. You fucked this shit up, Charlene. Fix it."

***

I didn't even realize how huge my bridal party was until everyone arrived that night at my family's church for rehearsal. There were about twenty bridesmaids and twenty-one groomsmen. We had about six flower girls and a ring bearer. My cousin Tyra was my maid of honor since Ne'Vaeh refused when I asked her at my engagement party. Ashton was Aaron's best man. There was tension between half of the bridesmaids and myself—the half that attended my baby slash bridal shower were uncooperative. Kelissa didn't show up with her man. Renée and Jennel didn't show up with their men. Autumn was a last-minute addition to the bridal party, but she hadn't shown up either. Alisha was sick as a dog, but she showed up with Ashton. Disappointed, she shook her head at me as Pastor Matthews showed Aaron and I where and how to stand, and the wedding planner showed me the exact way that she wanted me to hold the flowers.

It took nearly ten makeup artists to get my makeup right that night, attempting to cover up the stitches that I ended up getting the evening of my shower. The wedding planner tried to get me to stand in a way that took attention away from my right cheek. Aaron's parents looked so proud of him. Since my father was no longer with us, my father's brother, Ricardo, was going to give me away. My mother was a nervous wreck, just bracing herself for a wedding disaster.

The caterers did an excellent job on the dinner selection that night. Aaron sat next to me, looking so handsome and actually happy. He held my hand in his that evening as his father stood up to give a toast. To tell you the truth, the whole drawn-out speech was a blur. All I could see was Jamie sitting with his aunt and sister at the table directly in front of mine. He was the reason why there were twenty bridesmaids and twenty-one groomsmen—his plus-one hadn't shown up. Jamie's eyes glistened as he held up his glass to toast to whatever it was we were toasting to.

And then, there was another tapping of the glass to my left. There Ne'Vaeh was, walking into the reception room, dressed in a gray comfortable jumper and heels. Her hair was pulled up into a bun, sleek bangs hanging over her eyes. Gold hoop earrings hung from her ears. The "Heaven" necklace that Aaron admitted to buying her hung in her cleavage. Renée, Jennel, Kristina, Autumn, and Kelissa followed behind her.

"I'd like to propose a toast." Ne'Vaeh said as she held up her glass. One of the waitstaff must have given her a champagne glass at the door.

Aaron looked at me as I rose in my chair, then he looked at Ne'Vaeh and her entourage. I didn't even tell him what happened to my face that night. I lied to him, telling him that I fainted outside of the building where my baby shower was held, hitting my face on the cement steps. Yes, I lied about where we had the shower too.

Mother rose in her seat as well. Alisha, who sat comfortably in Ashton's lap, sat up at attention. I could hear her "oh, shit" from across the room.

"I have known Charlie since we were in elementary school. There were nights where the woman who gave birth to me would beat me and my brother until we passed out. She couldn't beat my sister. Oh, no, my sister was her money. Who else was she gonna sell for drugs?" It was obvious that she'd been drinking. "Juanita would leave us for months at a time with no food or lights. My family members tried calling social services, who barely came by our house to check on us. But Aunt Joyce, she took us in when she could. And Theresa never hesitated to take us in. When my brother was murdered, I went for weeks and weeks at a time without sleeping or eating. It took years for me to be able to sleep without seeing his face, or hear him screaming for me to help him. There were nights where I'd wake up, kicking and screaming because I kept having the same reoccurring nightmare of Juanita beating my brother unconscious. Charlie would hold me, telling me everything was going to be okay. She went to every therapist visit. The night that I tried to kill myself with an entire bottle of vodka and oxycodone, Charlie was right there with me at the hospital. I just knew that Charlie would always be down for me. That she would never do anything to hurt me. She was like a sister to me, and just a few days ago, I found out she is my sister."

My heart raced in my chest because I knew where the conversation was headed.

"Ladies and gentlemen, I made a mistake." Ne'Vaeh dried her face. "I let my guard down and gave into temptation. I needed love and affection, willing to accept it from anyone, even if it was my best friend's—my sister's—boyfriend."

All eyes shot straight to Aaron, who sat back in his seat, drinking his entire glass of wine. "Aw, shit" was written all over his face, but he remained calm.

Ne'Vaeh faced me. "Charlie, I never meant you any harm, and I never meant to come between the two of you. I should have done better because I knew better, and I'm sorry." Her lips trembled.

Jamie rose in his seat, clearing his throat. "Shorty, come on, you're drunk. Don't do this, sweetheart." He walked over to her, which was probably a bad idea.

"And you, don't tell me what to do," she exclaimed as Jamie walked toward her. She looked around at everyone. "I'm woman enough to own up to my mistakes. Mr. and Mrs. Whitehaven, you have an amazing son. Someday, he will make some woman happy and overjoyed beyond belief. He deserves a woman who will love him wholeheartedly and unconditionally, giving him her heart, mind, body, and soul. Aaron, you are awesome in every way possible. You do not deserve to be lied to," Ne'Vaeh cried.

"Aaron, what is this? Who is this girl? What's going on?" Aaron's mother, Ella, exclaimed. She knew Ne'Vaeh, and never really cared too much for her at all because she didn't fit into her little color-struck fantasy of her son breeding light-skinned children. Ne'Vaeh reminded Ella of herself, who she was more than ashamed to be.

Aaron looked at her, his eyes watering. "Heaven, what's up? What's going on? Why are you doing this?"

Ne'Vaeh looked back at Jamie. "Which one of you are gonna tell Aaron what's going on, Jamie? Or should I?"

Jamie shook his head at Ne'Vaeh, grabbing the wineglass from her hand before she tossed it in his face. "Shorty, calm down, yo. If you wanna hate me, then hate me. But don't do this shit in front of these people's family, Ne'Vaeh. You're really gonna air this shit out in front of all of these people?"

"Okay, I'll tell him—Aaron, Charlie is having Jamie's baby, not yours." Ne'Vaeh got straight to the point and aired our dirty laundry in front of my entire family and Aaron's family.

The room was in an uproar for a good three minutes or so before the noise died down to hear Aaron's family screaming at me from their seats.

I couldn't hear anything because all I could see was the look on Aaron's face as he snatched his hand from mine, rising to his feet, laughing to himself, probably to keep from choking the shit out of me or flying across the table on Jamie's ass. Aaron looked at me. "This is a joke, right? Where are the cameras? I'm being punked, right?"

"Aaron," I whispered, lips trembling, scared out of my mind. "Please, let me explain."

He looked at the expression on my face, realizing the rumor was true. "So, the shit I've been hearing about you messin' around on me is true? You were gonna marry me, knowing you're pregnant by this muthafucka? When, Charlie?" Aaron's temples twitched.

"Aaron, can we please go somewhere and talk about this?" I pleaded.

"Charlene, when did you fuck that mutha-fucka?" he yelled in my face.

"In Miami, back in August," I whispered, watching most of Aaron's family get up and leave the reception area.

"Oh, don't forget about the week of tryouts when the Memphis State dancers showed up. Remember, I caught y'all two cheatin' mutha-fuckas in the bathroom at the Q-Club?" Kelissa held up her wineglass as if she was giving a toast. "Oh, and don't forget about the day after Ne'Vaeh's birthday party when we caught y'all hoes fuckin' in your apartment. You were cookin' bacon, eggs, grits, and shit for the nigga."

Aaron took off his jacket, tossing it in his chair.

"Son." Aaron's father approached him.

"So, when you and Jamie caused that scene at Ne'Vaeh's party, y'all had already been fuckin' and you already knew you were pregnant by him?" Aaron got in my face, but his father and cousin held him back. He pulled away from them. "And when did you tell Jamie that you were having his baby?" He looked up at Jamie because I was taking too long to answer. "When did you find out, Jamie?"

"The day before your engagement party," he responded.

Aaron looked at him. "Dude, you were gonna sit here and watch me marry this girl, knowing she's pregnant with your baby?" Aaron looked back at me. "And you lied to me, telling me that the baby was mine when I tried breaking up with you back in October? You knew this baby wasn't mine."

"Aaron, I'm sorry. I panicked. You were leaving me. I didn't know what else to do," I cried.

"You should have just let me go, Charlie. You can't say that you were trying to get back at me for the shit I did because you lied to me before that shit even came out," he exclaimed. "You waited until our engagement party to spring this shit on him, and why is that? Because you found out that his relationship with Ne'Vaeh was serious. And you must have heard his radio interview, telling the world how much in love with her he is, huh? That shit had you feeling some type of way, didn't it?"

I shook my head, lips trembling.

Aaron shook with rage. "You're in love with him, aren't you?" H laughed a little, watching the tears sliding down my face. "You're in love with him, and he's in love with her. I'm in love with her, and she's in love with him. Ain't that a bitch?"

I looked around the room at everyone, feelings like the whole room was spinning under my feet.

"Ladies and gentlemen," Aaron faced everyone, "thank you for coming out tonight for our rehearsal dinner, but it seems like there's not gonna be a wedding. This shit is embarrassing, Mom and Pop." He looked at his parents. "Mom, Pop, I told you the day that I put that ring on Charlie's finger that I was making a mistake, that I was in love with Heaven." He looked back over at Ne'Vaeh. "My biggest mistake was not going after what I wanted back in high school."

Ne'Vaeh was instantly calmed, drying her face, speechless for a second or two. "Aaron, please, don't—"

Aaron looked back at me. "Charlene, I'm not even mad at you for fuckin' this dude. I'm mad at you for being so fuckin' selfish and conniving. You wanted that muthafucka just like I wanted her. You held onto me because you knew I always wanted her. Shit, you probably knew I was in love with her before I even admitted it to myself."

Aaron wasn't lying. I knew he had a fascination with that girl back in high school, the first day the two met. Though he didn't approach her then, I knew he wanted to. I should have known it would only be a matter of time before he built up the nerve to approach her, whether we were together or not.

"Yo, Jamie," Aaron laughed to himself, "you better fix that shit because I'm coming back for her."

Jamie laughed to himself too. "Aaron, yo, I know what I did was fucked up, but you know I won't let that happen."

Aaron could care less what Jamie had to say about shit. "I'm just tellin' you, dude, don't leave that door open for too long. You might as well get your little time in with shorty because I'm coming back for what's mine—I put that on muthafuckin' everything."

Jamie stood there, temples twitching, but he fell back. He knew he was in the wrong. There was no use fighting for Ne'Vaeh when it looked as though he'd lost that battle.

Aaron grinned at Ne'Vaeh. "Shorty, when you're tired of loving him, holla at me. I don't give a fuck who I'm with, who you're with, where I'm at, or what I'm doing—when you want me, just let me know, a'ight?"

Ne'Vaeh's lips trembled. "Aaron, I know you're hurting. I swear I didn't mean to tell you like this."

He tried to smile. "It's all good. Y'all enjoy the rest of the evening. Hey, the food is free. Mom and Pop, I'll pay you back for everything." Aaron turned to walk away.

I tried to grab his arm, but he pushed me away. "Aaron, I'm sorry," I cried, watching him leave the room. I stood there, drowning in pain and embarrassment.

"Now, you got a taste of your own medicine. Swallow that shit, bitch." Kelissa held up her glass, then drank from it. "Cheers, everyone."

I can't even begin to tell you how many curse words I heard that night from both families. I was threatened with a lawsuit for the cost of the engagement party and wedding from Aaron's mother. His aunt damn near snatched their mother's ring from my finger. Jamie's aunt Bethany had the lecture from hell waiting for me after she ate a whole plate of shrimp. She accused me of wrecking Jamie's life, destroying his dreams, ruining his career. She knew her nephew wanted nothing to do with me. Though she was angry with him, she was angrier with me because she said I had no business sleeping with her nephew who made it perfectly clear that he could have fifty of me if he wanted to. Supporting my child financially wouldn't be a problem, but we both knew that actually playing an active role in the child's life would be a different story.

***

I arrived back at my apartment that night to see everything that Aaron had bought for little August set neatly in my living room. I had been calling Aaron for hours, wondering if he was okay. I didn't want him to hate me. I just wanted to him know that I never meant to drag him into my mess.

"You're gonna have to get someone to swing by the house we were about to close on to get the baby's furniture set." I heard Aaron's voice coming from the balcony.

My heart beat rapidly in my chest as I closed the front door behind me and tossed my keys and purse down on the couch.

Aaron came in from off the balcony, closing the slide door behind him after tossing his cigarette. His eyes were red, as if he'd been crying and smoking weed at the same time. "I think this is everything."

I was speechless, not really sure what to say. I wondered if the terrified feeling that I felt inside was the same as those people in the movies who knew that the man they cheated on was just about to kill their ass.

"My family is pissed at both of us right about now." Aaron shook his head at me, not quite saying what I expected him to say. "Pissed at me for being in love with the girl who's in love with the man who you're having a baby with. And pissed at you for tricking me into marrying you. I mean, you timed everything just right. You had to have sex with me the moment you found out that you were pregnant—we didn't even have sex for months before you went to Miami, and we didn't have sex until like four weeks after you came back from Miami. I was too busy to go to any of your appointments with you, and I didn't even keep up with how far along you were. You knew I wouldn't even notice the shit. You're smooth with your shit, I can give you that."

I backed up a little as he approached me. "Are-Are you gonna kill me?"

Aaron laughed a little. "Kill you for what? You freed me, Charlie. I just came to thank you." He handed me the key to my apartment.

Taking the key from him, I said, "Aaron, I'm sorry."

His eyes searched my face. "You didn't have to lie to me."

"And you didn't have to love her," I exclaimed. "I would've never slept with Jamie in Miami if you would have slept with me every once in a while. If you didn't wanna be with me, you should have left me. Fuck your parents, I'm sorry—they're not gonna live your life for you. Everything you do isn't gonna make everyone happy, Aaron. If you wanted that girl, you should have told me to 'step' when I asked you out that day in Mr. Porter's class. So, she isn't the girl that your parents want you to be with—she's the girl that you want to be with."

"She loves that dude, man. He's done some serious damage that is gonna take more than me to undo."

I rolled my eyes. "Aaron, that girl needs someone like you. I need someone like you, but you have always craved, wanted, and needed her. I guess that's okay, but you should have been with her to begin with."

"I agree with that, Charlie."

"So go get her." I looked up into his face.

He nodded. "Oh, I intend to, but I'm gonna have to give her some time. She's been through too much. I gotta let her heart heal. And I gotta give my heart some time to heal too, ya know? I can't stay in Maryland and watch her chase after Jamie. This shit is embarrassing more than anything. I got played by my girl and her sister. Makes me look like a bitch, I tell you that much."

I really felt like shit. I knew what I did hurt Aaron more than anyone. He wanted someone to love, he wanted a family, he wanted to be happy. He put his heart on the line for a girl who was carrying someone else's baby. He gave up the girl he wanted to be with me just to make his parents happy.

"Aaron, I tried to love you even when I knew you loved her. I didn't mean to fall in love with Jamie. He just showed me the attention that no one else has ever shown me. For once, I just wanted someone to like something about me besides the way I looked. When I talked, he actually listened. Aaron, I need that. Your mind has been elsewhere for years," I whispered.

He nodded. "Yeah, well, all I can say is fix the situation with your sister. As far as Jamie is concerned, that baby inside of you isn't gonna keep him from loving her. Somebody will love you the way that you want to be loved one day, Charlene. Just don't fuck it up." He walked past me and out the door.

I don't think I slept a wink all night. All I could think about was the rehearsal dinner. My family was disgusted with me—there was no telling when my mother was going to speak to me again. Aaron was leaving the country in a few days just to avoid me or any reminder that he couldn't have Ne'Vaeh. I had to try to fix my situation with Ne'Vaeh the best way that I could so that Jamie would be in his child's life. I had no idea how I was going to make it work, but I had to think of something for the sake of little August Carter Green.

Chapter 12

My Fairy Tale Doesn't Exist

Previously, Ne'Vaeh

"Ne'Vaeh, sweetie, we can't just burst up in this meeting like this." Renée tried to stop me from marching straight into the conference room of Dollars and Cents, Inc. "Ne'Vaeh, please, don't do this." She tried to pull me in the opposite direction of the door as she eyed the receptionist calling security.

I pushed Renée off of me. "No, this mutha-fucka is gonna feel me today. I'm sick of this shit. I'm sick of being lied to. He didn't even tell me that he fucked her. All he did was make me feel guilty about sleeping with Aaron. He slept with the bitch an entire week. Then he fucked her in a club; then he went home with her on my got-damn birthday. Did he tell me this shit?

No. I had to find out at the baby's got-damn baby shower. He has some explaining to do."

"Oh, shit," my cousin, Tyreeka, sighed as I burst through the doors of the conference room.

Everyone in the conference room looked up at us.

Jamie stood from his chair as I came charging in the room, Renée, Jennel, and Tyreeka following behind me.

Renée laughed nervously, looking at the crowd of people. "Sorry. We seemed to have walked into the wrong room." She tried to pull my arm, to make an exit.

I pulled away from her. "Get off of me, Renée." I approached Jamie, who was shaking his head at me.

"Shorty, what's up? What are you doin' here, yo?" Jamie faced me, sitting down on the edge of the table.

"Oh, where am I supposed to be? Back at your house, catering to your baby's mama at the baby shower for your got-damn son?" I pushed him in his chest.

Jamie looked at me, breathless, not able to say a word for a few seconds.

"When did you plan on telling me that you fucked her, Jamie? Don't you think telling me that you fucked the bitch should have come before asking me to throw her a fuckin' baby shower?" I pushed him again.

"Shorty, this isn't the time or the place for this." Jamie caught his breath, though he was winded, scared, and nervous as hell. He knew how reckless I was when I was mad.

"Aunt Bethany, did you know that your nephew fucked my sister?" I faced his aunt, who just stared at her nephew like she wanted to smack the shit out of him. "Did you know she's supposed to be getting married to someone else who thinks the baby is his?"

Jamie got up from the table, grabbing me by the arm, trying to lead me out of the room. But I pulled away from him.

"No, I want your colleagues to know exactly what type of person you are," I cried. "You made me fall back in love with you when you knew what you did with her. I don't give a fuck when you found out that she was pregnant, Jamie—you knew you had sex with her, and you didn't even tell me. This whole time, that bitch has been smiling in my face, knowing she was carrying your baby. You couldn't even stand to see another man look at me, Jamie. I should have known the reason why you were so protective was because you were feeling guilty about what you did with her. I can't keep living like this. I'm tired of this pain. Do you love her?"

Jamie shook his head at me. "Nah, shorty, I don't love her."

"Why didn't you tell me about her?" I cried, pushing him in his chest. "You're supposed to be my man, my best friend, my soul mate. She said that you made love to her on the got-damn beach. They told me they caught y'all fuckin' in the bathroom at the club. Kelissa said they caught y'all fuckin' in Charlie's apartment the day after my birthday party. Did you kiss her the way you kiss me? Did you hold her the way you hold me? Did you fuck the bitch the way that you fuck me? Huh?"

Jamie just stood there, eyes downcast, hands in his pockets.

"Maybe we should reschedule this meeting, Jamie. I mean, if your private life is more important than your career, let us know." The man sitting at the head of the table looked agitated and annoyed with the situation.

Jamie looked at him, and then back at me. "Shorty, go home; wait for me. This isn't the time to discuss this."

"No," I cried. "We are going to discuss this now. I don't know one female outside of me that you have had sex with more than once. She must have really put in on you, Jamie, for you to take her in the bathroom at the club and fuck her. For you to fuck her in her apartment, in the same bed that Aaron has sex with her. For you to fuck her on three different occasions, the pussy must have been made of gold or some shit. Admit it, Jamie, you liked it."

Jamie looked at me, tired of me causing a scene so he said whatever he could to piss me off so I would leave the office. "Yeah, shorty, I did. I drowned my dick and my face in that pussy. Is that the shit you wanna hear? You wanted the truth, now, there it is."

My hand did the thinking for me that day. It went straight across his face. The next thing I know, Renée, Jennel, and Tyreeka were pulling me away from him and security was rushing through the doors. If my cousins hadn't pulled me away from Jamie, I would have scratched his face off that afternoon. He knew exactly where it hurt. He knew what he had to say to get me to leave him alone. He knew he fucked up, and there was no way he could take back the damage that he'd done.

My cousins had the hardest time holding me back. One of the security guards had to pick me up and carry me out of the room, kicking and screaming my ass off. The security guard carried me all the way out of the building, letting me down outside of the front door, kicking, screaming, and scratching like an alley cat.

"Come on, Ne'Vaeh, let's get out of here. You don't even know what type of meeting we were rolling up on, girl. You could have just ruined that boy's career. You're crazy," Jennel exclaimed, pulling me over to a bench outside of the building.

Renée and Tyreeka fanned me with their purses, trying to get me to calm down.

I shook my head, legs shaking, nerves jumping, tears racing. "How he could do this to me?"

"Eh, shorty," Jamie's voice called out.

I looked up to see him walking down the steps toward me. He was on defense mode, ready to get in my shit for embarrassing him in front of all of those rich white people. Renée, Jennel, and Tyreeka blocked him as he came up to me. His temples were twitching, face turning red. I stood up to confront him.

"Yo, ladies, get the fuck out of the way. Mind your business, yo. I need to talk to shorty." He huffed and puffed, face red where I had smacked him.

Renée folded her arms, shaking her head in defiance. "Hell, nah, Jamie. You're not gonna hit this girl. You deserved to get smacked in the face. What do you think you did to her?"

Jamie was pissed, but he tried to remain as calm as he could. "Just let me talk to her, yo."

Renée hesitated to move out from in front of me, but she held my arm because she knew I wanted to strangle him. She held on tight as I tried to pull away from her. "Ne'Vaeh, chill out."

I looked up at Jamie, watching the tears slide down his face. I shook my head, crying with him. "Go back in the building, Jamie. We really don't have anything to talk about."

"Ne'Vaeh, what happened between Charlene and I was months ago. I was seeing someone back in August. I was fuckin' a whole lot of girls outside of Charlene, shorty. I'm not sayin' that makes it any better; I'm just sayin' she didn't mean and she doesn't mean anything to me. I didn't tell you about her because what woman wants to hear about their man fuckin' other women? I haven't told you about any girl that I slept with except for shorty down in Mississippi who had the abortion."

I looked at him. The more he talked, the deeper he dug himself. "Why did you choose her of all people, Jamie? You must have always wanted to hit it, huh?"

He hesitated for a minute. "The old me did; I'm not even gonna lie and pretend that I didn't. When I ran into her in Miami, she was crying and shit, talking about Aaron didn't love her and how he was making her feel like he didn't want anything to do with her. I was just trying to show her some attention. I told her what she was wanted to hear, that she was attractive, and that she could have any man that she wanted. Yeah, I wanted to have sex with her before you and I got together in high school. I've been with a lot of girls, shorty. I'm different now, Ne'Vaeh. I love you—not her, not anybody else."

Tears raced down my face. With each word that he spoke about her, my heart grew weaker. "Well, thank you for playing Super-Save-a-Bitch, Jamie. Now the ho can't stop laughing at me. While you wanted to fuck the bitch in high school, apparently she was feeling you too. Do you know she bragged about having your baby, Jamie? Said that I'd taken everything from her that she wanted, including you. Said that this baby she's having with you is the one thing that I'll never be able to take from her. She wanted the key to your heart so bad, Jamie, so I gave it to her." I pulled from Renée.

Jamie looked down at my neck, where his necklace used to be and where Aaron's necklace still hung. He looked back up into my face. "You gave away the key to my heart, shorty?"

I shook my head. "No, asshole, I smacked that bitch in the face with it. Both of y'all mutha-fuckas lied to me. You knew my truth, you knew how bad I felt about sleeping with Aaron, and you knew I hated myself for falling weak. Instead of telling me the truth, you thought you could just break up with me before I found out. I told you not to make me fall back in love with you. I told you not to touch my heart if you didn't know how to treat it. You gave me all of these hopes and dreams that someday, you would be my husband, and your ass doesn't even know how to be a fuckin' boyfriend." I pushed him hard.

"Shorty, you're mad at me for fuckin' Charlie when your ass was fuckin' Aaron?" Jamie had the nerve to try to match my sin with his.

I pushed him again. "No. I'm mad because you fucked the bitch, and then lied about it."

He hesitated. "Shorty, I didn't lie, I just—"

"Didn't tell me, asshole—same muthafuckin' difference," I screamed.

"Well, it ain't like you told me the shit willingly. Your ass was caught. Everyone saw you with the nigga at the hotel. Charlie found the damn dress receipt in his pocket. There was no way that you could deny the shit," Jamie snapped at me. "You would've kept that secret inside for as long as you could too, shorty, so you can't really judge me or what the fuck I did. We were both in the wrong, which is why we should put this behind us and move the fuck on."

I couldn't deny the truth. I don't know if I would have kept the lie rolling like Charlie and Jamie had, but I wouldn't have been able to look Charlie in the eye after knowing that I slept with Aaron. Jamie showing up at my birthday party the way he did really pissed me off. That was the push I needed to go with Aaron that night to the hotel. Yes, I knew I was wrong. But that didn't change the fact that after Charlie and Jamie knew about us, they never admitted the truth about themselves.

"Jamie, you lied to me." I pushed him again. "Yes, I was caught. Fine, you wanna share the blame, I'll share the shit without you. But at least when I did make a stupid decision, I protected myself. You weren't supposed to fuck her with no protection. You weren't supposed to dump me just so I wouldn't find out who the bitch was that you got pregnant. And you weren't supposed to make the bitch fall in love with you. 'Fuck 'em and leave 'em'—wasn't that the shit you were talking back in high school before we started dating? What happened to all that, Jamie?"

"Shorty, I know I fucked up. I tried telling you. I swear I tried." Jamie tried his best to apologize to me, but I really wasn't trying to hear it at the moment.

"Well, you didn't try hard enough. You and that bitch better find a way to tell Aaron, because I'm not gonna let her go through with this wedding. I'll do whatever I have to do to stop this wedding. She's not gonna get to live happily ever after while I live fuckin' miserable. Aaron doesn't deserve this. He didn't do shit to deserve being tricked into giving that bitch and your son his last name." I dried my face.

"Ne'Vaeh, baby, I didn't mean to hurt you. I'm sorry. Baby, you know I love you." Jamie held my hand in his, not afraid of me slapping him dead in his face again.

Oh, I could feel his pulse through his fingertips, giving my heart a jolt or two. I looked up into his face, slipping my hand from his. "You made her love you, Jamie. You talked a good game, and her heart fell for it. Apparently, my heart fell for your lies too. And I will never forgive you for that. Please don't call me, don't text me, don't message me on Facebook. You don't know me; you don't fuckin' exist, Jamie. I'm done with you." I pushed past him.

The heart plays tricks with your mind. It took everything in me not to call Jamie that week. I didn't talk to anyone. I left Renée's apartment and went to stay in a hotel the day of Charlie's baby shower. I didn't want to be around anyone. I stayed in bed all the way up until two hours before Charlie's rehearsal dinner. I made sure to get as cute as I could that night, just to show that my life could go on without Jamie or Charlie in it. I called my backup to come with me to the church in case a fight or two broke out. And I called my sister, Autumn, to see her one last time before she flew back to California. You should have seen the look on Aaron's face when I told him the truth about Charlie and Jamie. I knew he was hurt, though his anger helped him play it off. I didn't want to hurt that boy, but he needed to know the truth before he made the biggest mistake of his life. My heart slowly but surely began to freeze again.

After breaking Aaron's heart, I convinced myself that it was time to give Anastasia Jones-Allan a call. It was time to take her up on her offer. I needed a change. She said that she was in D.C. for a few days, and if I wanted to fly back to Atlanta with her on January second, she'd be glad to pay for my ticket. She really didn't give me a lot of time to think it over, but the faster I left Maryland, the better.

Renée stood next to me, arms intertwined, lips quivering as I got off the phone with Anastasia.

It was December thirty-first, the day that was supposed be Charlie's bachelorette party and the evening of my holiday performance. Renée and her girls were taking my sister and me out for our last night together before Autumn went back home. We were going to bring the New Year in right.

"Ne'Vaeh, you're really leaving?" Renée exclaimed. "Leaving school, leaving your job, leaving your family?"

I shrugged. "Renée, I have to do this. I can't sit here and watch Charlie have Jamie's baby in my face. I can't sit here regardless of whether Jamie decides he wants to help raise her baby. The man I love is having a baby with my sister. I don't deserve that."

Renée said, "No, you don't. You're right, but going to Atlanta isn't going to change anything."

"Weren't you the one sayin' that 'she'll rock the hell out of that mic' shit to Anastasia on my birthday? What happened to that?" I asked.

Renée laughed a little. "Okay, okay, I get excited when I hear you sing. You're amazing. But . . . I don't want you to leave me. You're like my little sister."

I looked at her, eyes growing misty. "I'm scared, Renée. Scared of staying here and letting Jamie talk me into getting back with him. I'm like two seconds from calling that boy, asking him to take me back. I deserve better than this. Now, I've cried for four days straight. The boy blew up my phone so much that I just turned the bitch off. It took you four days to figure out what hotel I was staying in. The only reason why you even found me is because you purposely left your phone in my purse, knowing it had a GPS on it."

Renée laughed to herself. "Yeah, I am pretty smooth with my shit."

I rolled my eyes. "Renée, Jamie has showed up to your apartment five times in the past few days looking for me. I'm so not ready to see him, and I know he's gonna show up to see my performance tonight. I really wish you could be there."

Renée sighed. "Cuz, I'm not even gonna lie—I am pissed with Jamie's ass. I rooted for him, basically pushing you to give him a try again." Renée was really mad at herself. "Yes, he fucked up, but I really like Jamie. I can't just give up on him like that."

I looked at her. After everything that we'd been through, she still had faith in him. She still believed that we could work it out.

"He doesn't love that girl, Ne'Vaeh. You know he doesn't," she exclaimed.

"I know that, but he had no business fuckin' with her." I got pissed just thinking about the two together, fuckin' on the damn beach for the whole world to see.

"And you had no business fuckin' Aaron." Renée tried to turn the blame on me just like Jamie tried to do.

I folded my arms, pissed, when I should have known she'd choose Jamie's side over mine. "My situation is totally different, Renée. And Charlie was fuckin' Jamie damn near three months before I even touched Aaron. She was pregnant by Jamie, then had the audacity to throw shade at me for messing around with Aaron. She was dead wrong—wrong as fuck."

"And so were you, Ne'Vaeh." Renée was getting irritated with my rationale. "It's doesn't matter who fucked who first—it's all fucked up."

"Whose side are you on, Renée?" I squealed.

"I'm not on anyone's side," she hollered back.

"Tah! The hell you're not." I rolled my eyes.

"All I'm saying is you're just as much at fault as she is." Renée shook her head at me. "As much as you hate her, as much as you wish she wasn't, Charlie is your sister. And Jamie made a mistake."

I looked at Renée. She had a soft spot for Jamie. He'd been through hell his entire life.

Football changed his life. It took him places he'd never see otherwise. Jamie had seen the bottom, and once he got to the top, he was determined to stay there. Renée wanted me to forgive him, and a part of me wanted to, but he had crossed the line when he dumped me so I wouldn't find out he'd screwed around with a woman who was supposed to be my closest friend, let alone my half sister.

"Renée, a mistake is a one-time thing. He made a choice. A choice to leave me naked in that bed four years ago without saying goodbye, when he should have taken me with him. A choice to sleep with Charlie without any protection when he knew she had a boyfriend. A choice to fuck her on the beach, fuck her at that club, and fuck her in her apartment in the same bed where she had sex with Aaron. A choice to lie to me about ever sleeping with the bitch. And a choice to try to dump me just so he could hide the fact that the baby she was carrying was his." I dried the tears that I didn't even realize were sliding down my face until my cheeks began to sting.

Renée sighed. "With you, Jamie is complete. Without you, Jamie is lost. He doesn't give a fuck about anything or anyone without you. That's why he's such an awesome quarterback. He puts all that aggression and power into the way he plays. You are his motivation. Not Charlie. That boy needs you, and you need him. Don't let that bitch win."

Sadly, I said, "She already has, Renée."

Suddenly, Renée looked at her watch. "Oh, shit, girl, I gotta get back to work. I took an hour and half break to come here to get my damn phone back. I should get off around 9:00 tonight. There is no way I'm missing taking you and my girls out for New Year's." Renée gave me a tight hug before letting go. "I'll see you later, girl. Good luck tonight, and I hope you decide to stay here in Maryland."

Around 6:00, I was finally dressed and ready to head to campus for the choir's holiday performance. I had a bad habit of driving my car until the gas light came on. I stopped at a gas station to put the last twenty dollars that I had on me in the tank. Just as I was about to jump back in the car while the gas was pumping, I heard a familiar voice calling out to me.

"Heaven, I can't avoid you for nothing." Aaron's voice came from my left.

I looked up to see him approaching me, dressed to impress, in a brown hat, scarf, leather coat, and dress pants. He looked so good. And he always smelled liked he'd stepped straight out of the shower. I was speechless for a minute. "H-Hey," I stuttered.

Aaron smiled. It was good to see him smile. "What's good wit'cha?" He licked his lips.

"I-I'm just headed to my holiday performance tonight at Howard. What are you doing on this side of town?" I looked up into his face.

"My family's leaving today to go back to California. I just came from the airport to tell them goodbye. Not to mention my bachelor party is out here in D.C. tonight." He grinned.

I was confused. "Aaron, bachelor party? But—"

He laughed, "Just because Charlie and I called off the wedding doesn't mean I'm calling off my party. Your cousin's wife, P. Jones, hooked us up with some bad-ass strippers, yo. The party is gonna be off the chain, turned all the way up. You can come through, if you want."

I shook my head. "Oh, hell, no, Aaron."

He smiled. "You know you wanna show them strippers how to twerk."

I laughed out loud. "Whatever, Aaron. Twerk what?"

He grinned.

"It's really good to see you smile, Aaron," I nodded, fighting back the tears.

His smile faded. "Well, I gotta move on, Heaven. No use crying over a relationship that should have been over years ago. How are you holding up? You were the one in love."

"I'm just trying to get my life back. I gotta do something for me. I'm leaving in a few days." I looked up at him.

Aaron looked down into my face, eyes tracing my lips. "Where you headed?"

"Atlanta," I sighed.

His smile grew back. "You're doing it, aren't you? You're gonna sign a contract with P. Jones?" He was definitely more excited than I was.

I rolled my eyes. "Gosh, you sound like Renée. I'm really doing this just to get away from Maryland. But, yes, I'm meeting up with Anastasia, aka P. Jones, tonight after my performance. She's gonna watch me perform tonight. Let's just say tonight is my audition."

Aaron nodded, smiling from ear to ear. "Okay, that's what's up. You nervous, Heaven?"

"Am I?" I laughed. "My stomach is doing back-flips as we speak."

"You'll do good. You'll dazzle the crowd as normal. Shit, you dazzled the fuck out of me when you sang to a nigga at your boy's party a few months ago." His eyes searched mine.

I looked up at him. "What makes you think I was singing to you?"

He grinned. "But really, though," he avoided the question, "how are you doin'? It's gotta be tough knowing your own sister is pregnant by a dude you thought you would be with forever."

I started to feel warm all over again, a feeling I didn't want or need to feel at the moment. "Well, Aaron, it's obvious that my fairy tale doesn't exist. Love has never loved me, Aaron. I'm pretty used to this fucked-up, miserable, lonely feeling by now."

"I know how you feel, sweetheart; trust me, I do." Aaron shook his head. "I'll be leaving in a few weeks too. Luckily, we didn't close on that house that we bought. I have a hell of a lot of money to pay back to my parents for this wedding bullshit. Leaving the country is my new start. I'd ask you to roll with me, you know, if you weren't already going to ATL."

I looked at him.

Aaron grinned. "I didn't get a chance to thank you for letting me know the truth about the baby."

"You don't need to thank me. I couldn't stand by and watch Charlie make a fool out of you. You're a good man who deserves so much better than her—better than me. I just want you to be happy, Aaron. I'm hurt by this entire situation. The fact that they slept together, the fact that they both lied about it, the fact that she's having his baby, the fact that she told you that she was having your baby—everything."

He looked intently at me. "You know, I meant what I said at the rehearsal dinner, Heaven. Dude is trippin', like he's the only man made for you. When you want me, I'm yours. I'm not giving up on you, Heaven. You're my dream girl. These past few months have damn near killed me. I'm not gonna lie, I played myself when I got a taste of what it would be like to be with you. I had the best nights of my fuckin' life in that suite with you. I felt like I could be with you forever. I knew from the moment you fell asleep on top of me, in my arms, that letting that feeling go was gonna be damn near impossible." Aaron's emerald-green eyes searched every inch of my face. "I'm gonna miss you, Heaven."

The gas pump shut off.

Both of us went for the pump, his hand covering mine.

I looked up into his face, lips trembling.

He smiled, eyes tracing my face. "I got you."

I quickly removed my hand as he placed the nozzle back in its slot. Then I looked down at my watch. "I really have to get going, Aaron." I looked back up at him.

He smiled, nodding. "A'ight. I feel you. Good luck at your performance tonight. Show P. Jones she's got some competition."

I smiled nervously. "Have fun at your bachelor's party."

Aaron grabbed my hand, pulling me closer to him. Then he gently kissed my forehead, and my knees grew weak. "You can come through tonight if you want, sweetheart. And if you don't come, well, I guess I'll see you on TV, Heaven." After saying that, he walked away from me.

I was nervous out of my mind as I got out of my car and made my way down the walkway to the auditorium. Anastasia P. Jones-Allan and her entourage met me at the entrance. She was so beautiful . . . hips, big booty, copper skin, long hair and all. I wasn't sure if the house was crowded because she was making a guest appearance, or if our choir was just that good. She watched as I was sent to hair and makeup. "You were made for the spotlight," she told me before going on stage that night. I put my heart, body, mind, and soul into my voice that evening. I just channeled all that pain and hurt that I was feeling and put it into my performance. Anastasia wowed the crowd with her surprise performance. I looked out into the crowd that night and saw Jamie and a few of his boys sitting in the audience, in the first row. My heart pounded in my chest as our performance came to a close that night.

"You were absolutely, positively amazing tonight," Anastasia gushed as she changed in the dressing room.

I sighed, rolling my eyes, sitting on the sofa. "Girl, please, whateva. The crowd went wild when you surprised them with your appearance. I'm not even sure how you're gonna get out of here tonight without getting trampled. I hope my cousin has you armed with at least fifty bodyguards tonight."

Anastasia laughed out loud. "Girl, it's all good. I'm used to the crazed fans by now. So, what about you? You ready for all of this?"

I looked up at her, shaking my head, feeling the tears coming. "Nah, girl, but I gotta get away from here. I'm sure you heard what happened."

She sighed, pulling her hair back in a ponytail. "Sweetie, you can't run from love. I tried once. I could tell you some thangs, girl, believe dat. Love always finds a way to get through to you. We are all human. We make mistakes. Don't leave that boy if that's not what you really wanna do, sweetie."

My lips trembled as Anastasia's assistant handed me a cup of hot chocolate. "Anastasia, I love him, but he made me look like a fool. He knew the entire time that he had sex with Charlie. Not just once, but for days and weeks at a time. He tried to dump me before I found out the truth. He's really got me wanting to show up and show out at Aaron's got-damn party tonight."

Anastasia laughed a little, sitting down on the couch next to me. "Girl, just let it go. I'm not saying that he didn't fuck up by getting your girl pregnant, but he really loves you. He gave up his lifestyle for you. Any man who does that when he really doesn't have to is a keeper. Do you know how many hoes he had? How much pussy he could have had? How many bitches he had suckin' his dick?"

I cringed. "Okay, Anastasia, damn; I get it."

"I'm just sayin', cuz," she rolled her eyes, "the only reason why that bitch told him that she was pregnant was because she wanted to keep him from you. Which is the exact reason why she told Aaron that she was pregnant by him—to keep him from running to someone else. She's dirty. I don't think I'd ever forgive her. But her child shouldn't have to suffer for this shit."

I looked at her. "What do you mean?"

Anastasia's eyes searched mine. "You and I are really not that different. I lost my entire family, Ne'Vaeh. I lost my mother and my grandparents who left me. My mother was a ho, running the streets. I didn't find her until I was damn near an adult. I found her on stage, at this strip club in Atlanta. She was the whole reason why I worked at that bitch. I would have given anything just to have a normal life, with a normal mother, who talked to me about boys, who helped me with my homework, who helped me shop for a dress for prom." Her eyes glistened under the vanity mirror lights. "Ne'Vaeh, I'm saying this because Jamie is not going anywhere near Charlie because he lost you because of her. Now, do you want this sweet innocent little baby not to have his father around?"

I shook my head, eyes swollen with tears. "Anna, that doesn't have anything to do with me."

She disagreed. "Boo, it does. Just talk to the boy, let him know you still love him and that you forgive him. I'm not saying get back with the muthafucka if you don't want to. Just don't leave here hating him; that's all I'm saying. You love this boy, right?"

I sighed. "Of course I do."

"Then stay with him."

"Love isn't always enough, Anna," I replied.

"The only reason why that boy lied to you in the first place is because he didn't wanna hurt you. I don't know Jamie, but what I do know is that you're his everything. I'm sure that nigga is suffocating right now being away from you."

I rolled my eyes. "He'll be all right, really."

"No, he won't. And neither will you," Anastasia sighed. "He needs you to save him. I'm not trying to run your life, but I'm telling you, he needs you. I want you to be a part of my crew bad as muthafucka, I really do, but I don't want to come between love."

There was a knock at the room door. Her assistant hurried over to the door, pulling it open. Jamie stood there, a bouquet of flowers in his hand. He was dressed in all white, from his baseball cap to his shoes.

Anastasia got up from the chair, walking up to him, moving her assistant out of the way. She looked up into his face. "You know, after hearing so much about you, this is the first time that we actually meet face-to-face." She looked him up and down, from his face to his shoes. Then she looked back up into his face. "Yeah, the bad boys are always the best looking."

Jamie grinned a little. "What's up, P. Jones?"

"I don't appreciate you breakin' my cousin's heart. You better do what the fuck you gotta do to mend that shit, muthafucka." Anastasia rolled her eyes at him, then looked back at her assistant. "Come on, Natalie. Let's let them talk alone." Anastasia looked at me. "We'll be right outside this door." She winked her eye, then left with her assistant.

I stood from the sofa, clearing my throat.

Jamie walked toward me, standing before me, handing me the bouquet of roses. "Shorty, you were amazing." he couldn't help but exclaim. "I mean, you and the choir took it to church for real, had the whole crowd in tears. It took everything I had in me not to bust out crying. You put your all into that performance. I know there had to be some record producers out there tonight seeing this. You'll get some calls this week, no doubt."

I looked up into his face, taking the flowers from his hands. "I already have. Anastasia is taking me to Atlanta in two days."

Jamie just looked at me, not really sure what to say. He just sighed deeply, putting his hands in his pockets. Took him a few seconds for his breath to catch back up with him. "I don't want you to go," he admitted.

My heart melted just a little. "It's not up to you, Jamie. I have to do this for me."

His eyes glistened. "You're leaving because of me?"

I looked up into his face.

Jamie shook his head. "Shorty, I know you hate me, but you don't gotta go."

I sighed, placing the flowers down on the sofa. "Jamie, I don't hate you. I said everything that I said to you the other day because I was pissed at you. I'm hurt, I'm not gonna pretend that I'm not. But I don't hate you. I told you that I could never hate you. I forgive you, I just . . . I don't wanna ever see you with her. I can't believe that y'all are having a baby together. You know that I always wanted to have your baby. What you gave to her was supposed to be mine." I cried out.

Jamie tried to hold my hand, pulling me toward him, but I jerked away.

I dried my face. "I'm tired of love hating me. I'm through with love. Your love has always confused me, Jamie. I can't be your fool anymore. You need to help Charlie raise that baby. You lay in that bed, now you need to help make it up. As much as I hate Charlie for what she did, I can't stand by and let you just act like you didn't get that girl pregnant. Ignoring the baby doesn't take away anything that happened between you two. That girl put her guards down when you came around, showing her some attention in Miami. I can't even blame her for falling for you because I fell too. I'm pissed at you because you didn't have to make her love you. You could have just fucked her like you did the other girls and left. Take her to a hotel or some shit, and then dismiss her. No, you made love to her, spent time with her, made her feel important, and then dissed her as soon as you thought you had me back.

You can't do a person like that, Jamie. That's why the girl did what she did. You need to promise me that you'll be there for her and that baby."

Jamie's lips quivered as he tried to fight the tears. "Shorty, I'll be there. I'm not gonna leave my son."

I was so disappointed in him. "I love you, I have always loved you, Jamie, but now it's really time to let go."

Jamie tried to be strong. He fought the urge to continue to beg me to stay. He cleared his throat. "So, when am I supposed to see you again, Ne'Vaeh? When you comin' back?"

I shrugged. "I don't know."

"What does Renée have to say about all this? I know Mrs. Mouth-Almighty, Never-Shuts-the-Fuck-Up had some shit to say about you leaving," he said.

I rolled my eyes. "You know she did, but like I just told you, I have to do this for my own sanity. I'm thinking of asking Alisha to come with me."

Jamie looked at me. "Alisha? Why?"

I shrugged. "I don't know. She's got a brain tumor. She doesn't know how much longer she has to live. She loves dancing. She's a great dancer. I'm sure she wouldn't mind dancing for Anastasia on tour for a little while. It would be a great present for her."

Jamie smiled a little. "What about Ashton? I don't think he'd want his girl to leave his side."

"Well, it's not about him. It's about her. She needs to live her life before it's gone, the same way that I do," I said, looking up at him.

Jamie looked down into my face. "You headed to P. Jones's party tonight?"

I looked at him. "Are you talking about Aaron's bachelor party?"

He nodded. "If you wanna call it that. Everybody is gonna be at the spot. I figured I might as well go with the rest of my boys from the team. It ain't no party if I'm not there, you know that." He grinned, teeth gleaming.

I rolled my eyes, heart racing in my chest. "Oh, please. I'm goin' out with the girls tonight. Autumn leaves tomorrow, so we're gonna bring in the New Year tonight at Club Heat. Really not trying to see that shenanigans tonight. Anastasia's girls fuck niggas on stage, okay? Not tryin' to see that."

Jamie laughed out loud. It felt so good to see him laughing, to look into his face, to see those lips, to breathe in his air, to smell his cologne, to look into his brown eyes. He held my hand, pulling me closer to him, looking down into my face, eyes tracing my lips. "I gotta see you before you decide to leave me, shorty. Make time for me, that's all I'm sayin'."

I nodded, looking up into his face, lips quivering, trying to fight back screaming out that I wanted him back.

My heart kept screaming, "*I love him. Look at that face. Look at that smile. No one makes you feel like this. Why are you leaving him when you know he needs you?*"

But my mind just rolled its eyes, saying, "*Girl, bye. You crazy as hell. You don't deserve the shit that he's put you through. Why should you have to share him with Charlie?*"

We are so stupid when we fall in love. It's like when your heart starts beating, then your brain eventually stops fuckin' working. I was slowly coming to my senses, though my mind and heart were still in conflict. The biggest mistake I made that night was when I looked into Jamie's eyes. Had not Anastasia come back into the room when she did, I would have told Jamie to "fuck that club—take me to your place."

"I have an announcement to make." I stood from the corner booth where I sat with my girls that night at Club Heat. We were in the VIP section that night, drunk as hell.

There we were—me, Renée, Kristina, Jennel, Alisha, Kelissa, and Autumn, together for the last time.

"I have decided to take my cousin's wife up on her offer," I said.

They all just looked at me for more of an explanation.

"I'm moving to Atlanta on the second. Anastasia Jones is flying me back to ATL with her to start recording in the studio. I'll be staying at her place until I can get a place of my own," I stuttered.

"What?" Jennel asked, trying to look happy, but she cried instead. She looked at Renée. By the look on Renée's face, Jennel knew that Renée had heard the news already. "Renée, you knew about this and didn't tell us?"

"She just told me this afternoon," Renée replied.

"I hope you're doing this for your career and not just because you wanna get away and forget about Jamie's triflin' ass," Kelissa said.

"Man, y'all heard the girl blow. She's got skills. Fuck Jamie." Alisha looked at me. "We will all miss you, but congratulations. Girl, nobody deserves this more than you do."

I smiled at her, taking an envelope from out of my purse.

Alisha looked at me as I handed her the envelope. "What's this?" she asked, lips already trembling.

"A plane ticket to Atlanta." I smiled, watching her fight the tears as she opened the envelope, taking out the one-way ticket to Georgia. "I talked to Anastasia, telling her that you are the best dancer in the area. She said that she'd love to see your skills, and she could use another dancer."

Alisha fought back the tears as she placed the ticket back in the envelope and handed it back to me. "Babe, you know how bad I want this. You know that dancing is everything to me. But I can't leave Ashton. As much as I would love the chance to dance for P. Jones—got-damn it—I can't leave him."

"Girl, you are crazy as fuck," Kelissa exclaimed. "You're sick. You deserve to live your dream. Shit, I'll go with you. I'm sure Ashton will understand."

Alisha shook her head, the tears beginning to stream down her cheeks. "I can't make that boy give up on his goals, just to see me achieve mine. I'm good, y'all. Thank you, cutie, for thinking of me. Just hold it for me unless I change my mind."

"What did Jamie say about you leaving?" Autumn just had to ask me.

"Don't nobody give a got-damn what Jamie thinks or has to say about it." Alisha dried her face and retorted.

"He-He wants me to stay," I sighed, sipping from my glass of Long Island Iced Tea.

Alisha rolled her eyes. "Of course he does. He doesn't want some other nigga snatchin' you up. He knows he fucked up. He knows it doesn't get better than you."

"When did you talk to Jamie?" Jennel asked.

"He showed up at my show tonight and brought me flowers."

"I'm sure the bitches had thorns in 'em." Kelissa rolled her eyes, watching us giggle.

"Have you seen Aaron?" Kristina asked.

Renée looked at Kristina, and then at me.

I glanced at Renée. "Yeah, we ran into each other at the gas station today."

"Aaron must be devastated. He bought that baby everything, do you hear me?" Kelissa said.

"No, he ain't devastated, shit," Alisha scuffed. "That nigga sees this as an open opportunity. Don't think he's not gonna come for you, Ne'Vaeh. You heard what my boy said at the rehearsal dinner. That boy always does what he says and says what he does."

I looked at Alisha, trying my best not to grin.

She smiled at me. "Y'all would make the cutest little couple," she teased.

Renée rolled her eyes. "Please."

Alisha made a face at her. "The fuck you mean 'please'? Did you not see that shit that went down at the baby shower? You didn't see your cousin smack that bitch in the face, splitting her face open with that key? Charlie is having Jamie's baby. Don't nobody got time for that 'Sister Wife/Flowers in the Attic'-type shit. Cutie Pie ain't got time to be babysitting her nephew. Suppose the two were to get married. That little boy would be her nephew-stepson. Y'all muthafuckas crazy."

I giggled a little. If I could count on someone to think like me, it was crazy-ass Alisha. "Omg, you're a trip, Alisha. I'm gonna miss you so much."

She winked at me. "Go and getcha money, girl. Fuck Jamie."

Renée's phone vibrated in her purse. She took it out, looking at the screen. Her eyes lit up. "It's a text from Tyreeka. Y'all know Anastasia's throwing that party tonight? The party that was supposed to be for Aaron and Charlie?"

"Maybe we should go." Kristina shot me a quick look.

I shook my head. "Oh, hell nah. Y'all know Charlie's ass is dumb enough to show up. Not to mention Aaron will be there, and Jamie mentioned that he was going to the party tonight. That's a setup for disaster right there, y'all."

"Man, fuck Charlie, fuck Aaron, and fuck Jamie," Jennel snapped, getting her purse. "Man, Renée, call a ride to come pick us up."

I sighed. "Here we go again."

Chapter 13

End of the Road

Ne'Vaeh

The party was packed that night. Anastasia's assistant, Kira, caught sight of us hoping out of Renée's boyfriend's/fuck-buddy's/whatever the hell he is Expedition that night. She signaled us to bypass everyone else in line, and we headed through the double doors. People were lined up and down the hallway entrance to the club. And just when I thought I made it through the tunnel to the light, someone snatched me in the opposite direction by my hand. My heart nearly stopped as I looked up to see Aaron's light eyes smiling at me. I looked back to see Renée and the rest of my girls strolling through to the party. Renée looked back at me, grinning, shaking her head.

"Heaven, you came." He pulled me closer to him.

I looked up at him, struggling to catch my breath. Oh my goodness, that boy looked *so* good. "You really gonna hem me up in the hall-way like this, Aaron?" I stuttered.

He laughed a little, letting go of my hand. "Sorry. I'm just glad to see you. Man, you have my heart racing. Come talk to me real quick." He stood from leaning back against the wall, and I followed him to the bar.

I'd never seen so many 34Ds and muscle-en-hanced asses in all my life. Anastasia's girls put the "werk" in twerking. Those girls almost had me throwin' dollars at them. Most of the girls could clap their booties louder and harder than most people could clap their hands. They had those men falling in love that night. You know how stupid men are—they actually enjoy getting tricked out of their money. Franklins were raining all over the place.

Aaron sat down at the bar after signaling the bartender to come over. "Fix whatever you think I might like, shorty." He grinned at the cute bartender, then looked back at me.

I sat there in my tight-fitted silk blouse and short gray skirt. I looked something like a sexy lawyer. My hair was pulled up into a bun, with hair added for fullness. My bangs were swooped to the side.

Aaron looked me over before his eyes met mine. "You came to see your dude before you leave town? Or did you come here to see me?"

I shrugged. "Well, I knew you both would be here, so why not kill two birds with one stone, right?"

Aaron laughed a little as the bartender handed him his drink. "Regardless of who you came to see, it feels good to see you."

I looked up at him as I reached behind my neck to unhook the "Heaven" charm necklace that he'd given me for my birthday. I sighed as I took his hand in mine and placed the necklace in his palm.

Aaron looked at me, eyes sparkling under the club lights. "Sweetheart, why are you giving this back?"

"I can't take any reminder of Maryland with me to Atlanta. I'm leaving everything that hurts here, Aaron." I looked at him. "I love this necklace, but I gotta give it back."

Aaron's feelings were hurt, but he understood. "Well, at least you didn't smack me in the face with it . . . not literally anyway."

I laughed a little. Seems everyone heard about how the key print ended up on Charlie's cheek.

"You did a number on that girl's face." Aaron shook his head, eyes searching my face. "Must have been something she said."

"Well, you know that mouth of hers is always writing checks she can't cash." I rolled my eyes.

He grinned. "So, how did your performance go?"

I nodded. "Good, good. She loved it. She's dying to get me into the studio to record with her. I really can't believe this is even happening. It doesn't even feel real, ya know?"

Aaron understood. "Yeah, I feel you, sweetheart. I say the same thing every time I look at my new jersey hanging up in my closet."

"So, you all packed, ready to go to France?" I watched him sip from his glass.

Aaron nodded. "Hell yeah, I need this vacation like a muthafucka. You know, my mom's is actually excited for me. Never thought she'd accept that this is what I wanna do, but she does. Dad is still warming up to this, but he'll come around. He really doesn't have a choice."

I smiled, happy for him. "I'm really happy for you, Aaron. You turned a negative into a positive. I'm sorry about the wedding, but you'll find someone in Paris. A guy like you will never have a problem getting a girl."

He looked at me and said, "I'm not going to Paris to get a girl—I'm going to Paris to get away from a girl."

I blushed a little, taking his drink from his hand, and sipped.

"Yo, Aaron." One of Aaron's teammates called him from a crowded corner in the club. His teammates were surrounded by strippers who were ready to trick their thirsty asses.

Aaron looked back at me, his eyes sparkling. "I'm really gonna miss you, Heaven. There's no one like you on earth. Please, never change for anybody. I'll see you again—I know this ain't goodbye, so I'm not even gonna say it." He pulled me closer to him by the hand that was free. "Give me some love. I know it's still there somewhere."

I hugged him around his neck, feeling his lips grazing against my neck. His smell was intoxicating, hypnotizing, breathtaking.

"Heaven, I will always love you. When you need me, just call me. There's always room for you in Paris," he whispered, lips grazing against my ear, breath causing the hairs on my neck to stand straight up. He held me close for a few seconds, his heart racing in his chest. "If you don't come to me, I'll come to you, and that's a promise."

My heart smiled. *Oh, I love him. Look at those eyes. Look at that smile. The way he holds you feels amazing. Oh, he smells so good. Our hearts are in sync.*

My brain scoffed. *Bitch, didn't you say some similar shit about Jamie?*

I unwrapped my arms from around him before I let my emotions overrule my intentions. "See you around, Aaron." I looked up into his face as I let him go.

He nodded, light eyes sparkling. "I meant what I said, Heaven. I'm coming back to getcha. Anyway, have fun tonight."

I walked away from him, not having to go far to catch up with my girls, who stood alongside the dance floor, watching Anastasia and her girls perform a sexy dance routine in the middle of the floor. Renée eyed my profile as I stood next to her, folding my trembling arms. I was feeling some type of way after seeing Aaron. I knew he was hurting just as much as I was, but he played it off much better than I did.

I was actually having a decent time that night. No drama, no crying, no fighting. I hadn't seen Jamie, thank goodness. But I ran straight into Charlie that night when I came out of one of the bathroom stalls. She stopped in her tracks. We just stood there, face-to-face for a few seconds, each of us hesitant on making the first move.

Renée came out of the bathroom stall next to the one that I came out of. She stopped in her tracks when she saw us standing there. "Now, Ne'Vaeh, be cool." She saw my hands clinch into a fist for a second or two. "We came to party, not to reminisce with drama, remember?"

My eyes searched Charlie's powered face. Whoever did her makeup must have been a magician. You could barely see the wound that I imprinted on her cheek.

"Yeah, the stitches and the fuckin' key print are still there." Charlie folded her arms. "I never had to wear this much fuckin' makeup in my got-damn life, Ne'Vaeh."

I laughed a little, folding my arms right along with her. "Well, it could be worse. I mean, you could be wearing a body bag, so I'd just accept having to wear a little makeup if I were you."

Charlie approached me.

Renée hurried to stand between us. "Charlie, you need to—"

Charlie rolled her eyes, moving Renée to the side by her shoulder. "What are you—her got-damn bodyguard? Back off, Renée, okay? Damn." She took a necklace out of her pocket, then took my hand in hers, placing the cold necklace in my palm. It was the key charm necklace that I had stamped her face with.

I looked up at her.

"I tried giving it back to Jamie, but he wouldn't take it. It really hurt him when I tried giving it back to him, after telling him what happened at the baby shower." Charlie looked at me. "Yeah, I deserved these stitches. Yeah, I wrote a check that my ass couldn't cash. Never saw you hitting me in the face with the key to that boy's heart, though. He loves you so much that he won't have anything to do with my baby if you have nothing to do with him. I know you hate me, I know I messed up, but please . . . This is my baby's life. I know I don't deserve your forgiveness after everything that I said and everything that I did to you, but I don't have anything left, Ne'Vaeh. My mother won't speak to me. Aaron's parents are suing me. Aaron is going on about his life in Paris. I barely have any friends left. I lost everything and everyone. This is Jamie's baby too, no matter how much he wishes this baby wasn't. Just don't let him abandon his baby." Her lips trembled. "Please, Ne'Vaeh, just talk to him for me."

I looked at her, necklace clinched in my hand. "He'll be there for that baby, Charlie. I won't let him walk away from his responsibility. He made his bed, so he needs to lie in it. I just won't stick around to see you two together, raising this baby.

I don't know if I can handle seeing the product of the two of you."

Charlie looked at me. "You're leaving?" She looked happy—too damn happy.

"In two days."

"Anastasia's signing Ne'Vaeh to her label." Renée had to rub my opportunity in her face.

Charlie grinned, actually looking happy to hear the news. "Y-You're actually doing something with that voice of yours? That's awesome."

Oh, I couldn't even hug her and cry in her arms. I missed my best friend. Circumstances had driven a wedge between us, and our friendship would never be the same. There was no turning back the hands of time or undoing the pain that had been caused on both ends.

"Ne'Vaeh, five minutes until the countdown begins." Renée yanked on my arm.

I looked at Charlie. "We gotta get going."

Charlie smiled, tears in her light eyes. "Congratulations, sis. I love you, I miss you, and I'm sorry."

"Happy New Year, Charlie." I backed away from her and walked out of the bathroom before the tears started coming.

Our girls were waiting over by the bar, watching the flat-screen TV behind the bar. Every year, we'd watch the ball drop in Times Square. The one New Year's Eve that Juanita wasn't drunk or high, she took me, my sister, and baby brother to see the ball drop. I had to be about nine years old. It was my favorite memory of Juanita. It was the only time I remember her telling us that she loved us and actually meaning it.

The countdown had begun. "Nine, eight, seven . . ."

I felt someone's warm fingers slipping in between mine. Looking up, I saw Jamie's eyes staring straight back into mine. I happened to glance up, not even realizing that I was standing directly under some mistletoe. Instantly, before I can even say "wait a minute, muthafucka, hold up now," Jamie pulled me close and embraced my lips in his as the confetti sprinkled over everyone in the club. No one other than Jamie existed the moment our lips were interlocked. The boy had my knees buckling, nearly knocking me off of my stilettos. He gripped my waist in his hands, kissing me until I tore my lips from his. He made it so that I'd have no choice but to start my year off with him in it.

I wiped my mouth, looking up into his face. "Stealing kisses, are we?"

He grinned, grill gleaming under the club's white lights. "You coming home with me tonight?"

I looked up at him, folding my arms. "Now why would I do that?"

"So, you didn't come here to be with me tonight?" His eyes searched mine.

"No, I didn't," I lied.

"So, you were just gonna leave me without saying goodbye, then?" Jamie held my hands in his.

"Jamie, I'm here with my girls. My sister leaves tomorrow. Who knows when I'll see her again. My girls came here to have some fun tonight. Just leave me alone, Jamie, okay? We already discussed this. It's over." I shook my head at him.

Jamie's eyes sparkled. "Just come by the crib and spend some time with me for a little while. You're leaving me tomorrow, shorty. I can't just let you go without a proper goodbye. Just come home with me tonight. Please?"

I felt a slight push forward behind me. I looked over my shoulder to see Anastasia's ass nodding at me to go with him. "Go, got-dammit," she mouthed.

I looked up at Jamie, hesitating a little, but nodding. I guess he thought he was going to change my mind from leaving Maryland.

We stood there face-to-face in his kitchen that morning around 2:30. We didn't say anything the entire ride to his place.

"Shorty, you really leaving me?" he finally asked.

I sighed. "So, what . . . I'm supposed to miss the opportunity of a lifetime because you're too selfish to let me go? The fact that I came home with you tonight doesn't change anything that you did to me. I gave you my heart, and you shit on it. Not once, but twice. First, when you left me four years ago; then this past year when you got Charlie pregnant. If you wanted to fuck bitches and play football, Jamie, you could have stuck to that and left me to the books and the choir. I was living my life just fine without you. I had gotten used to the fact that you were never coming back. Your love hurts, Jamie, and I'm tired of hurting. We need to just go our separate ways once and for all. Once we moved on, we should have never looked back."

Jamie held my hand, pulling me closer to him. He knew that he held my heart in his hands, and he played on that. "What am I supposed to do without you? I need you. You can't leave me." His eyes traced my face. "Ne'Vaeh, I apologize. I didn't mean to hurt you."

I nodded, trying to keep from crying. "Jamie, I know that, but I'm still leaving."

He just looked at me, breathing heavily, not sure what he could do or say to convince me to stay. "What do I have to do, shorty, to get you to stay?"

My heart jumped in my chest as he pulled me closer.

"She doesn't mean anything to me, Ne'Vaeh. I should have never touched her, kissed her, slept with her, looked at her—nothing." He looked at me beseechingly. "Please, don't go."

"Jamie, if she didn't mean anything to you, you wouldn't have slept with her for three months." I lost the battle with my tears. "She's having your baby, Jamie. My sister is having your child. How do you think that makes me feel? If I was pregnant by some dude—no, if I was pregnant by your brother—how the hell would that make you feel? Would you take me back? Would you want to have anything to do with me?"

Jamie didn't know what to say.

"Don't expect me to do shit for you that you wouldn't do for me." I shook my head at him angrily, drying my face. There was really no use crying over him.

He said, "I know I fucked up, shorty. You've been my boo since preschool. I have loved you all of my life. I'm sorry if sometimes I don't know how to show it, but I do love you, and I am sorry. You're my world, Ne'Vaeh, and I'm lost without you. I'm not just saying this shit, girl, I mean it."

I was so angry with the boy, but I loved him so much. I couldn't get the image of Jamie singing to me at his Thanksgiving party out of my head. I wanted to hear his voice again just one last time. "Just-just sing to me. Sing anything. I just wanna hear you sing to me."

Jamie's smooth ass already had a song memorized, and he began, "What should I do, what should I say? My girl says she's leaving when I need her to stay.

"Just stick around and you will see, I am the man you need me to be," Jamie sang to my soul. "I can't see you with anybody else; baby, you're all I ever wanted. I wanna keep you to myself. I know I hurt you, I didn't mean to make you cry; I should have just told you the truth, I didn't have to lie. I can't picture my life without a girl like you; I need you to stay, just tell me what I gotta do."

I looked at him, shaking my head, trying to pull away.

"You're the best thing in my life, I haven't told you in a while; I'll do anything to keep you happy, do my best to make you smile. I love you, I need you, I crave you, I see you. Won't hurt you, won't tease you, I just wanna please you." Jamie stopped singing, looking down into my face.

"Why did you stop singing?" I asked.

"Because when I was writing the song, I started crying on this part and couldn't think of the words to say how much you've changed me." He dried his tears. "I just want you to stay with me, shorty." He pulled me closer to him by my blouse and gently kissed my lips. "Stay the night with me. Stay forever with me. I wanna be with you, gotta be with you, and need to be with you." He started to unbutton my blouse. "Don't leave me."

I cried out loud. I wanted to stay with him forever. Everything in me wanted to forgive Jamie for what he had done. He was human. He was entitled to make mistakes. I wasn't perfect either. Just like Renée said, I'd played an equal part in ruining Charlie's life as she did in mine. I slept with her boyfriend; she didn't sleep with mine. Jamie and I weren't together when they slept together, but Charlie and Aaron were together when I thought it was cool to sleep with him. The only difference between my sister and me was that she carried the evidence of her mistake.

Jamie pulled my shirt from my arms as I began to unbutton his. His lips devoured mine as he pushed my skirt up around my waist. I gasped as he lifted my body up, wrapping my legs around his waist. And just when he sat me on top of the counter, about to lay me down, my cell phone rang in my purse. I reached for it, but Jamie pushed my hand away.

"Nah, shorty, don't get it." He kissed my lips.

I gently pushed him away. "It might be important. Who calls someone at this time of night, Jamie?" I grabbed my phone from my purse, taking a glance at the display screen before answering it. It was Renée. "Renée, sweetie, what is it? It's really not a good time."

"Ne'Vaeh, where are you?" Renée sounded like something was seriously wrong.

I looked up at Jamie, who stared straight back at me, sensing my heart beginning to race for a reason other than him. "I'm with Jamie. What's wrong?"

"I just got a call from the hospital in Glen Burnie. Your mother has been stabbed ten times," she exclaimed.

My heart stopped. I wasn't even sure what to say. I wasn't sure how to feel. I wasn't sure what to do. How could I cry over someone who has never cried over me? It's hard to feel anything but hate toward someone I feel has always hated me.

"Ne'Vaeh, are you still there?" she asked, crying through the phone.

"Shorty, what's wrong?" Jamie's eyes searched my face.

I looked up at him. "Renée, where are you?"

"I'm on my way to Glen Burnie right now. The doctors are saying she lost so much blood and is going to need a transfusion. I'm a universal donor, aren't you? Won't you give your mother blood to save her life?" Renée had the nerve to question my morals.

"Renée—"

"While you're with Jamie fuckin' his brains out, your mother is dying. I don't give a fuck what she did to you in the past—she needs you now. Now you get here. Tell Jamie to pull his dick out of the pussy and take you to see your mother." Renée hung up in my face.

I looked up at Jamie as I took the phone from my ear. "Juanita is in the hospital."

"Well, let's go to her."

My mind was taking me in all types of directions that night. When Jamie and I arrived at the hospital, nearly all of my family was waiting in the lobby. Out of everyone in the room, Renée and I were the only universal donors. Juanita was O+ which made her very limited in who could give her blood to. Both Renée and I had our vitals checked and filled out questionnaires. We had our blood type confirmed by giving a sample of our blood. It felt like an eternity before the doctor called me back into her office to discuss the procedure.

I sat in a chair alongside Doctor Hicks's desk.

She eyed her computer screen for a few minutes before turning to me.

I looked into her pale face. "Well?"

"Well, we can't use your blood, Miss Washington."

I looked at her, heart racing. "Why not? Is it because of my heart condition? I'm fine. I can give Juanita my blood."

The doctor grinned. "Your heart is actually doing pretty good. Your vitals are perfectly fine. Based on your records, you haven't had blood pressure this good in years. I didn't hear your heart skipping any beats. Your heart valves are opening and closing when they should."

"Then what's wrong?"

"Based on the blood test we did this morning, your urine sample, and the last date of your menstrual cycle, I'd say you are about three weeks pregnant," the doctor smiled.

I immediately stood from the chair, heart racing like it was a NASCAR driver.

The doctor stood with me. "Sweetheart, calm down." She saw that I was about to hyperventilate. "Sweetie, you have to calm down." Gently, she placed her hands on my shoulders.

"I-I don't wanna have his baby," I cried out.

"Well, that's something you need to discuss with your OB-GYN." Doctor Hicks said, looking into my face.

"I mean, I want his baby, just not now." I dried my face.

"Either way, sweetie, I'm not the one to talk to about this. I'm here to talk about Juanita," she replied. "Your cousin Renée is just fine to give her aunt blood. And you will be fine."

"And my mother?" I finally caught my breath. "How will she do?"

"We don't know yet. Only time will tell." Doctor Hicks patted me on the shoulder.

I couldn't face my family that morning in the waiting room. I couldn't face Jamie. Pregnant? How could I be pregnant? I had an IUD. Shit, I had a fuckin' tilted uterus and an ovary that didn't even produce eggs. God was punishing me for my mother's sins. God kept me in pain because of her. There she was, dying in the hospital, and despite everything she'd taken me through, I showed up to try to rescue her. I hadn't seen the woman in six years, and the only words I had for her were "fuck you." Renée was Juanita's only immediate chance at survival. I couldn't save Juanita if I wanted to.

We all sat in the waiting room for hours, pacing the floor. Jamie didn't leave my side. He knew I wanted to bail. He didn't even ask me why the doctors decided to let Renée donate her blood instead of me. I think he was more concerned with my state of mind and how I would react when I saw Juanita's face. My entire family forced me to stay there until she woke up. As soon as Autumn got the word that the surgery was over and the transfusion was successful, she kissed me goodbye. She didn't want to see Mother and really had no words for her other than "fuck you."

Jamie wanted to go into Juanita's room with me, but I wouldn't let him. I didn't want anyone in the room with me when I said what I needed to say to her. I had no choice about whether I wanted Renée in the room. After the transfusion was over, she sat with Juanita, talking to her about the incident. I walked into the room right in the middle of the conversation.

"Aunt 'Nita, you ain't got no business fighting anyone over a fuckin' security guard," Renée exclaimed, sitting at the foot of Juanita's bed.

"The muthafucka raped my cell mate. When I went to confront him, he had three other inmates jump me in the kitchen, Renée. What would you have done? If that bitch didn't get ahold of that steak knife, I would have killed her." Juanita struggled to sit up. She looked up when she saw me standing in the doorway. She had been beaten up, head bandaged, cheek bruised, torso bandaged, and wrist broken, but she looked 100 percent better than I remembered her.

Renée looked at me as I hesitated to come inside. She looked back at Juanita, who sat up in the bed, trying to smooth down her hair with the one hand that was free. She was handcuffed to the bed with the other hand. A correctional officer stood in the corner of the room.

Juanita hesitated. "Ne'Vaeh, I-I heard you were flying to Atlanta tomorrow to sign a record deal with Passion Studios."

I just looked at her, still standing in the doorway. My feet wouldn't move, when every thought in my body was telling me to run straight out of the room.

Juanita's eyes sparkled. "You know, I named you Ne'Vaeh because from the moment you came out of me, you had this unique cry." Juanita laughed to herself. "I said I have never heard a baby cry like this. It was almost like you were singing. I said to myself, she has got to be from heaven. So precious, so unique. Since my life was the exact opposite of heaven, I named you Heaven spelled backward, Ne'Vaeh."

Tears slid down my face. I couldn't speak. I couldn't do anything but just listen.

"I know you hate me, babe, but you have to listen to me when I tell you to stay with Jamie. Don't leave him. The music industry will chew you up and spit you out as soon as you don't do what they want. I know because I've been there. Yeah, your mother was a backup singer for a few artists that I won't name. Had me going to all sorts of wild parties, got me hooked on all sorts of drugs. I started using drugs when I was pregnant with Autumn, and it was downhill from there. I was fourteen when I had your sister, and I had just signed a recording contract. I was raped by the executive producer for my album, and when I tried telling on him, my career was over." Juanita's lips trembled. "Just stay here with Jamie and let him take care of you."

I finally regained my senses, shaking my head at her. "Juanita, that was your life. The fact that you couldn't control yourself and put yourself in a fucked-up situation doesn't have shit to do with me."

Juanita chuckled. "Oh, it does, sweetie. My mother was a drug addict, always in jail, never taking care of the eight children she had. I can't tell you how many of my own uncles and cousins she allowed to rape me. I can't tell you how many trash cans I ate out of looking for food to feed my younger siblings. I know how you feel, Ne'Vaeh."

"If you knew how I feel, how could you put me in the exact same situation that your mother put you in?" I screamed. "You didn't have to abuse us, you didn't have to abandon us, you didn't have to pimp your oldest daughter, you didn't have to do drugs, and you didn't have to kill my brother. You chose that lifestyle, Juanita."

She nodded. "Yes, I did. I felt like I didn't have a choice. I looked for love in all the wrong people. And when I didn't get the love in return, I turned to drugs and alcohol, something I knew I could always depend on as long as I had the money. I don't expect you to forgive me. You shouldn't. I don't deserve it. But don't punish that boy because of me. He won't hurt you again, baby. That boy loves you."

"Juanita, I know what's best for me. I have to leave this place and everything that has to do with it. You don't know shit about Jamie. The muthafucka didn't even want me until he saw someone else was interested in me," I screamed.

"You know that's not true," she said.

"And how the fuck would you of all people know what love is?" I cried.

"Because I know what it's not, Ne'Vaeh." Juanita held her side, face cringing like she was in excruciating pain.

Renée instinctively pressed the nurse call button on the side of the bed.

I rushed to Juanita's side. "Mama," I cried as she collapsed in my arms. I looked up at Renée as nurses rushed into the room.

Juanita had an allergic reaction to the blood. The doctors weren't really sure how to handle the situation, so they just let time be the deciding factor. The family stayed at the hospital all day, waiting until Juanita was stable to decide whether to leave. I still hadn't packed up my bags for the following day, and Anastasia was blowing up my phone. I hadn't told anyone that I was pregnant. I didn't feel pregnant. I felt hung over. I hoped that the heavy drinking that I'd been doing hadn't affected the baby, regardless of whether I'd decide on keeping the baby. Jamie had enough problems than to have to deal with two baby mamas. I wanted to leave Maryland more than ever once Doctor Hicks said that I was pregnant. I couldn't even look Jamie in the eye.

"The doctors said that Aunt 'Nita is stable, so y'all can leave if you want," Renée told everyone as she stood in the middle of the waiting room.

"They're going to take her back to the prison in two days, after making sure her body fully accepts the transfusion."

Jamie looked at me. "Can I take you home?"

I hesitated. "Ummm, Jamie, I think it's best that I just go home with Renée."

He looked hurt. "Shorty—"

I shook my head. "I love you, Jamie, but I gotta go." I stood from my chair, hurrying over to Renée, locking arms with her as we headed out of the waiting room. Renée didn't ask any questions; she just took me home.

Renée watched as I packed my clothes into two suitcases the night we left Juanita in the hospital. I hadn't said a word all day to her about Juanita or Jamie.

"So, you're really not gonna stay? Does Anastasia even know what's going on with your family right now?" she asked, sitting beside my suitcase on the bed.

I looked at her. "Renée, we've been through this. I'm leaving. Anastasia doesn't have to know my business. I'm sure she has her own problems dealing with Darryl and his groupies than to worry about me and my small world."

"You could have at least talked to Jamie. That boy stayed with you all day in the fuckin' hospital," she protested. "I'm sure he had better things to do. I mean, he is star quarterback of a fuckin' NFL team. He's got better things to do than to chase around a girl who's dissin' him."

I rolled my eyes. "Renée, please, shut up."

"You don't wanna leave him." She stated again, "You know you don't."

I stopped packing for a second. "No, I don't."

"Then why are you doing this? Anastasia will understand. As bad as she wants you, I promise you, this won't be your last opportunity," she assured me.

I looked at her. "Do you even know why I couldn't give blood to Juanita?"

Renée rolled her eyes. "Because you're pregnant."

I nearly swallowed my gum. Not because she knew what was going on, but because she had kept her big-ass mouth shut about it all day. "Renée, you knew?"

She pursed her lips at me. "Really? I'm a nurse. I have access to your hospital records. You think I wouldn't find out or even ask the doctors why you couldn't give your own mother blood when you have the same blood type?"

I felt terrible leaving that boy, but I had to. I looked at my cousin. "Renée, I'm having Jamie's baby. You know I always wanted to have that boy's baby."

She held my hand. "Sweetie, it's okay. He wants you to have his baby. Just tell him you're having his baby. Don't just leave, Ne'Vaeh."

I slipped my hand from hers and started packing again. "He already has enough on his plate. He's got Charlie to deal with, and she's gonna give him hell. I know her. She's not gonna stand there and watch him take care of me and mine when she needs to be taken care of too. I'm leaving, Renée, and there's nothing that is going to convince me to stay here. I need to do what's best for me, and what's best for me is to leave all of this hurt and pain in the past and move on."

"How the fuck are you gonna move on, Ne'Vaeh? You're having this man's baby. If you plan on keeping this baby, when do you plan on telling Jamie about it?" she had to ask.

I looked at her. "Plan on keeping it? I've wanted his baby from our very first kiss, Renée. I would never kill a part of Jamie, but I don't wanna tell him about it, either. Not right now."

"Girl, you're making a mistake leaving him. He's been through a lot. How are you gonna explain this shit to Anastasia? When you're throwin' up and shit during rehearsals, she's gonna know. When you're stuffing your face with pickles and ice cream, Ne'Vaeh, she's gonna figure the shit out."

I looked at her. The more she talked, the more sense that she made. "Renée, I'll cross that bridge when I get to it. Right now, I need a break from Maryland. I need a break from Jamie, from Charlie, from Juanita, from school, from doctors' appointments, from sleepless nights, from crying, from pain, and from heartache."

"You need to tell that boy that he's got a baby on the way. I know this situation is fucked up, but leaving isn't going to fix that. You didn't create this baby alone. Your health isn't all that great to be having a baby in the first place, and you wanna do this shit by yourself?" she asked. "You don't know what you're getting yourself into. Have you even been paying attention to how hard Anastasia works? That girl dances flawlessly, and her dancers are always on point. She's multitalented, so you already know she's gonna push you. You don't even know if your body can even handle all of this."

Now, I shook my head at Renée. "Renée, something in my heart keeps telling me to go. That I need to do this."

"What you need to do is get to know your mother. Not the crackhead," she cut me off before I cursed her the fuck out. "Not the murderer. Not the woman who abused you. But the woman who's very sorry for what she's done. Promise me you'll accept her calls because I gave her your phone number."

My eyes widened.

Renée smiled sheepishly.

I rolled my eyes. There was really no use getting mad at her. She always thought she could help fix my heart.

"Cuz, I can't watch you leave tomorrow, okay?" she whispered. "I just can't."

I nodded. "I know."

"You're my best friend, and I don't know how I'm gonna make it without you. Your trouble-making ass is the best thing I have in my life right now. The only true relationship that I have. I know I'm always acting like your mother, but it's only because you need one." Renée wanted to cry, but she didn't.

"You know I appreciate you, girl." I tried to smile. "I'm gonna miss your bossy ass."

Renée sighed. "You sure you don't wanna stay? I mean, the least you can do is go say good-bye to him." She wasn't letting go of the subject of Jamie.

"If I go say goodbye to that boy, I might not leave."

"That's the point, sweetie. Don't go," she begged.

I zipped my suitcase. I had called Anastasia, asking her to come by and get me so that I could stay with her in her hotel room for the night. I knew Jamie well enough to know he'd pop up over at Renée's house sooner or later to try to convince me to stay. Renée couldn't possibly understand the way that I was feeling. I was tired of losing. I was tired of hurting. I was tired of crying. But most of all, I was tired of love being so disappointing. When Anastasia came to pick me up that night, Renée had the hardest time letting me go and not begging Anastasia to convince me to stay.

I stayed up the entire night, sitting in the window at the hotel, looking up at the stars. Anastasia knew something was wrong, but she didn't question me until the following morning when we sat down at the kitchen table in the hotel to eat breakfast.

She looked up at me from her plate. "So, what was it like seeing your mother in the hospital yesterday?"

I looked up at her. "Renée has got to have the biggest mouth on earth."

Anastasia laughed. "Nah, actually, I ran into Jamie yesterday at a gas station. I saw him filling up his car, and I got out of the Navigator to say hello. You can imagine his shock when he saw me standing before him at the gas pump, sayin', 'Eh, nigga, where's my cousin?'"

I tried not to laugh. You had to love her sense of humor.

Anastasia looked at me, finishing her laugh with a sigh. "He said he was tired as hell, had been up with you all night and half of the day at the hospital. Said your mother needed a blood transfusion because she had been stabbed. I know you don't have a good relationship with your mother, yet when she needed you, you tried to be there."

"Yeah." I stuffed bacon in my mouth. "Story of my life."

"That man, Aaron, is really feeling you too." Anastasia laughed out loud. "Girl, even if you wouldn't have told the truth about Charlie and Jamie at their wedding rehearsal, I'm sure he would have left Charlie standing at the altar. He was so not gonna marry her with all of those feelings he harbors for you." She looked at me. "Trust me, I know what you're going through. My life was like yours a few years ago. Loving Darryl or getting him to admit to loving me was a battle, sweetheart, believe that."

I looked at her. "Why do my mind and my heart have to always be at war, Anastasia? My mind is telling me that I have to go, but my heart is telling me that Jamie needs me to stay."

"Boo, yes, Jamie does need you to stay, but you have to do what's best for you." Her eyes searched my face for any sign of feelings about what she was saying. She saw my facial muscles tensing, fighting back the tears. "Sweetie, I told you already, if you wanna stay, it's okay. I'm not going anywhere. The contract will be waiting for you when you get there if you wanna be with your bae."

I shook my head. "He doesn't know what he wants, Anna. He's a playa, a bachelor, a playboy, a dog, a ho—anything but what I want him to be. I love that asshole with everything in me, but I can't watch him help raise that baby when I need him just as much as Charlie does."

Anastasia nodded. "Okay, sweetie. I won't try to change your mind. It seems you obviously have your mind made up. I just want you to know that the ticket you have goes both ways in case you wanna come back to him."

Anastasia, her entourage, and I checked our baggage that afternoon at the airport. We all sat down together, waiting for our departure time to be announced. I was so nervous, I was shaking.

My leg was shaking a hundred miles per hour until Anastasia put her hand on my thigh to stop it.

I looked up into her flawless face.

"You good, ma?" Her brown eyes searched mine.

I hesitated to nod. "Yeah, Anna, I'm straight."

"Darryl just texted me, asking about his baby cuzzo." She nudged me. "Oh my goodness, that dude is so excited about you moving to ATL. Girl, I'm just warning you ahead of time that he is not gonna let you get any rest for at least a week. My tour starts in a few days too. Our first show is in Cleveland. We gotta put in work if we wanna give a great performance. You are now rockin' with the best, Ne'Vaeh, so you have to be at your best. My crew will tell you, I works my people hard. And just 'cause you are family doesn't mean I'm cuttin' you any slack. You won't need that much vocal training, so that won't be an issue. We just have to teach you the songs. Your voice is so powerful, boo. I don't plan on keeping you in the background for long. As soon as my tour is over, we're gonna have to put some of those songs that I've written into you. You are gonna bring so much sassiness and classiness to my label, boo. This is so exciting."

All her plans were making my got-damn head spin.

"Oh my God." Anastasia's hairstylist, Courtney, looked over my shoulder, then back at me. "Ne'Vaeh, isn't that your man?"

I looked over my shoulder to see Jamie strolling over to us. I sighed, sitting back in my seat. "Oh my goodness, why doesn't Renée know when to shut up? She is always—" I stopped, then looked at Anastasia. "Wait, Renée didn't even know what airport we were flying out of or what time my flight was leaving, because when I tried to tell her, she kept cutting me off. Anastasia, you called Jamie? Why would you call Jamie?"

She grinned. "He's coming over, boo, so you might as well talk to him."

Defeated, I shook my head at her, and then rose to my feet as Jamie approached all of us. My heart beat out of control in my chest as he walked up to me, looking down at me. He took me by the hand, leading me away from everyone, over to the middle of the walkway.

"Why are you doin' this?" he asked, looking at me. "You know I don't want you to leave. Why are you leavin' me?"

"Jamie, you know why. We already talked about this."

"The only reason why I even signed with the Ravens is so that I could be close to you again. I shouldn't have messed around with Charlie, I'll admit that. I shouldn't have messed with any of those girls—I'll admit that too. I'm sorry, shorty. I'll do whatever you need me to do, just don't leave me," he begged, still holding my hand.

I shook my head. "No, Jamie, there's nothing you can do or say to convince me to stay."

"Passengers headed to Atlanta, Georgia, please proceed to Gate 37E." The passenger services agent finally made the boarding announcement over the intercom.

Sadly, Jamie looked down into my face. "I'm a better man because of you. Yes, I've made some bad choices—okay, a lot of bad choices. And I don't want letting you just leave me be another one. Ne'Vaeh, baby, I love you." He pulled me closer to him.

I slipped my hand from his. "Jamie, I have to go." I turned to walk away.

"Ne'Vaeh, marry me." He grabbed my arm, pulling me back to him.

I looked into his face as he let go of my arm and pulled a small velvet box out of his pocket. He got down on one knee, flipping the box open. Inside was a brilliant, vintage princess cut diamond. Blue and white diamonds wrapped around the band. I held my hand over my heart, looking into Jamie's face.

It was as if the entire terminal got quiet, waiting on my response.

"Baby, please, marry me. There's no other woman out there for me. You complete me. You are everything and the only thing that matters to me. Spend forever with me. Grow together with me. Be mine, please, Ne'Vaeh." He held my hand.

I cried out loud, looking up at Anastasia, who stood there crying herself. She nodded at me, mouthing, "Say something, got-damn it."

I looked at Jamie. I loved him, but I knew in my heart that if I stayed in Maryland, he would hurt me again. Maybe not intentionally, but he would. I was having his baby, and he didn't even know. And I know I was wrong for not telling him about the baby then, but he didn't need to know.

Anastasia's crew headed toward the gate to board the flight, walking past us. I watched as they walked down the terminal, tears streaming down my face.

Jamie stood from the floor, holding my hand. "Baby, please, come home," he begged.

I looked at him, sliding my hand from his. Then I reached into my coat pocket and took out the necklace that held the key to his heart. I held his hand, placing the necklace in it. The hardest thing I had ever done was look up into those gorgeous brown eyes of his and tell him, "Jamie, I have waited a long time for you to ask me to be your wife, but we're not supposed to be together. Everything that's happened between us proves that we should have left things the way that they were. I have never tried to change you, and I'm not about to start now. You just keep being you, Jamie. If I stay, I'll only be holding you back. You need to have fun, enjoy your life, and not let anyone hold you down. You're young, you're gorgeous, you're sexy, you're a got-damn professional football player. Live your life, Jamie. Give this ring to someone when you're really ready, and not just because you don't want to see her with anybody else. And give the key to your heart to someone when you're really ready to give your heart to her. I refuse to share you with my sister, Jamie, and I shouldn't have to."

Jamie bit his lip to stop from crying out loud. He closed the box, clinching it in his hand. Then he looked down into my face, at a loss for words.

"Goodbye, Jamie." I backed away from him, and then turned around, hurrying after Anastasia and her crew.

Anastasia shook her head at me as I caught up with her. She grabbed my hand, holding it tightly in hers. "Come on, sweetie. If you're really leaving this boy, you can't look back. Just keep on walking."

I sat down in a seat next to the window in first class.

Anastasia sat down beside me. She watched my every move, from positioning my seat, to wiping the tears from my face. "You know, that ring would have looked amazing on your tiny little finger." She teased me too soon. "And you could have at least kept that necklace, girl. You know he's not gonna give that shit to anyone else after the way you just dissed him in front of everybody."

I looked at her. I couldn't stop the tears from rolling down my face. "Too soon, Anna." She shook her head. "I would say that you'll be fine, but I'm not so sure. I would say that he'll be fine, but he put his heart out there on the line for you, and you dismissed him. I don't know what the future holds, but I doubt that boy will ever love like this again. Love is never easy. You have to work to keep a relationship together. If you hurry, you can still catch him before he leaves the airport."

"I wasn't gonna stick around and wait for him to hurt me again, Anna. You know I wanted to say yes to marrying him. You know I wanted Jamie to take me home. These past few months dealing with Jamie have been some of the hardest months of my life. He was gone for over four years, Anastasia. I have felt more pain these past three months than I did the entire time that he was gone. I don't have time for his lifestyle."

Anastasia laughed to herself. "You're trying to convince yourself that Jamie is bad news when you know that he's not. You're afraid of love, Ne'Vaeh. All I'm saying is don't think that once you leave a man, you can just run back to him when you're ready. Remember, you're the one who set him free. Like I said, once you walk away from a man like him, there's no turning back."

I left Maryland that day in hopes of leaving everything in my past behind me. I couldn't stay in Maryland and listen to my family tell me that I needed to reach out to Juanita. I hadn't seen the woman in six years and to my family, one conversation with her meant that we could fix what had been broken for nineteen years. I couldn't stay in Maryland and watch Charlie chase after Jamie for the next eighteen years. Jamie wanted to settle down, but at the same time, he wanted to live that playa lifestyle.

I knew it took everything in him to sleep with just one woman every night when he was used to having multiple women every night. He was a ladies' man. True, he gave up a lot to be with me, but who was I to stop Jamie from living his life? He didn't need to be tied down to me. When I thought I had him to myself, turns out Charlie had a piece of him too.

Yes, I was carrying Jamie's little boy or girl, but so was Charlie. Two women in his ear, naggin' him about diapers and well-baby checkups? Not to mention my child was going to be Charlie's son's cousin and half brother or sister. My life was screwed up. My relationship with Jamie was over. Seeing Aaron that night at the club lit something inside of me. He was flying halfway around the world to get away from all of us, and I didn't blame him. He was starting over, starting fresh, trying his best to let go of what could have been. I had to leave Maryland, but I had no choice if I wanted to keep my sanity. I couldn't handle any more disappointment. I didn't know then what Anastasia meant, but I would soon find out. ATL, here I come. . . .